PENGUIN BOOKS

The Unvisible

The story you are about to read came to Fredrik Haren at 2 a.m. one night in Bangkok. It came like a gift. A gift with a message.

The story came fully developed, ready to be written down. And it demanded to be told.

This book is that story, written down as it was told to the author.

Fredrik Haren lives in Singapore with his wife and three children. His middle child, Maria, had invisible friends until she was five.

The Unvisible

Fredrik Haren

PENGUIN BOOKS
An imprint of Penguin Random House

PENGUIN BOOKS

USA | Canada | UK | Ireland | Australia
New Zealand | India | South Africa | China | Southeast Asia

Penguin Books is part of the Penguin Random House group of companies
whose addresses can be found at global.penguinrandomhouse.com

Published by Penguin Random House SEA Pte Ltd
9, Changi South Street 3, Level 08-01,
Singapore 486361

First published in Penguin Books by Penguin Random House SEA 2022

10 9 8 7 6 5 4 3 2 1

ISBN 9789814954556

Typeset in Adobe Caslon Pro by MAP Systems, Bangalore, India

www.penguin.sg

To Elaine, Lucas, Maria and Sophia—for making life beautiful.

'To be willing to give up everything, in order to find yourself, is life's biggest challenge.'

– Amanda Ma

Prologue

'A question that sometimes drives me hazy: am I or are the others crazy?'
– Albert Einstein

A person fighting for her life is not afraid to die. She is afraid of life coming to an end.

The woman desperately trying to break free from the two nurses confining her, clearly had no intent of seeing her life come to an end. The staff at the St Lucia Mental Hospital tightened their grip as the woman tried yet another way to escape. The annoying woman did not seem to realize just how senseless resisting was. The determined look on the faces of the two men should have been enough to make her give up. Undeterred, she continued her struggle and screamed. 'They are going to kill me!'

The two nurses lifted her slightly so that her feet just touched the ground. Or rather, they would have touched the ground if she had not been kicking so wildly. They could restrain her body, but they could not control her mind. Nor her vocal chords.

'The voices. Can't you hear them? They are here!'

As the nurses finally were able to restrain her with the additional help of a pair of hand- and leg-cuffs in leather, a pale-skinned male assistant, who had been observing the commotion from a distance, approached the woman and gently took her hand. In a calm and soothing voice that seemed to defuse the tension in the room he said, 'It's all right, Alexandra. We can hear them. Of course we can.'

Alex gave him a confused look. 'You have to let me go. Listen to me—they are here. And they know that I know! That I've revealed the secret. That I've revealed them. That . . .'

The two nurses leant over Alex. One of them straightened her left arm, while the other got a syringe out of the bag around his waist.

'No! No injections! I'll calm down. I promise!' she begged.

The nurse found a vein on the inside of her arm and plunged in the needle.

Alex mumbled, almost whispered. 'They are here. Save me . . . Please save me . . .'

Her eyelids grew heavy. She fought against the tranquilizing effect of the medicine but did not stand a chance. Slowly, but surely, the world around her became blurred.

As she relaxed, so did the tension in the nurses who had been pinning her down. The younger nurse loosened his grip a little and wiped the sweat off his face.

'Do former employees often come back here as patients?' he wondered.

The nurse asking the question had only been working at St Lucia for a couple of months. There was not a hint of irony in his question. He was genuinely worried that his new workplace might make him mad.

The question hung in the air.

'Poor Alexandra!' the young man said, still waiting for someone to answer his question. His face expressed something else: that the one he really felt bad for was himself.

Alex's head fell forward as she seemed to black-out. Just before losing consciousness, her eyelids flew open to reveal two eyes that were suddenly fully alert. She gazed into the baby blue eyes of the man holding her hand. Their eyes locked in a moment of mutual understanding. To one of the nurses it seemed as if Alex had winked, but that must just have been a spasm in her eye muscles right before she drifted off into sleep.

Just outside the door, stood two people. A man and a woman. The man was tall and athletic; the woman short and slight. Their fair and smooth skin made them look young. Their wise, narrow, eyes made them look old. It was frankly difficult to tell how old they were. They could have been twenty-five or forty. The woman might have been petite, but she was clearly in charge.

The two observed the group.

The man whispered to his colleague, 'The sane have no idea, whilst the aware are seen as insane.'

The woman nodded in agreement.

Six months earlier

Chapter 1

'At the innermost core of all loneliness is a deep and powerful yearning for union with one's lost self.'
– Brendan Francis

Torture. That was the best way to describe the feeling of once again walking up the gravel path to the large, familiar house with its well-kept garden. This was the house she had grown up in. It was also, unfortunately, the house she had occasionally been forced to move back to a few times over the years. Most recently two years earlier, during her failed studies in medicine, when she had been so overwhelmed with school work that she just hadn't been able to also hold down a part-time job. Her lack of financial resources had stopped her from renting her own place. Instead, she had had to move back in with her parents yet again.

To move back into your old girls' room as an adult had been bad enough. To do so as a failed thirty-year-old medical student when your father was a highly respected doctor had been Alex's definition of humiliation.

Many were the nights when she had had to sit and study for exams while putting up with her mother's sympathetic comments. 'I'm sure you'll do well.' When Alex could see in her mother's eyes that she knew very well that it would not go very well at all. Her mother knew Alex was going to fail. And it was not just her mother who knew that; her father knew it too. And he told her so. To her face. 'You're going to f-a-a-i-l.' He stressed the word 'fail' by elongating the syllable to emphasise that he knew just how badly she was going to fail.

Alex also knew. She was not meant to be a doctor; she was not suited for the job and she did not want it. This combination of unsuitability combined with lack of talent and lack of interest was a recipe for failure. In spite of this, Alex believed that she had really tried her best. For the sake of her father. To prove that Dr Johansen's daughter really had inherited some of his medical genius. She had also done it for her mother, even though she did not really understand why it mattered so much to her mother that her daughter become a doctor.

So, she had failed. And as in an evil plot of a Greek tragedy, her father had died of a heart attack the very day after Alex had stood in the living room and explained that she had decided to quit her medical studies. When she had told her parents that she was thinking about studying journalism instead, her mother had started to cry.

Her father had thumped down his glass of whisky and spluttered, 'Journalist?! Report about war and disasters? Probe into other people's misery? Describe, in detail, the obscene ways that people have met their demise? Do you know what doctors do? We save lives. What do journalists do? Gossip. They gossip about death! You—a journalist? Over my dead body!'

Her father had expected his thirty-year-old daughter to accept her parents' decision. She had felt as if she had been eleven again asking them for permission to go on a sleep-over. Out of the question. End of discussion.

Alex had conceded, went to her room and sneaked out early the next morning to avoid the tense atmosphere. And then, later on that day, her father had had a heart attack and dropped dead on the spot.

'Alexandra—how could you? It was all that nonsense of you becoming a reporter that killed him. 'Over my dead body!' he said. Over his dead body!'

The words her mother had screamed at her from a haze of sorrow and despair when she had come home later on that day still hurt. Alex cursed her father for how fate had decided those would be his last words to her.

While her mother had apologized for her choice of words Alex knew that her mother still blamed her for the death. Alex could see it in her eyes. The shame stuck to Alex like a bad smell she could never wash off. That the doctor later had explained that her father's death could not have been caused by anything Alex had said should have made it easier for her. But it hadn't.

And now, here she was again. Standing in front of her parents' house. Her mother's house, she corrected herself. Ready to once again be exposed to the judging glares of her mother. To be tortured. This time as a guest.

The air felt heavy. She rang the doorbell.

Mrs Johansen opened the door donning a clean apron.

'Alexandra!'

Her mother was more or less the only person who still insisted on calling her by her full name. She had long given up trying to get her mother to understand that she had never felt comfortable with a name like Alexandra. She felt it was a name better suited for a young model with ambitions to marry rich. Perhaps that was the reason for why her mother had chosen that name—and why she insisted on using it. As if she was still hoping.

With impeccable make-up on and not a hair out of place she could be cast for the role of Mrs Perfect Housewife.

'No need to ring the doorbell! Come in! We've been waiting for you.'

Her mother had the ability to make the words 'We've been waiting for you' mean 'We've been looking forward to seeing you' while at the same time implying 'You're late. Why can't you come on time like your brother and his adorable wife?'

Watching her mother disappear into the kitchen, Alex took a deep breath and walked into the living room where Daniel sat on the sofa playing with his son.

Alex held up two fingers towards her brother, a private greeting between them of which origins neither of them could remember. She ignored Laura on purpose. Laura had 'doctor's wife' written all over her.

There was not really anything wrong with Laura and perhaps this was why she got on Alex's nerves. People who did not have any faults were scary. It was always the most perfect ones who turned out to be paedophiles or drug dealers. Laura was one of those perfect, good-natured people that made you want to go looking for a flaw.

'Well, hello there, Alex!' Laura called out, a little too friendly, from her default position next to her husband. 'How're your media studies coming along?'

Alex managed to squeeze out a 'Fine, thanks' before going up to Daniel and Laura's youngest son, whom they, annoyingly, still called Junior. They must have left Eric with the nanny.

'Hi there, JR!' She called him JR to tick off Laura. 'How's my favourite nephew?'

Junior obviously could not answer since he was only eight months old, but Alex refused to use baby talk when speaking to babies. She could not understand why you could not use normal words just because the babies themselves could not talk. 'So, should we crawl around on all fours because they can't walk—or drop our food on the floor because that's what they do?' she had once wondered when, for some reason, Laura had brought up the subject.

Junior was lying in one of those multi-functional baby chairs that you could use both as a carrier and as a car seat. It looked exclusive—not that Junior cared. He just lay there, gazing up at the ceiling as Alex looked down at him. It always surprised her just how relaxed a child's face could be.

Everyone talked about the smoothness of a baby's bottom, but Alex was more fascinated by the natural peacefulness of a baby's face. Alex stood there, looking at her little nephew, fully aware that the proud parents were expecting her to say something about how sweet he was, or how fast he was growing.

Instead she said, 'Did you know that children have blue eyes when they are in the womb?'

Laura threw a questioning look at Alex. 'But that cannot possibly be . . .'

Daniel interrupted his wife. 'Melatonin is the protein that gives us our eye, skin and hair colour. Before the protein develops, however, our eyes are blue.'

Alex wished that her brother would stop talking to his wife as if she were a student. That was a bad habit he had:

talking to others as if they were students—or patients. It was the occupational hazard of a profession where you were used to others listening to you.

Ignoring Daniel, Alex decided to have some more fun with Laura and added, 'I recently came across an article that said infants, in their first few months, always look more like their mothers than their fathers. It's nature's way of protecting illegitimate babies so that the man who thinks he is the father doesn't get suspicious if the baby looks like someone else. When the biological father's genes make an appearance, the other man has already developed fatherly feelings towards the baby. This makes it more difficult for him to reject the child, even if they don't look like each other.'

'You shouldn't believe everything you read on the Internet,' Daniel broke in. 'Personally, I think Junior is a carbon copy of me. Same high, intelligent forehead. Same charming smile.'

Daniel got up to take the baby and Alex happily abdicated the job of making sure that Junior was always the centre of attention, but just as Daniel picked up the child Junior jolted his head backwards. The baby opened his eyes wide as if he had just seen something terrifying right behind Alex's shoulder. The fear in the baby's eyes was so intense that Alex instinctively turned around. But there was nothing there. Alex moved away and flopped into an armchair. At the very same time, the fear moved down into the lungs of the child and emerged as a terrified scream.

'He certainly knows how to scream,' Daniel said to Alex, while glancing over at Laura and stroking his son's forehead in an attempt to quieten him down.

But the baby kept screaming. Alex shifted in her chair. There were few things as heart-wrenching as an infant shrieking out of fear.

'He's probably just tired,' Daniel tried to justify the behaviour. He rocked the baby, paced around, spoke soothing words to him and kissed the little bawling bundle, but nothing helped.

Laura's gaze shifted between her child and the kitchen door as if, on the one hand, she wanted to show what a modern and responsible husband she had, while on the other hand, she was terrified of looking like a bad mother, especially in the eyes of her mother-in-law. Finally, she could not stand it anymore and went over to comfort her son.

Just then, the little child suddenly went quiet, just as unexpected as it had started screaming earlier.

A couple of seconds of complete silence reigned while everyone inhaled: the adults in relief that the difficult situation had passed and the child in order to get some fresh air into his lungs.

Laura sat back down, Daniel placed Junior in the baby carrier and Alex made herself more comfortable in the armchair. Everyone smiled, especially JR. His fury had come and gone as quickly as a thunderstorm in summer. Now, he cooed happily in his seat.

Mrs Johansen cooed in her own special way from the kitchen, 'Alexandra, can you come and help me with the roast?'

But before Alex had a chance to react, Laura—that always so perfectly annoying Laura—chirped, 'Let me help you!' She ran into the kitchen to save the roast as if she were saving a child from a burning building.

Alex deliberately sighed a little too loudly as if to invite her brother to jump in with a diplomatic comment about her sister-in-law's fawning over their mother. But instead, he just blurted out, 'While the women take care of the food, I'm left to deal with the kids . . .'

They both made their way to the dining room.

Alex snapped back, 'Don't you forget who's the baby in this family.'

'Baby? Please call me Doctor Johansen—"the perfect family man".'

Alex stopped for a moment and let her brother walk a few steps in front of her. She did not want to go into the dining room with the golden boy of the family. 'Black sheep tend to graze alone,' she said quietly.

She already knew that it was going to be a long dinner.

The man watching the family breathed a sigh of relief. He had to admit that the child's screams had made him nervous. To be on the safe side, he had withdrawn. When the family went into the dining room to eat, he seized the opportunity to sneak out of the door and he would do the rest of the watching through the window.

People who were not conscious about someone observing them were much easier to work with. His job was to make sure that this mission was carried out smoothly. Watching was a balancing act: you had to be close, and at the same time you had to be open. Open to take a step back.

Chapter 2

'Believe those who are seeking the truth. Doubt those who find it.'
– André Gide

Two women were sitting in the far back corner of the main lecture hall of the College of Media Studies. They were Alex and her friend Jade. Jade was wearing an oversized college sweatshirt, which looked as if she had borrowed it from her boyfriend. Alexandra also was wearing a college sweatshirt, but whereas Jade's big shirt gave her that sexy, girl-next-door look, Alexandra's shirt just made her look like someone who had woken up with nothing better to wear.

Today's lecture was called 'The Perception of People's Perceptions'. 'A perfect topic after last night's awkward family dinner,' reflected Alex. As soon as the teacher, Patrick Gardener, begun his lecture Alex's attention had been drawn to the stage where Patrick was preaching in front of the class. He seemed to enjoy giving them a performance rather than a class.

'Some myths talk about creation as a process with an active God as the creator. These are called creation stories. Myths and rituals are a part of the social legacy handed down from generation to generation via upbringing and peer pressure. The German theologian, Paul Tillich, defined the relationship between a myth's symbolic and historical content with the concepts of unbroken and broken myths respectively.'

Alex leaned towards Jade and whispered, 'The unbroken myth is literally true . . .'

A second later, Patrick continued, 'The unbroken myth is accepted as a statement of literal truth, while the broken myth can be regarded as a historical truth.'

Jade gave Alex a resigned look. 'Again?'

'Again,' Alex replied.

Alex thought back to the beginning of the term when she and Jade had been dazzled by their teacher's ability to tell stories and how they had been impressed by the breadth of his knowledge. Teachers could generally be divided into two categories: those who knew a lot, but could not teach. And those who were good at teaching but were not that knowledgeable. Patrick Gardener was one of very few teachers who could successfully combine knowledge and inspiration.

But their respect for Patrick had been dented when, one day on the spur of the moment, Alex had googled what Patrick was saying. It turned out that he was reading almost verbatim from Wikipedia. She had told Jade and since that day Alex and Jade had made it a game to try to catch their teacher ripping off content from the Internet.

Jade had lost a lot of respect for Patrick, while Alex was more pragmatic. She had tried to get Jade to understand that all teachers memorized knowledge from some source or another, so why should it be any worse to quote from

Wikipedia? Alex was impressed that Patrick could present dull facts from Wikipedia in such an inspiring way.

Alex looked up from her computer and instead rested her eyes on the teacher. She could not help being drawn to his dynamic style. She found it attractive. Jade might frown at the idea of Alex getting involved with a teacher, but Alex's mother would most likely get very excited about a professor. OK, he was not a doctor, but a professor's title was status too. Alex made a disgusted face, and quickly tried to wipe away the thought of what her mother would think about who she was dating. Why should what her mother thought have an impact on who she liked? But yes, her mother would like his title. Alex liked his confident style on stage. And he was cute. Perhaps she should work up the confidence to ask him out on a date. Or not. She forced herself to focus on the teacher, instead of thinking of him.

While Patrick, a few minutes later, once again read out someone else's text as if it were his own, Alex decided to bookmark the site so that she could read the text later on. She started writing down several ideas for the project the teacher had assigned them. It was an assignment about myths and rituals, but she was not really that interested in writing an essay on the subject. She needed to try to find an angle that would help her feel more enthusiastic about the topic. After all, what did a course about myths and rituals have to do with her journalism studies? She found it difficult to see how she would become a better journalist by studying something that wasn't true.

The more she thought about the assignment, the more convinced she became that if she had to write about a myth, then it should at least be a myth that some people believed to be true.

Sitting on the floor at the very back of the hall, behind the last row of chairs, with his back to the wall, sat a young man. He seemed oblivious to the lecture. Instead, he studied a bumblebee that was flying around in the room. He followed it with his eyes. Every time the bumblebee took off and flew for a bit, the man smiled. It was as if the insect's movement was the most beautiful thing the man had ever seen. No one else in the room had even noticed that the little critter was there.

Chapter 3

‘Faith is your belief in the evidence of things unseen.’
– Shri Tulshi

Spring arrived early this year. The sky was crystal clear. It felt as if the sun was brighter than usual and as if everything in nature had become sharper and clearer.

This is a day for walking, Alex thought to herself, as she looked out of the bus window.

Alex could walk alone, for hours—enjoying nature and letting her thoughts wander. She had done a bit too much studying lately, and she could really use a break. If she would have realized how long it would take to find children with imaginary friends, she would probably have chosen another topic for her assignment. When Alex first had the idea to write her assignment about myths on stories about children with imaginary friends, she had loved how this would allow her to write about something contemporary—actual children with actual stories of invisible friends. She had classmates who wrote about old myths from hundreds of years ago, like trolls or elves, and Alex found that utterly uninteresting. At least she would be doing real interviews with real people about stories they thought were real. But now that she had started to do research on her selected topic it still did not excite her. She still could not understand how writing an assignment about myths would make her a better journalist.

To be honest, she was sick and tired of college assignments that she only had to do in order to give the teacher something to grade. Actually, she was fed up with studying. Of being in the intellectual vacuum that school really was. Of waiting to get the chance to do something for real. She really needed a break, even if it was only a short walk. But more than a break, she needed money. So a walk in the woods would have to give way to her weekend job. She decided to compromise with herself by getting off the bus a few stops too early and walk the rest of the way to work.

Alex had taken the job at the mental institution after dropping out of medical school, perhaps, she thought, it was a subconscious choice of employer to somehow show her family that she still had some connection to the medical field. Or just a way to feel sane by being able to be exposed to the people who were really mad.

She could see it now, the large, white, main building with the smaller wings standing on each side like bridesmaids next to a bride. The house gleamed palely.

'Why are mental institutions often so grand and beautiful?' she wondered. 'And why were they so often found in stunning locations? Was it to let the calm of nature cure the deranged minds of the mad? To use the peaceful environments to heal chaotic minds? Or was it just a perk to get people to want to work in these harsh institutions?'

She suddenly remembered a conference centre for the blind that she had once heard about. It was located at the top of a hill with, what must have been, amazing views. She still could not decide if it had been brilliant or absurd to construct a centre for the blind on a spot that had a breath-taking view. It's not like the blind would ever know. Her own conclusion had been that a venue with amazing scents and smells would have been more thoughtful of the blind than a venue with a great view.

The bus she had recently got off was starting its return journey from the last stop at the hospital. The driver looked at her grouchily. She smiled back. She was not going to let a bus driver with a bad day affect her own mood at work. Alex had noticed that it was much easier to work with the mentally ill if she was having a good day herself. The patients seemed to be especially good at sensing the emotions of the employees, and bad moods spread quickly. If there was one thing you did not want while working in a mental institution it was a situation where people were in a bad mood.

Looking after mental patients was hard enough on a good day. You should do everything you could to avoid the bad days. So Alex had to convince herself that she was having a good day. She stopped to breathe in the view while filling her lungs with fresh air. On the other side of the gate, the air was heavier. 'It'll be okay,' she said to convince herself. As long as she did not have to look after Gunnar.

She was afraid of Gunnar.

The man who had been in charge of watching the woman on the bus had gotten off at the same bus stop as her. But he did not follow her for long. Instead, he sat down on the grass some distance away from the hospital. No point getting too close to the Subject and scaring her. His colleagues in the main building would take over.

He would no longer watch the woman, but she would still be under observation. The man who had just finished surveillance duty wondered how long it would be before one of the people he was watching would make a mistake and reveal too much.

Chapter 4

'The sons of this world are more shrewd in dealing with their own generation than the sons of light.'
– Luke 16:8

'Alexandra, you get Gunnar.' Birgitte did not even look up from her papers as she allocated the day's duties to those just starting the Saturday morning shift.

'Why me? Can't someone else get him?' Alex said half-heartedly. A small part of her had to object, but deep inside she knew there was no point in trying to change Birgitte's mind. Birgitte had been working at the hospital for twenty-five years and she just wasn't the kind of person who would change her mind. Especially for someone who was not even a trained nurse, just some temporary staff. Alex's colleagues had told her to ignore Birgitte's rude and often downright nasty behaviour. That was just the way she treated new employees. But Alex sensed that Birgitte was especially tough on her because she was the daughter of the famous Doctor Johansen.

Instead of waiting for a degrading comment from Birgitte, Alex muttered, 'Never mind, I'll take Gunnar.' Then she left the room and headed over to her assigned ward. Alex told herself it would probably work out. It was a lovely day and she was going to have a good day at work.

A few minutes later Alex stood outside Gunnar's and Benjamin's room. She took one last deep breath to relax, and then she stepped into the room. The patients lived two-and-two in rooms as big as lecture halls. Well, to be honest, they were not really that big—they just felt like they were. Perhaps the high ceilings and large windows created the illusion of classrooms. Then there were plenty of things about the rooms that made them look nothing like classrooms. The fact that the beds, chairs and all the other large items were screwed to the floor, for example. Or that there were alarms installed on every window. Alex called them 'break-out alarms' as they were installed, not to catch intruders, but to detect if someone from within was trying to escape.

One of the patients, the one called Gunnar, sat hunched over a table in the middle of the room. Noticing her, he quickly put an arm over some papers. His piercing eyes made it quite clear that he did not want anyone to interfere with what he was doing. But Alex was not going to let herself be controlled by her patients. She was the one in charge, she was the one with the keys and it was she who decided if someone should be punished for bad behaviour or rewarded for behaving well.

'Hi, Gunnar, what are you working on?' she asked. 'Can I see?'

'Fuck off!'

'I don't think he wants to show you,' came a quiet monotone voice from the other end of the room. Gunnar's roommate, Benjamin, was curled up in a recess of one of the large windows. He sat with his elbows resting on his knees and his chin cupped in his hands. Benjamin was Gunnar's opposite: a very calm and small scrawny creature. If you did not know that he was mentally ill, it would have been easy to mistake Benjamin for a silent and contemplative young man. A poet perhaps. You wouldn't think he could hurt a fly. The fact that he had violently stabbed his mother to death with a sharpened toothbrush was something Alex still had problems comprehending.

Alex smiled at Benjamin. 'No, it doesn't look as if he wants to show us. What do you think he's hiding?'

Benjamin sank into his seat, glanced out of the window and said even more quietly, 'I don't think he wants to show you ... the drawings ...'

'Shut up!'

Gunnar got up and walked towards the window where Benjamin curled into a ball. Alex instinctively stood up to get ready to intervene, but after just a few steps Gunnar stopped, as if realizing that if he went after Benjamin the drawings would be exposed. Protecting the drawings was clearly more important than putting Benjamin in his place. He sat back down and covered the table with his arms while staring at Benjamin.

Alex tried again 'Come on, Gunnar, can't we see your nice sketches?' She took a step towards him. Gunnar leaned over the table even more and stuck all his pieces of paper under his chest.

Then the world seemed to explode. He pulled the drawings closer, even crunched one of the papers up and put it in his mouth. Alex reacted instinctively. She leaped forward, trying to get him to spit it out. But Gunnar did not back away, as she expected him to. Instead, he rushed up, took two quick steps towards her, grabbed her arm and dragged her over to the table before Alex even had a chance to react.

'Don't you fucking dare take things that isn't yours!'

As he roared, Gunnar pushed Alex harder and harder against the table. She panicked and tried to fight her way out of his grasp, but Gunnar was big. And strong. His thick, hairy arms pushed against her back and neck. It was becoming difficult to breathe. When she tried to scream, nothing came out. She sought to meet Gunnar's eyes but could not. In desperation she looked for Benjamin, but could not see him either. She cursed the fact that she had not taken her portable security alarm with her. She had meant to fetch it earlier, but then decided to look in on 'her' patients first. She could hear Birgitte's scornful comments about how important it was to follow procedure, but right now, Birgitte felt very insignificant. The only thing that mattered was to figure out a way to get out of Gunnar's grip. Quickly.

But she really had no defence left. He was stronger than she imagined. Or maybe she was weaker than she thought. She was fighting for her life and he was not even out of breath. Strangely enough, her mind decided to create a mental note to exercise more—self-defence, karate, perhaps. No, judo, she scribbled in her sub-consciousness while the conscious part of her brain tried to find a way for her to survive.

Suddenly her head slipped out of Gunnar's grip and she could breathe. Life-giving oxygen flowed into her lungs for a second. She also could see Benjamin. He was sitting in the window, looking out. Apparently utterly unaffected by what was happening just a few metres away.

It even looked as if he was smiling.

I'm going to die here, she thought. What an annoying way to die: strangled by a patient because she needed the money to pay the rent so that she would not have to live with her mother. She sighed inwardly while her lungs screamed for air. A devastating insight hit her: Someone like Gunnar, who was locked up indefinitely, had nothing to lose by killing someone on the staff. She felt sick and decided to make one last attempt to escape. To fight for her life not to end.

Then everything went black. The last thing she heard was the alarm screeching. She might also have heard footsteps outside the door as well as the door opening and the man screaming at someone to move away from the table. But maybe that was all just a dream. Because by then, everything had become very dark.

She was probably only unconscious for a few seconds, but before she really understood where she was and what had happened, her colleagues had overpowered Gunnar, taken him out of the room and even brought her a glass of water.

She was still sweating. Cold sweat. The drops of sweat lay like pearls on her forearms and she could feel them all over her face and neck. 'Why were they called beads of sweat?' she wondered, 'They don't look like beads. More like semi-circular balls of glass.' She smiled at her brain's way of dealing with a crisis by changing the topic of her inner dialogue.

She dried her face on the sleeve of her uniform.

'Are you alright?'

It was the new guy, whose name she had not learnt yet. She nodded and tried to look as if she meant it. She obviously wasn't all right. She was terrified. It was only now that she realized just how close it had been. She reflected on how our brains have evolved to let us ignore danger in the moment, only to reflect on the peril we were in once a crisis has passed.

'Miss Johansen!' Alex's thoughts were interrupted by Birgitte's shrill voice. 'Tidy up in here and make sure there are no objects left behind that can be used as weapons. Who thought it was a good idea to give them pencils?! And don't forget: we have an alarm procedure for a reason. The alarm is useless if you choose not to use it.'

Of course that bitch had already heard about the incident and, obviously she had come running to dole out some unhelpful advice. 'Here I nearly die and you order me to clean up?' she wanted to say. But she did not. She could not help wondering how Birgitte had become so heartless. Had she endured twenty-five years here because of that personality, or had she become like that after spending twenty-five years in this madhouse?

The stench of violence still hung in the air. She sat down and drank some water. It hurt when the water went down her throat. Alex glanced towards the spot where Benjamin had been sitting. The window was open. Benjamin must have opened it to set off the alarm and bring the security guards to her rescue. She wanted to thank him but that would have to wait. Right now she needed to be alone.

Alex declined all the thoughtful questions from staff that kept rushing in. Instead she asked to be left alone to clean up. She knew she probably needed to talk to someone, but her ambition to be a good girl had tricked even herself.

The thought of what would have happened if Benjamin had not opened the window buzzed around in her head and her heart raced even faster. The stress was pressing against her chest and she did not even notice that her legs had started to shake. When the tears finally came, she let them run down her cheeks until the first drops were just about to fall from her chin. Then she wiped the tears away, sniffed, took a deep breath and stood up.

She talked out loud, mimicking the tone of Birgitte, 'Now, Miss Johansen. Tidy up this room and make sure there are no objects that can be used as weapons.'

For the first time since the incident—that was what she decided to call it, 'the incident'—she noticed that some of the papers that Gunnar had tried to protect were still lying on the table. There were four empty, white sheets of paper that were slightly wrinkled. Gunnar must have managed to put the drawings face down when she came in. She turned over the first sheet.

In her hands she held a wonderful pencil drawing. She saw that the illustration was of the park outside the hospital. Judging by the angle, Alex guessed that the sketches were drawn from one of the windows in the room, perhaps the window that Benjamin had just opened.

The drawings were amazingly detailed, almost photorealistic. It seemed as if every leaf was included. A rake lay on the lawn with a garden hose next to it; a wheelbarrow was leaning against a tree. Every small object was painstakingly drawn, down to the smallest detail. Even the coloured flags on the old white park benches were included. But something was off. There were people in the pictures that Alex did not recognize. Two athletic men were sitting up in a tree and a small, slim woman rested on a bench. Alex could not stop looking at those people. They had something angel-like about them. But also, something disturbing. It was as if they did not quite fit in, as if they did not really belong there. And yet they looked so naturally comfortable there.

She did not know how long she sat there looking at the drawings, but she would never forget how she was jerked back to reality. A young nurse—she had not learnt his name either—tore open the door, looked at her with fear glued to his face. He screamed, 'Come and help!' The nurse was probably not aware of what she had just gone through.

Before running out to help, she quickly gathered up the drawings, put them inside her waistband, and pulled down her shirt over her trousers. Only Gunnar and Benjamin knew about the drawings and it was only right that they should now be hers. Confiscating the drawings was her tiny revenge for Gunnar trying to kill her.

When she rushed through the door, she saw a group of colleagues huddled down at the end of the corridor. Benjamin was gazing out of the window while two nurses pressed him up against the wall. Gunnar was lying motionless on the floor with three men piled on top of him. But Alex ignored all of that. The only thing she really saw was Birgitte. How she lay on the ground face down and with arms spread out in an unnatural position. Her white coat had ridden up at the back and you could see almost all of her flesh-coloured tights. Alex saw all that, yet it did not sink in. Instead, she stared at the irregular deep red stain that Birgitte was lying in. It took her several seconds to understand that Birgitte was lying in a pool of her own blood.

When she caught sight of the sharpened blue toothbrush lying next to the dead woman, she looked worriedly at Benjamin, who was still looking out of the window. Alex's gaze was drawn back to the dark pool on the floor and to the lifeless body that had shouted at her only a few minutes earlier. It was obvious that Birgitte would never scream at anyone again. The comprehension of what had happened rolled over her like a shockwave. Birgitte was dead. Murdered just a few metres away. Alex marvelled at the way her eyes went all blurry. She was going to faint again. When her knees gave way, she let out a surprised moan as she made a half-hearted attempt to protect her head with her hands as she fell to the floor.

A few months later, an internal investigation would come to the conclusion that Benjamin had probably given the sharpened toothbrush to Gunnar, who had then stabbed Birgitte eight times in the throat and back. At least three of the stabs had hit the jugular vein. Neither of the two suspects had ever talked about what happened so it could never be proved which one of them had struck the fatal blows.

The investigation also noted that if Birgitte had been carrying the prescribed alarm button at the time, she most likely would have survived the attack.

While everyone in the corridor was staring at the dead body, a woman grasped the opportunity and slipped out without anyone noticing. She had hidden in the stairwell when panic broke out and now that everyone thought it was over, she saw her chance. She had to report what had just happened; this news was far too important to send via a messenger. She had to deliver this in person.

The woman knew she had reacted too late and that she would be criticised for doing so. It was unfortunate that someone had died, but it was even more of a problem that that woman had managed to get her hands on some of the drawings. Physical evidence in the wrong hands was never a good thing.

The woman knew she had made a mistake. But if she could report it quickly and come up with a suggestion as to how to solve the problem, then perhaps she could come out of this situation okay.

She thought about what she had been taught: *To make a mistake is not to err. But to not correct your mistakes is the biggest mistake you can ever make*. And this was one mistake she was definitely going to correct.

Chapter 5

'Pray that your loneliness may spur you into finding something to live for, great enough to die for.'
– Dag Hammarskjöld

Time off had been good for Alex. She had been offered eight days' leave with full pay in order to 'work through her feelings'. That she had eagerly accepted. She had also been invited to talk to a psychologist. That she had annoyingly declined. She did not want to sit down with a psychologist and be treated like a mental case when all she wanted to do was to get as far away as possible from the world of psychiatric care.

Instead of using her paid leave to work through her feelings, she had thrown herself into her school assignment. It had felt like the best way to get over what had happened would be to concentrate on something concrete. She had been very productive and her assignment was coming along really well. The project web site was up. It featured a request to get in contact with children who had imaginary friends. It was a fairly simple site with a page describing the background to her project and another one outlining the kind of stories she was interested in. She also had a contact page encouraging people to send in their stories via e-mail. Alex had included a picture of herself to make the whole thing a bit more personal.

By mailing various children's organizations and asking them to help spread the word she had quickly been able to build up a respectable number of visitors to the site. She also joined a mailing list for former journalist students and explained what her project was about. After that, a few of them wrote articles about her project, which meant that the number of visitors to her site increased even more.

Today, however, she was not going to work on her website. Today, she was going to have her first interview since the incident.

She had put off her interview with Eric for almost a week, not because she would have any problems conducting it, but because she just could not face meeting Laura. Eric was Alex's brother's oldest son and the reason for why Alex had chosen to do her project on imaginary friends. Eric lived in a world that was richer than everyone else's. He had a vivid imagination that Alex found fascinating. Alex saw it as her duty to do what she could to make sure that her nephew never lost his unique ability to make up stories.

How a child with a father as logical as her brother, and with a mother as nervous as Laura, could have such an inventive brain was a mystery. Alex often teased her brother by asking him if their mailman had been unusually good-looking and creative.

'Laura says hi and hopes you're feeling better,' Daniel called out to his sister after showing her to the living room and going to the kitchen to fix something to eat.

Alex had deliberately chosen a Thursday evening for the interview as she knew Laura took Junior to his baby swimming classes then. At least now she did not have to hear her sister-in-law's sympathetic comments about how 'terrible' it was to have experienced such a 'terrible event'. With Laura out of the house, Daniel could play the part of bantering brother instead of playing the more annoying part of family man.

'The next time some madman threatens to kick your ass, just tell him your brother will come over and beat him up.' Daniel had said to her the first time she told him about what had happened. Her brother had some personal development work to do in the area of having difficult conversations. But he had offered to give Alex a prescription for tranquillizers if she was finding it difficult to sleep. While she had turned him down, she had appreciated the gesture. She had felt that he was looking out for her.

Daniel came in with a tray full of cookies and Eric walked beside him carrying a large jug of juice. Eric poured the drink into the glasses himself, his tongue poking out of his mouth as he concentrated on not spilling a drop. He served Alex with a tea towel on his arm. 'Bon appétit,' the boy announced as if he were the headwaiter in a fancy restaurant.

Alex played along. 'Everything looks absolutely charming!'

Daniel rolled his eyes, 'I'll leave you two actors here to play with each other. If you want anything, I'll be in my study.'

'The Master Chef seems to be in a bad mood today,' Alex laughed. But then she cleared her throat and prepared for a more serious and formal interview with her nephew.

It probably was not very professional to interview a relative for her assignment, so she had decided to conduct the interview as the journalist student she was—and not as Auntie Alex. No one at the college needed to know that one of the children in her research group was her relative. She asked the child to sit down, turned on the recording function on her phone and gauged that her nephew was now ready to be interviewed. Alex asked Eric to tell her about those imaginary friends of his.

Eric immediately became more serious, the playfulness in his eyes was gone. When he showed her how his invisible friend usually sat in the living room during the day while his father was at work, he was not role-playing anymore. He was demonstrating. He sat down on the floor crossed legs, and arms down by his side. His face showing no emotions.

'Are you meditating?' Alex smiled. Eric jumped up. And ran around the apartment as fast as he could.

'What are you now? A jaguar?'

Eric stopped. 'You said you wanted to know what my secret friends do, so I'm showing you. They can run really fast.'

The boy stopped and took small, careful steps towards the sofa where Alex was sitting. As he tiptoed, he held out his hands to keep his balance better.

'What are you now? A spy?'

'He likes to be secret,' the four-year-old boy explained to his ignorant aunt.

Then, without any warning, he put his hands around Alex's neck and started to squeeze, first gently, then harder and harder.

The feeling of having a pair of hands around her neck brought back nightmares from the incident with Gunnar. Her heart raced while her mind black-outed. She broke free and yelled, 'Eric! What are you doing?!'

Eric shrugged and whispered, 'Do or don't. Die or live.'

'Don't say that. Who taught you that?'

'He did. He's here. Everywhere. All the time.'

Alex asked him to sit down and explain what he meant. The longer the interview progressed, the more uncomfortable she felt. As if she was eavesdropping on something she was not really meant to hear.

In the room next door, Daniel crouched behind the door he had left slightly open. He could hear his sister without any problem but Eric spoke unusually softly and he really had to strain to hear what his son was saying. He wrote as much as he could on a pad of paper on the floor. As the conversation progressed, his handwriting got more and more aggressive.

As he wrote 'He is here. All the time,' he underlined the words with thick, heavy lines.

His suspicions had been right . . . That fucking bitch! He was too upset to think about a strategy. But that could wait. After all, they said revenge was a dish best served cold.

'We'll need reinforcements. I suggest sending a Mediator. Better to be cautious today than sorry tomorrow. The woman looked straight ahead as she spoke. Her white hair was tinged with gray strains and her long fringe framed her face so that you could hardly see her eyes.

She looked at her two colleagues sitting next to her and they nodded in agreement. They moved on to the next item on the agenda. So many decisions still to be made.

Chapter 6

'The important thing is not to stop questioning.
Curiosity has its own reason for existing.
One cannot help but be in awe when he contemplates the mysteries of eternity, of life, of the marvellous structure of reality.
It is enough if one tries merely to comprehend a little of this mystery every day.'
– Albert Einstein

'Who are you?'

The voice behind Alex was sharp in the way a short person tries to raise her voice to create authority to compensate for her lack of height. And sure enough, when Alex turned around, she saw a woman in her thirties with her arms crossed, trying to look stern. She could not have been more than one and a half metres tall.

'And whom may you be yourself?' replied Alex a little too sharply as she looked down at the woman standing in front of her.

Alex was not particularly tall herself at 1.7 metres, but she felt much taller in this moment. Alex was not merely another insecure parent whom the kindergarten teacher could run circles around. No, Alex was a journalist—well, technically she was just a journalism student, but this was a good time to practise creating some authority. Even if Alex understood the importance for reporters to probe, investigate, push for answers and never be intimidated, that kind of behaviour was not really her style. She had to become better at it, and to become better she needed to practice. This tiny little kindergarten teacher seemed an appropriate person to practice on.

The little woman spoke again, 'My name is Charlotte and I am actually in charge here, and we don't just let strangers wander around. As far as I know, you're not related to any of the children here, so I'd like you to leave now, please.'

Actually in charge, Alex thought. *What do you mean by 'actually'?* Here was yet another insecure person who had to make up excuses for her leadership and who thought that she would get the upper hand by talking in long, rapid sentences so that the other person could not reply without interrupting. How very tiring. So, this would be yet another difficult interview? All the interviews she had done, apart from the initial one with Eric almost a week ago, had been difficult to do in one way or another.

Well, this was the eighth school Alex had visited, so she had heard one form or another of this lecture many times before. She also knew how to deal with the teachers to get them on her side. Instead of snubbing the woman, Alex explained that she was studying journalism and that she had chosen to write about children because 'children are the most treasured assets in our society' while all her classmates were writing about global warming, the stock market or world trade.

After that, all she had to do was to wait for the obligatory sermon about how wrong it was that men who worked with machines were better paid than women who worked with children. Finally, she just needed to agree to that and the kindergarten teachers and she were best buddies.

Today's teacher was no exception. After just a few minutes she had gone from angry foe to cooperative friend wanting to help in any way she could to get more media attention on 'the very important work of women who work with children'.

Alex explained that her project was about children with imaginary friends. A few minutes later, the woman returned with a list of children's names and the phone numbers and addresses of families that might be interested in her project. Alex was surprised by how easy it had been to get hold of the home addresses of children, especially when considering the current fear of paedophiles. To be fair: a female paedophilic journalist was probably rather unlikely but it was still unsettling to think how easy it had been.

After a day of wooing kindergarten teachers, Alex had managed to contact eleven parents with kids who had imaginary friends. Five of them had agreed to meet her.

The first interviews had frankly not been very fruitful, partly because Alex was not that experienced in doing interviews. Some of Alex's classmates had chosen journalism because they liked people. Alex did not belong to this group. She wanted to see connections and use the media to focus on the injustices of the world. And she was curious. However, she was not the type of person who would stop an old lady on the street to interview her because she believed that 'everyone had a story to tell'. Alex needed a larger context if she was to get really involved in an interview and the interviews she was doing for this assignment just did not give her that. Alex could get along well with the kids, but it was the parents that were the problem. And if you were going to interview a child, then you could be absolutely certain the parents would want to sit in.

Standing outside the house where the child for her next interview lived, Alex started questioning her whole project. The thought of having to interact with yet another over-protective parent in order to hear the views of a child was becoming increasingly off-putting. For this interview she decided to just ignore the parents and concentrate on talking directly to the child.

A woman with her five-year-old daughter clinging shyly to her legs opened the door. Alex introduced herself to the mother and said, 'You must be Mary.' Then she bent down, smiled at the girl, and said, 'And then you must be Saga.'

The interview was conducted in the kitchen with milk and cookies as props. The kitchen was meticulously cleaned and organized. Alex noticed small crucifixes above both doors leading into the room, as well as one hanging over the oven, and one—a cheesy fridge magnet cross-sitting on the refrigerator and holding a pamphlet from a church. As predicted, the mother had to hang around.

At first Saga answered Alex's questions in monosyllables, but after a while, she relaxed and her answers got longer and more detailed. She spoke with a soft and quiet voice, but it was a voice that invited you to take her seriously.

She told Alex why parents could not see the invisible creatures under the bed. 'If adults sit down to put their hands under the bed, the invisible have already crawled out from under the bed,' she explained. 'And besides, you can't see them anyway, because you have stopped looking.'

Alex did not know why she thought this was such an interesting answer; perhaps it was because the girl said it as if she were revealing a secret.

Unfortunately, Saga did not get the chance to say much more. Her over-protective mother, who had been sitting just next to the girl during the interview, raised her hand to cut the interview short. 'Let's stop here. It can hardly be healthy for a child to recite her daydreams.'

While the mother turned her back on them to put away the milk in the refrigerator, the girl sneaked up to Alex and pulled her out of the kitchen and into the hallway. She had a drawing in her hand. 'Here,' the girl whispered. 'You can have this. So you can see what they look like. But don't tell anyone you got the drawing from me. If they find out you have the drawing, you could die. Killed by the Killers.'

Alex looked at her in surprise.

'But Saga, don't talk like that.'

Saga looked down at her own hands. 'I'm just telling you the truth. Tell anyone about the drawing, and you die.' Then she ran up to her room.

Had a little child just threatened to have her killed? Alex did not know whether to laugh or cry. Part of her wanted to reprimand the mother for having such a rude child, while another part of her strongly felt that the right thing to do was go after the girl and ask her some more questions. While she stood there wondering what to do next, Saga's mother came into the hallway and walked straight to the front door. She opened the door demonstratively. Alex had overstayed her welcome. She thanked the mother for being part of her project and left.

On the bus home, Alex looked at the drawing. The first thing that struck her was how expressive it was, even though it was clearly done by a child. The drawing was full of people and, in the background, there were some pyramids floating upside down. Some of the people walked hand in hand; others seemed to be sneaking around a corner. One person was standing and praying towards the blue sky. The praying woman had a snake around her neck and dark rings under her eyes, as if she had not slept for a very long time. In one corner of the picture, with a big smile on her face, stood a little girl. Everything felt unreal. The feeling was strengthened by the fact that while all the objects in the picture were coloured in bright colours, all the humans—and the snake—were left uncoloured. Their skin and hair shining white as the paper. All the people were left uncoloured, all, except the happy, little girl in the corner, who had been given a light-yellow skin tone and some red cheeks.

Looking at the drawing made Alex uneasy. She felt as if she had done something wrong, as if she had stolen the drawing from someone or that someone was observing her with disapproval. She folded the drawing away and turned around. No one was paying her any attention, so why did she feel as if someone was watching her? The girl had given her the drawing as a gift so why did it still feel so wrong to have accepted it?

Saga gazed out of her window. Next to the girl, on the window ledge, sat a white dove. Saga patted the bird on its head and it cooed softly.

'Thanks for hiding up here,' the girl said. 'I don't think I could have pretended to be so normal if you had been downstairs with us.'

The door swung open and the girl's mother stood in the doorway.

'Saga, who are you talking to?'

'I'm not talking to anyone,' the girl replied. 'I was just singing.'

Chapter 7

'Vision is the art of seeing what is invisible to others.'
– Jonathan Swift

Alex had suggested meeting at her favourite Starbucks, which was located on a side street near the university.

She did not have any problems locating the person she was supposed to meet, even if they had never met. Sometimes you got a picture in your head of what someone looked like by just hearing their voice. And when the man she was meeting had called her the previous day, she got a picture of a dark-haired, handsome and slightly mysterious person.

The dark-haired bit turned out to be completely wrong, but the rest was spot on. The man sitting at the table looked undeniably mysterious. Or, to be more precise, he looked intriguing in an unusual way. It was not exactly normal to go into a coffee shop and see someone wearing a completely white three-piece-suit. What was it about certain people that meant they could wear the strangest things and get away with it, when nearly everyone else would look ridiculous in the same outfit? It made Alex think of a photo she had once seen of a sexy, manly, David Beckham wearing a skirt.

The man she was meeting had that same aura of being comfortable in his own skin. As if he was surrounded by a protective layer of self-confidence. Or would that be self-esteem? Or was it both? It was not only his white suit that made him stand out, however. His unusually pale skin made you look twice.

After receiving her order from the barista, Alex hesitated to go and meet her appointment. Instead she just stood and looked at him for a little bit too long, while she tried to convince herself to walk over and introduce herself. Finally, taking her courage in both hands, she approached his table.

'Is it okay to be blind as a teacher?' Alex had noticed his white cane leaning against the table.

The man looked up and smiled behind a pair of sunglasses. 'Alex, I presume?'

She swore in silence over her habit of talking without thinking.

'Oh, I'm sorry! I just . . .'

'It's OK. Sit down.'

Alex sat down, and put down her cup of coffee on the table.

'Adam. But I'm guessing you already knew that.'

The man stretched out his hand over the table. Alex hesitated for a fraction of a second, before accepting it. His pale skin had distracted her. It was unfamiliarly white. She noticed that he was wearing a silver ring shaped like a bamboo pole that coiled itself around his right ring finger.

'Um . . . yes. I'm Alex. And I am really very sorry for . . .'

Adam interrupted.

'Your reaction is quite common. A lot of people can't wrap their heads around the idea of a blind albino working as a kindergarten teacher.'

'But . . .'

'Well, first off, I'm not blind. I'm severely visually impaired. And secondly, the kids at my school have absolutely no problem with the fact that one of their teachers can't see so well.'

'I was thinking more of the parents. That they . . .'

Adam broke in again. Alex had a tendency to get annoyed at people who interrupted her, but this man did it so unobtrusively that she found herself not minding.

'You're right. The parents are a bigger problem than the children. Ironically, most often their biggest problem isn't that I'm visually impaired, but that my skin, and hair, is unusually white.'

'Anything unusual makes people uncomfortable. And you albinos are uncommon.'

Was the phrase 'you albinos' really politically correct? Alex became more and more annoyed with how her words decided to come out of her mouth.

'Yes. And there is a lot of ignorance about albinism. Like the common misconception that all albinos have pink eyes, or that we are all blind.'

'I really don't have any problem with the fact that you're . . .'

Once again, Alex heard how her words kept jumping out of her mouth in the wrong order. With every sentence she completed she seemed to be digging herself a deeper hole.

'I know.' Adam said before continuing. 'But can we stop talking about the prejudices people have about my skin, and get onto the topic we're both here to talk about?'

Alex was grateful for the lifeline she had been thrown. She took her notebook out of her bag and, while she kept looking for her pen, she took a closer look at the man.

There really was something unusual about him. It was not just the fact that he was an albino, or that he worked as a male kindergarten teacher. He was just so different from the other men she had met at the kindergartens. Actually, he was different from any other man Alex had met. He was stately. That was an unusually old-fashioned word to use when describing a person. But she could not help it, because that was what he was: Stately. Beautiful in a magnificent way. When she thought that she had never met anyone quite like him she meant that as a compliment.

Adam had contacted her via e-mail after discovering her website. Alex could divide those who contacted her about her project into two groups: the interesting and the uninteresting. The interesting were parents, or teachers, who had kids with imaginary friends and who were willing to discuss the topic with her. Everyone else ended up in the uninteresting category. Like the man who had asked her to send him photos of the children she had interviewed. He had quickly hung up once she asked him what his name was. Then there was that angry woman who wondered if this was where all her tax money was going. In other words, nutcases with too much time on their hands. Uninteresting.

When it came to today's interview, she found it difficult at first to decide which category Adam belonged to. On the one hand, he was 'interesting' because he said he worked with children who had lively imaginations. On the other hand, after introducing himself, his first question had been, 'How many people know about your project?' Unlike the others, he had not asked a lot of check questions or demanded references. Quite the contrary—he had been a little bit too eager to be interviewed. Alex had quickly learned that people who were too eager to meet up were usually people to be avoided.

However, Alex had been captivated by his voice on the phone. His voice was tender, yet persuasive. His choice of words thoughtful and deliberate. Apparently you could be soft-spoken, without coming across as soft.

When he asked her if they could meet, she answered, 'Sure. When works for you?' It was only after they hung up that she reflected over how anxious he had been to meet up. And how eager she had come across as well.

While she was looking through her bag for that pen, and remembering their phone conversation, she missed the first part of what he was saying. ' . . . so adults have a tendency to over-interpret children's stories. For example, it has been shown that children who are witnesses at the trials of paedophiles often make up large parts of their stories.'

She found a pen and refocussed her attention on the conversation. 'You mean the victims of paedophiles lie?'

He answered, 'We hear what we want to hear in stories. That's what makes paedophile trials so treacherous. Since the crime is so horrifying, the police do everything they can to convict the accused. Unfortunately, the interrogating officers can sometimes try too hard, so they ask leading questions and only hear the answers they want to hear. Children desperately want to give the right answers. And later on, they cannot back down. Impressions become fantasies and fantasies become the truth.'

'So are you saying that the kids are making up stories?' Alex was confused.

'You're not listening. I don't mean that—quite the opposite. But as I just said, paedophile cases are so serious, which is why it's vital that we do things right.'

'We'? Do blind albinos work in teams? Alex thought to herself, taking a sip of her coffee.

Adam continued, 'I sometimes train the police in how to interpret children's stories. Some children suppress the truth and make up another reality because the truth hurts too much. It's important to be able to see through these imaginary walls of self-defence.'

'So how do you know when a kid is telling the truth?' Alex moved a little closer to Adam. She wanted to understand what he said; she enjoyed listening to him.

'Everything a small child says is true. For that child. Whether it's true in our world is a different matter. My advice to you is: don't overanalyse children's stories to make them fit your hypothesis. Just like horoscopes, you can make children's stories mean anything.'

'So you don't believe my theory that children have a universal imaginary world?'

'Let me put it this way—I think you're being too ambitious in trying to find a truth in a collection of fantasies.'

'So, you're implying that I'm just making it all up?' She put down her cup abruptly, spilling some of her coffee.

'Let me ask you something: do you believe in UFOs?'

'Of course not!' She took a deep breath. 'I think the likelihood of life on another planet is statistically probable. And if I'm not mistaken, ten years ago we hadn't even identified a planet similar to Earth, whereas nowadays we find a couple of Earth-like planets every month. So yes, I do believe there's life on other planets. But that doesn't mean I think they come here in spaceships to leave messages in wheat fields.'

Adam kept his cool and spoke as calmly as he had before. He chose his words with care. 'Nearly everyone who says they have seen a UFO describe it as a fast-flying saucer-like ship that emits a strong light. Just because everyone says the same thing—does that mean there really are flying saucers full of aliens? Or does it mean that a myth has become a truth and that UFO enthusiasts are just connecting their stories to an established truth that makes those stories truer?'

'So now you're calling me a crazy UFO believer?' Alex smiled and crossed her arms.

Adam looked at her serenely. His arms rested confidently on the table. 'All I'm saying is: don't be too eager. Marvel at what the kids have to say, but don't destroy the magic of their stories by looking for a logical pattern that doesn't exist. Your college assignment is to describe a myth—not to find a truth.'

Alex leaned back in her chair. She lowered her rhetorical defences. 'You have a point.'

'It's getting dark, Alex. I have to get home.'

Alex could not help asking, 'How on earth can darkness affect a blind man?' Then she bit her lip.

Adam explained that sighted people seemed to find it more difficult to notice his cane in the dark, and that drivers could not see him as well. They decided to meet again soon and Adam left the restaurant with surprising ease, leaving Alex alone with her thoughts. His words about not looking for patterns that were not there hung in the air, like mist on a field.

Perhaps her imagination was really running away with her. Perhaps she was trying too hard to hear what she wanted to hear in those stories the children told her.

On the other hand, she could not ignore the feeling that the picture that these children were collectively painting for her made her uneasy. One night she had woken up in the middle of a dream with the feeling that there was someone else in the room. Sitting there in the café, she thought back to that night, to that strange feeling in her stomach. The feeling had been so intense that she had switched on the bedside lamp to convince herself that she was really alone. And, of course, there was no one there. But neither the bright light of the lamp, nor her nervous laughter, had dispelled that uncomfortable feeling of being watched. As she tried to go back to sleep, she remembered the last part of her dream. In her dream, Eric had looked at her with serious eyes and said, 'He's here. Everywhere. All the time.'

Alex lay there in the dark, remembering the boy's serious eyes, and what he had said. She would not be able to sleep if she did not find the answer to what was keeping her awake.

She got up, found the notes from her interview with Eric, and started to read:

Eric: 'He's here. Everywhere. All the time.'

Me: 'Eric, are you all right? You look scared. Who are these invisible people?'

Eric: 'It's not me who's afraid; it's you, the adults, who should be afraid. Afraid for your lives.'

Me: 'Can you tell me a bit more about them?'

Eric: 'They don't want us to know that they exist. But they do. Because I've seen them. But I'm not going to tell.'

Me: 'Please—I want to know more. Tell me more.'

Eric: 'Can we stop now? I'm tired. I don't want to talk about this anymore. Can we stop? Daddy!'

The next day, as she had sat looking through her notes and remembering her dream, she had the uneasy feeling that the stories she had listened to weren't just stories. All the children talked about their invisible friends with a respect she had not expected.

There was something about the stories that was not right. Was she too logical and single-minded when interviewing the children? Or was it a lack of imagination from her side? She decided to change tactics at her next interview. To ask more intimate questions.

And she would update her website with a text saying she was very keen on hearing stories from children whose imaginary friends were very pale or transparent. That is how a lot of children described their friends. Was it just coincidence or were the stories connected?

Earlier on, she had uploaded one of the drawings that Gunnar had tried to hide. There was something about it that conveyed so well what the children described. Underneath the drawing, she had written: 'Artist's reconstruction of a child's imaginary world.'

Something touched her hair and in the blink of an eye she was pulled away from her thoughts and found herself back in the café. Someone had walked by too close, and she looked up. No one was there. She tried to come up with a logical explanation, and saw a young man, who was obviously annoyed, slamming the door shut. 'Close the damned door, people!' a man yelled after a couple that had just left the café without closing the door behind them.

Alex zipped up her hoodie and carelessly wound her scarf around her neck. She felt cold. She wanted to get home quickly—and yet she did not. She wished she had someone to cuddle up with. The thought of going to bed alone bothered her. It had never bothered her before.

She walked out into the darkness. It did not rain. But it felt like it did.

When the woman got startled, the man watching her knew he had come too close. He had been forced to lean against her to let some people pass. When she had reacted to his presence, he had withdrawn.

It was important that humans perceived the world as normal. That their trust in 'the real world' was strong enough to blind them from seeing 'the true world'. That they did not understand how unreal their real life was.

Chapter 8

'You cannot depend on your eyes when your imagination is out of focus.'
– Mark Twain

Someone knocked on Alex's door. The doorbell to her apartment did not work, so she had put a note on the door that read: 'Doorbell out of order. Do what they did in the 1800s: knock!'

Before she got to the door she heard another knock. This time a little harder. A little longer.

'Alex!'

The person was calling her name through the door. She looked through the peephole and could make out the outline of a man. He looked old and was wearing brown corduroy pants. The kind professors wear.

Her initial reaction was disappointment. She had hoped that it would have been Adam. She had thought a lot about him since their meeting the night before.

She opened the door. The man really did look like a professor, also without the distorting lens of the peephole, and he seemed harmless. She relaxed a little.

'Are you alone?'

Alex quickly closed the door a bit. 'Who are you?'

'My name is Charles Williams, but my friends always call me Mr Williams. I've seen your web site where you ask people to send in stories of children with imaginary friends. I especially noticed your interest in stories about pale imaginary people.'

She opened the door a little more, but showed no signs of wanting to let him in. The man who stood outside the door looked uncomfortable—like an awkward door-to-door salesman on his first day at work. It was obvious that Mr Williams belonged to the uninteresting category, so Alex decided to finish off the conversation as fast as she could.

'If you have some examples you want to share with me, then you can send me an email like everyone else. Don't take this the wrong way—but what made you think it was a good idea just to turn up on my doorstep at ten o'clock at night? And, by the way, how did you get my address?'

'It isn't exactly difficult to find someone's address in today's digital world. Surely you, a journalism student, would know that?' The man held up a smartphone. 'All it takes are a few quick database searches and a couple of well-chosen phone calls and you can find a lot of interesting information about a person—if you just know where to look. For example, I was not surprised to find out that you decided to study medicine as you're a doctor's daughter, but flunking so many of the courses was, perhaps, more unexpected.'

Alex scrutinized him. 'What are you doing here?!'

'I'm here to save your life.'

She had had enough. 'Look—it's not funny. I'm going to shut the door. And if you don't go away, I'll call the police.'

The man started talking faster in order to say as much as possible before getting the door slammed in his face. 'Have you started wondering if the white people are more than just myths? That there is some truth in these stories? That . . .'

Alex slammed the door and put on the safety chain. Through the door, she called, 'I'm calling the cops now. Can you please just leave?'

But Mr Williams did not seem to take her words seriously. He kept on talking even faster and louder. 'I guess that the drawing you put up on your site, the one with the very pale people, isn't really drawn by an artist, is it? I'd say that it was done by a mental patient. And perhaps you're wondering if that someone is really mentally ill or just pretending?'

'Go away or I'll call the police! I mean it.'

Alex heard a noise outside the door and hoped that he had finally gotten the message. She ran into the kitchen and turned off the light before going to the window to look outside. If she hid behind the curtains and peeked out through the small gap between the curtains and the window, she could see the entrance to her building without being seen.

The man calling himself Mr Williams opened the main door and walked out. But, before the door slammed shut, he put something between the door and the frame. Was he trying to prop open the door so that he could sneak in later? Alex was furious. It was one thing to come to her house unexpectedly, but quite another to prepare for a crime. Who the hell did he think he was?

When he saw him walking across the street to stand at the entrance directly opposite hers, she had had enough. Alex hurried out of her apartment and sneaked out of the building through the back door. She then ran around the building, across the street and into the garden of the building opposite, where she unlocked the back door. All the doors on the block could be opened with the same keys as some of the tenants had their storage rooms in different buildings.

The man was still leaning against the wall next to the entrance. He was so preoccupied watching her apartment that he did not notice her coming.

When she was less than a metre away she burst out from behind him: 'What the hell do you think you're doing?'

Mr Williams was startled. 'You scared me!'

'I? Scared you? And what do you think you did when you knocked on my door in the middle of the night to threaten me?'

Alex expected him to start arguing back, but instead of defending himself, Mr Williams took out an envelope, opened it and held out a piece of paper that he gave to Alex. 'Here,' he said.

She stared at the paper he had unfolded. It was another incredibly beautiful drawing.

In the foreground, among some trees, were a group of soldiers standing attention. Next to a road winding away into the landscape was an entourage on horseback riding towards a large open field. Over the field hoovered two structures that looked like enormous upside-down pyramids. They were at least fifty metres tall and balanced on their tips. Out of the pyramid tips—the parts resting close to the ground—a stream of people was pouring out and running into the woods. All the people in the picture were white. Not white as in Caucasian white, but white as in white as snow. Some of the people had beautiful white snakes coiled around their necks. The drawing made Alex's heart beat faster.

Her brain started to think about something vaguely related and less threatening, as it often did when she was stressed or afraid. She remembered that the Chinese sign for 'afraid' consisted of the sign for 'white' and the sign for 'heart'. *A white heart—that really is what it feels like to be afraid*, she thought. And right now, she was terrified, her hands shaking. She did not really understand what made her so uncomfortable, and that uncertainty made her even more uneasy.

Her first reaction was to run back home, but strangely enough, the idea of being at home, alone, scared her even more. And it obviously was not Mr Williams she was afraid of anyway—it felt more as if he had come to warn her. She felt more tense by the fact that she had such an inexplicably strong reaction to a drawing. Was it because of the snakes? Was it an exaggerated fear caused by a phobia?

'It must have been easy to find out about my weekend job at the mental institution, but how could you know that I wasn't sure if the person who did the drawing was sick or not?'

'Because it looks just like my painting, and I got mine from a patient in a mental institution too. There are many like these. Alex, I believe we have a common interest in these drawings. And I'm serious about your life being in danger. But we can't talk out here in the open. Let me come in and I promise I'll explain it better.'

Alex hesitated for a while, but then decided to listen to the man. Perhaps she was curious to know more. She led Mr Williams back across the street and into her own building. When they got into her apartment, she saw how messy it was. Somehow this fact made the whole situation less tense.

She went into the kitchen to make some tea. When she came back into the living room, Mr Williams was sitting on her sofa with his hands on his knees. He had not even dared move the clothes that she had thrown over the back of the sofa. Instead, he perched on the cushions like a little boy visiting his Sunday School teacher. Perhaps she should have served milk and cookies instead?

However, when Alex put down the cups of tea and curled up on the sofa, Mr Williams gradually changed personality. He looked at her gravely and said, 'Now it's your turn to listen to me.'

A frustrated Watcher sat on the steps outside the Subject's building. He knew that it was in the mission's nature that he would not always be able to follow his Subject. A Watcher was supposed to watch and watching meant seeing. But to not be seen was more important than to see. If he had to choose between taking a risk to follow his Subject, or to wait to avoid any unnecessary confrontation, his orders were crystal clear: wait rather than watch.

As a Watcher you just had to accept that sometimes you temporarily lost contact with the Subject. Temporary loss of control was nothing compared to the risk of potentially losing the whole operation. At all cost he had to avoid creating a situation where the Subject became a Knower. In this case it meant he had to step down and stand by.

He silently repeated the words: 'Courage can mean being patient. And being patient requires courage.'

Chapter 9

'Man is equally incapable of seeing the nothingness from which he emerges and the infinity in which he is engulfed.'
– Blaise Pascal

Maternity wards are usually a hospital's most buoyant place, with their life-giving energy and loving beginnings. But when something went wrong there, they became, not only the saddest place in the hospital, but the saddest place on earth.

Today was one of those days. The perfect little baby-girl got to live for less than a day.

The ward was wrapped up in a black fog of emptiness. The infinite silence of a newborn child that had just passed away is eerie.

Two nurses who were trying to comfort the grieving parents explained that nothing could have been done to save their baby.

Daniel, who had stood a bit to the side to let the nurses do their job, felt he had to step in and save the situation.

'Nothing you could do?!' the husband of the woman who had just lost her child was furious. It felt wrong for Daniel to think of the man as 'the father'—the man hadn't really gotten a chance to step into the role of father before the child had died—so Daniel thought of him as 'the husband of the mother'. Women became mothers as soon as they got pregnant. Men became fathers first after the baby was born. That's why losing a child was often much harder on the women.

'Of course there were things we could do. Please forgive my colleagues.'

Daniel's body language gestured to the two nurses that he would take over, and they gratefully backed-off from the awkward situation.

In a voice that was calm and trust giving he continued speaking to the man, 'I think what the nurses were trying to tell you was that we did everything that we could.'

Daniel, who had been on duty, had been called in to help. But as a surgeon there really was not much he could do. Surgeons could save lives, even sometimes bring people back from the dead, but they could not save a life that was gone. And this tiny life was long gone. He was partly there so that the hospital could later say it had called on all its possible resources. But he also knew that one of the reasons he was called into situations like this was because he was good at dealing with grieving parents. The hospital thought it was because he was empathetic, but Daniel himself thought it was because of his rhetorical skills. He knew, for example, that if you said 'There was nothing else we could have done' all the parents heard was 'We did nothing'. But if you said: 'We did everything we could' the parents heard 'We did everything'.

How you said things was as important as what you said, if not more important. While no words could make things better in a situation like this, some words could make it worse.

'Every death in a hospital is a failure,' he reminded himself, as he left the grieving parents and went back to take a last look at the dead baby. Those words had been the words of his father to him every time one of Daniel's patients had passed away. Dr Johansen Senior had insisted on having Daniel share every single fatality that happened during Daniel's shifts so that they together could evaluate what had gone wrong and how it could have been prevented. And every single time his father had started with categorising the death as a failure. With his father now dead, Daniel continued with the process in his head.

'What could have been done differently?' 'Who had made a mistake?' 'What procedure would have to be changed?' Nothing was too small, or irrelevant to be scrutinized. And that included which words to use when consoling a patient's family.

To Daniel the Hippocratic Oath was a binding document. One of the oldest binding documents in history in fact. And it deserved respect. As did all contracts.

He had, obviously, memorized it by heart. Not only the modern version, but also the original version translated from Greek by Ludwig Edelstein in 1943. His favourite parts were the parts that read:

'I swear by Apollo Physician and Asclepius and Hygieia and Panaceia and all the gods and goddesses, making them my witnesses, that I will fulfil according to my ability and judgment this oath and this covenant:

To hold him who has taught me this art as equal to my parents and to live my life in partnership with him.

I will apply dietetic measures for the benefit of the sick according to my ability and judgment; I will keep them from harm and injustice.

In purity and holiness I will guard my life and my art.

If I fulfil this oath and do not violate it, may it be granted to me to enjoy life and art, being honoured with fame among all men for all time to come; if I transgress it and swear falsely, may the opposite of all this be my lot.'

Daniel knew it was a very special privilege for a son to get to learn about being a medical professional from his own father. It had not always been easy, but life was not here to be easy.

The line 'being honoured with fame among all men for all time to come' was what pushed Daniel forward. Few professions had such status amongst men as Doctors, and for good reason. In the words of his father: 'We save lives!'

And now the hospital had failed. A life had been lost. It was not his fault, but Daniel still took it upon himself to be in charge of the investigation into what had gone wrong. Daniel thought back to the first young child that had died on this watch. How his father had screamed at him for letting it happen. About what an epic failure it had been. It was years ago but still gave Daniel shills. Since then, saving the life of young children was of extra importance for him. Doctors saved lives, and the lives of babies were the most important. Babies were humans with their whole lives in front of them. Save a child and you saved more life.

A couple of flies insisted on landing on his forearms and Daniel annoyingly waved them away again and again.

Their buzzing sounded louder than usual in this silence and sorrow.

Daniel stood in front of the little girl still lying in her bed. She looked as if she was sleeping. It felt wrong to call her a corpse. She had not even started to live, so how could you call her dead?

Their first child, thought Daniel. *It can't be easy*.

A few minutes earlier, Manda had stood and looked down at the little girl who slept peacefully in the hospital crib. When she put her hand over the child's mouth, it covered most of the girl's face. The baby had opened her eyes and locked eyes with Manda: the newborn's eyes filled to the brim with fear. Manda could not help to think how she herself had once been a newborn child like this little girl. How she was born a Killer.

Then Manda had pressed down harder onto the baby's face with her hand. Made sure the child did not have a chance to breathe. Watched the child struggle until she did not live anymore.

When the nurses and doctor gathered around the child, Manda had already left the scene discreetly. She found a closet to hide in until everything had calmed down again. There, in the narrow space, under the cover of darkness, and all alone, she read her poem of death:

Black. The Kingdom of Sorrow.

An eternal darkness growing before me.

Who are you to judge.

The frustration ripped at Manda's heart without mercy. Snakes cannot be blamed for striking. Bees not for stinging. Predators prey. Thus was Nature. And Killers kill. Yet another mission completed. The humans called it Sudden Infant Death Syndrome. That was an exceptionally fitting description.

Suddenly the infant saw Death.

Chapter 10

'If the doors of perception were cleansed everything would appear to man as it is, infinite.'
– William Blake

Alex gave Mr Williams a sceptical look. 'I'll give you one hour. And I reserve myself the right to throw you out at any time if you're unpleasant or rude.'

'The only thing I ask of you is that you promise not to tell another living person what I'm about to share with you.'

'Sorry, but I can't promise that. I'm no priest sworn to any sacramental seal.'

'Can it at least be off the record, then?'

'OK. As long as you're not going to confess to a crime, I promise not to share your story with anyone without your permission. You have fifty-nine minutes left. Better get started.'

Alex made herself comfortable in the armchair, with both of her hands cupped around her tea cup and her legs curled underneath her.

The first ten minutes felt like a well-prepared lecture. It was apparent that Mr Williams had held this lecture before, and he started off by talking about subjects that were not in any way controversial.

'Historically, we have made many interesting discoveries where the invisible or impossible have become visible or possible. The common factor of great discoveries is that it takes time before the masses fully understand what has really been discovered. In other words, it takes time for an idea to become accepted.

'Before we knew there was something called air, air already existed. The ancient Greeks then proved the existence of air by showing that a vase put into water upside down remained dry on the inside. Something—air—must have stopped the water from coming in.

Or what about gravity? It's a long-established truth today that a powerful force stops people from flying off into space and that the same force keeps the moon in orbit around the earth. But in Isaac Newton's time, asserting this was to turn the established view of the world on its head.

And if you ask me, Newton's discovery of the law of gravity is one of the greatest discoveries in history. He showed how an invisible force that we can not see is affecting our world.'

Alex interrupted. 'The clock's ticking. This is all very interesting, but what's your point?'

'Well, even though we know that earlier truths have been shown to be wrong, we still find it so difficult to accept that many of today's truths will turn out to be false in the future. You're probably more right if you say 'Everything we know is false' than if you say 'Everything we know is true' as most of what we know today will be proved to be false in the future. Everything—from how the universe works to what love really is.'

The introduction was over. Mr Williams became more serious. His body language changed and he started to talk more slowly. Like a lawyer who has presented the facts in a case and then glides over to his closing arguments, so too did Mr Williams start to convince rather than explain. The change was subtle, but Alex noticed it.

'The big question is: are you ready to have your view of the world turned upside down forever?'

'Give me your best shot,' returned Alex with a voice that quite clearly showed she had no illusions of soon surrendering to a new world-view.

Mr Williams lowered his voice so that he was barely audible. 'At first, you won't believe what I'm about to tell you, but give me some time to explain.'

He breathed deeply and dove into his revelation. 'Alexandra. An unknown species of human beings is living amongst us right here on earth. We cannot see them as they are not visible to the human eye. But they are here.'

Alex felt how her body tensed defensively. Mr Williams carried on talking without giving Alex a chance to interrupt. 'We call them The Unvisible, but they call themselves Yangyang. They are people of flesh and blood just like us, but because their cell structure makes light reflect against their bodies in a slightly different way our eyes can't detect them. They exist—but we can't see them. But they are very much physical animals. They look like us—well, nearly—laugh, love and eat as we do. They're people—even if we can't see them. And they are living in our midst.'

Alex cast a doubtful look at the man she had let into her home. 'Are you seriously telling me that a bunch of invisible, human like, animals are running around and playing hide and seek with us?'

Mr Williams shifted uncomfortably on the sofa. 'They aren't animals—at least, no more than you and I. They're people or human-like beings, if you like. Apart from being shorter than we are and having platinum blond hair, they look like us.'

'I thought you said we couldn't see them? So how can you know what they look like?'

'Some people can see them. Not many have been given this gift but they exist. And no, I can't see them either. But I do know quite a few people who can. I have, however, seen them with the help of a technology that, for obvious reasons, isn't well known. Most people refuse to believe that The Unvisible exist before they see them physically. And there are gadgets that let us do that—just as X-ray equipment and radar let us see things we otherwise can't see with the naked eye. Those of us who have seen The Unvisible are called Knowers. That's the name they call us—and the name we give ourselves.'

More like Knuckleheads, Alex thought to herself, but she didn't say anything because the journalist in her had woken up. She was curious about Mr Williams. Why was he sitting in her living room and telling her fairy tales? Instead of dismissing the story as a tale spun by a compulsive liar, she decided to treat Mr Williams as if he were one of the children with imaginary friends that she was interviewing for her assignment. Come to think about it, their stories were pretty similar to the one he had just told her. She probed, 'So, what language do they speak?'

'They rarely talk and often use sign language with each other instead. When they do speak, they talk in the language of the country or culture they are living in. The Unvisible can be found all over the world. But they do keep away from places with Arctic climate.'

'Sign language? Do you mean they're deaf?'

'No, not at all. But the advantage of using sign language is that they can communicate between themselves without revealing themselves even if they're in the same room as humans.'

'So they're like a kind of ghost that only certain people can see?'

'They are not ghosts. Ghosts don't exist. And neither do spirits, trolls, gnomes or fairies. But your reaction is understandable, and quite normal. After all, there are many similarities between these mythical creatures and The Unvisible. Their skin and hair are completely white and a surprisingly large number of myths about supernatural beings are also depicted as white—from angels and spirits to ghosts or fairies. These myths are stories created by The Unvisible to explain unplanned contact between them and us. Think of these myths as stories that are made up to hide the truth.'

'Ah, gaslighting? It's a classic trick to launch alternative stories in times of crisis so that the public isn't sure which story is really true,' Alex said.

Mr Williams nodded in agreement. 'Ghosts and spirits are creatures living in another dimension; they're creatures that can go through walls, fly and disappear into thin air. But, of course, this is all nonsense. And none of this applies to The Unvisible. They are subject to the ordinary laws of nature—just like all living creatures. If they trip, gravity pulls them down; if they do not eat they will starve and they will die without air. A shot to their heart is as fatal to them as it is to us—except that it's harder to hit them as a target when they cannot be seen . . .'

He paused for effect and smiled foolishly, waiting for her to get his joke before continuing. 'You could arm wrestle with an Unvisible and . . .'

Alex interrupted him. 'Can you have sex with them?' That probably was not a question she would have asked a child with imaginary friends but she could not help it.

'The short answer is yes, although it isn't common, and breaks their code of conduct. But yes, it does happen.'

For once his answer was short. They sat for a few seconds just looking at their teacups. Alex felt she had gone too far, so she changed the subject. She had jotted down a few bullet points in her notebook while thinking about the next question.

'I still don't understand. How can they exist and yet not exist all at the same time?'

'Oh, they exist, we just cannot see them. Just because a blind person can't see someone coming into a room, doesn't mean it hasn't happened, right? Colour blindness is a better example. Most 'normal' people can see all colours. But there are some people who are colour blind. They are normal in every other way but just lack the ability to perceive colours. The concept of colour that you and I share doesn't exist for these people. Have you ever wondered what it feels like to be colour blind and have to hear others saying how the world is a symphony of colours that you can't see?'

She shook her head.

Mr Williams continued. 'But how can the colour blind know that those of us with normal sight can actually see all these colours? How can the blind trust what the seeing see? Why should they trust what others are assuring them over relying on what their very own senses are telling them? Colour-blind people accept that colours exist because most other people can see them. But imagine if almost everyone, apart from a select few, were colour blind! Would the majority, the 'normal' colour-blind people, then accept that there were these strange people who could perceive colour? Or would the colour-seeing people tell themselves that there was something wrong with their eyes; that they were oversensitive to colour so that they saw things that did not exist? Does something become a truth only when the majority believe in it?

Alex, it's like people are partly blind. There are parts of the world we just can't see. Like when an Unvisible enters a room and we can't see her. But just because we can't, doesn't mean she doesn't exist.'

'So you're saying they can walk around here? Inside my apartment, without us noticing?'

'We can't see them, but sometimes, we notice them. If they get too close, for example. You know that feeling when you can feel the presence of someone else in an empty room? Or when you think someone is watching you? That's an Unvisible who physically got too close. When that happens they usually notice quickly and move away again.

But you can relax. There are no Unvisible in your apartment right now. I checked when you were in the kitchen making tea.'

'You mean one of The Unvisible people could get into my apartment?'

'Not could. They do. Most people get a visit from them every now and then and since you started getting interested in kids with imaginary friends, their interest in you hasn't diminished. I can say in all probability that you have an Unvisible in your apartment most evenings.'

Alex surprised herself by reacting as if she really did believe that invisible people sneaked around her home. This annoyed her.

Just then, Mr Williams dropped his nearly untouched cup of tea, and the tea spilled onto the floor and under the coffee table.

The old man kneeled down, watching helplessly as the puddle of tea got bigger and bigger. Alex sighed and went into the kitchen to get something to clean it up with. After putting a pile of paper towels on the floor and picking up the teacup, she came eye to eye with Mr Williams and got a whiff of wine on his breath.

'Are you drunk?'

Avoiding eye contact with Alex, he replied a little bit too quickly, 'No, definitely not!'

'I want you to leave. Your hour is almost up and I've listened to what you wanted to say. I'm tired and want to go to sleep.'

Mr William looked like a child who had been promised he could stay up late and then was suddenly told to go to bed. But the message was clear: he would not get any more time with her, so he went out into the hallway, put on his coat and opened the door.

He turned around and looked at Alex. 'I know you think I'm just an old drunk with crazy ideas—and maybe I am. To come here and tell you my secret without planning it better was not very smart. But think about what I've told you. Promise me that.' Then he moved closer and whispered in her ear. 'You won't be alone when I leave. And you won't sleep by yourself tonight.'

His words—and especially the way he said them—gave Alex the chills. She took a couple of steps back and crossed her arms.

Mr Williams turned around and walked down the stairs with heavy steps. Alex stood watching him for a few seconds before sighing deeply. Disappointed, she shut the door. Here she had given Mr Williams an hour of her time because she really thought he had something worthwhile to say and then it had turned out to be just another uninteresting story. And a creepy one at that.

She quickly got ready for bed and, after a few minutes, she was asleep. But it was a troubled sleep.

The Watcher crept under the bed. In recent years it had become fashionable to have beds with build-in storage. That had forced them to frequently fall back to an older technique that they still used in many parts of the world: to sleep directly on the floor. But the bed in this room was of old style and he could still sleep under it.

When the light went out, he made himself comfortable and used his arms as a pillow. Before going to sleep, he wondered what topics had been discussed here before he was able to get in. He did not like the fact that he had not managed to sneak in earlier as he had missed her coming home as well as when the old man entered. But she did not seem to believe the man's story.

The Primary Queen was probably right to order extra surveillance of the woman. She was getting too curious. But that was not his problem. His assignment was to watch. And with the Subject in bed everything was under control.

If someone was going to be killed, that would be the job of a Killer.

Chapter 11

'Now faith is the substance of things hoped for, the evidence of things not seen.'
– Hebrews 11:1

Alex had managed to get a meeting with Patrick, and she had been positively surprised when he had prioritized her and given her an appointment in just a few days. Alex had framed her request as if she needed some guidance on her assignment, so technically it was a student meeting her teacher, but it was also a woman having dinner with a man.

Initially Alex had considered picking a dress for once, but in the end she had gone with a pair of black pants. But she had put on some make-up and, after some deliberation, chosen a glittery top.

When Patrick arrived, she saw that she had misread it all. Patrick had not dressed up. He came wearing his work clothes: chinos and a shirt that was not tucked in. The first thing he said when they met outside the fancy restaurant with prices that she really could not afford, was, 'Look at you, are you going to a party later?' Even though she had thought of this evening as some kind of date-like event, it was clear right from the start that, in all likelihood, he would not be paying the bill. And that in the worst case he might see it as a tutorial and expect her to pay for both of them. But he could not be that cheap, could he?

They ordered and waited for their food mostly in silence. Whatever conversation there was, was initially short and forced. A dinner between a student who thinks she is on a date with her teacher, and a teacher who realizes that what he thought was a tutoring session, was probably something quite different; was bound to be strained. When the food arrived Alex did the only sensible thing she could do: she started to talk about her project.

After going through the questions she had prepared, Alex decided to show Patrick the drawing she had received from Saga, the little girl. She wanted to know how to deal with it. She could not help thinking how the girl's sketch resembled the drawings she had taken from Gunnar and the one Mr Williams had given her. Alex then continued to show him the two drawings done by adults, and Patrick wondered why. So Alex decided to tell him about her encounter with Mr Williams.

'These drawings are made by patients at a mental hospital. The man who gave them to me says they are illustrations of a phenomenon that allows certain people to see things in nature that normal people can't see. He claims that he himself has seen them.'

'Are you trying to tell me that your friend seriously believes there are people who can see things in nature that we can't? Alex, there's a reason we put people into mental institutes—it's because they are crazy . . .'

'I'm not saying I believe it. I'm just sharing a theory. After all, isn't it interesting how these drawings have so much in common?'

'So these people are supposed to be invisible? And if they do exist, but we can't see them, then why don't we at least see their footprints?'

Alex did not reply. She did not have an answer to that, and made a mental note to ask Mr Williams.

A gigantic pause covered their table. Alex had nothing more to say. Patrick had made his point. The silence from a conversation that had reached its end could be deafening. They finished the meal in silence.

Finally Patrick cleared his throat and said: 'Well, well. Time to call it a night. This is a tutorial, right? The best thing about being a tutor is all the free meals you get with nice students requesting extra help. I'll go to the toilet while you pay.'

And there she sat in her top that was a little bit too glittery, and with a bill that was definitely too high. She had hoped that he would at least split the bill, and frankly that he would pick it up. What hurt the most was the revelation that this had not been close to being a date. He had even had the audacity to order a cognac with his coffee, knowing full well that he was going to let a poor student pay for it.

They left the restaurant together and Patrick neither held the door open, nor let her take the first taxi. Before getting into his taxi, he leaned forward as though he was going to give her a hug. As Alex lifted her arms to return the embrace, he shouted, 'Boo!', startling Alex. 'Watch out for invisible ghosts!' he laughed, as he jumped into the back of the taxi.

Leaning out of the open door, he added, 'But seriously. As your tutor, I have to advise you not to listen to everything people tell you. You're going to be a journalist. That means learning how to tell the difference between fact and fiction. This is precisely what this course is all about. I have to say, I'm a little bit disappointed in you, Alexandra.'

He slammed the door shut without saying good-bye.

Alexandra? He had called her Alexandra. Like her mother. Like she was a little girl who had done something wrong. She stood there motionless, and emotionless. When the next taxi arrived, she waved it away. She would walk home instead. To save money but also because the forty-minute walk was just what she needed right now. Alex silenced her phone, turned up her collar, thrust her hands into her pockets and started to walk. She completely ignored the fact that it had started to rain.

In another part of town, a Watcher studied his Subject. The lady he was watching had set the table for two, fully aware that her husband would not be joining her. That he would never come home for dinner again. The white tablecloth was freshly pressed and the cutlery was perfectly laid out. The tulips in the large crystal vase were freshly bought. The fish was swimming in a beurre blanc sauce. The baked potatoes steamed in their cases of aluminium foil. It was the details that made the experience.

The chair opposite her was empty. The fish on the plate was untouched; the baked potatoes too, and the bread roll waited to be buttered. The chair belonged to Dr Johansen. Across the table from his empty chair sat Mrs Johansen. She ate slowly. Put small pieces onto her fork and chewed gracefully. It was impolite to rush your food. The Watcher thought that if the woman had had the ambition to be an author she could have written a book on etiquette.

The Watcher observed the lady from the other side of the table. He had played the part of dinner guest many evenings when Mrs Johansen ate dinner without her husband. Far too many people ate dinner alone. The least the Yangyang could do was to keep the lonely people company when they ate.

He did not touch the food although it looked delicious. Perhaps he would eat some of it later on before she threw it away. But here, at the dining table, he did not touch the food. He just sat in the chair that had been Dr Johansen's and that Mrs Johansen thought was now empty. The chair she had raised her glass towards in a toast almost every evening for thirty-five years, regardless of whether her husband had been in it or not. How many dinners had she eaten alone while her husband had been on call or while he was away on some medical conference? The fact that her husband was dead and would never join her for dinner again would, perhaps, not make such a big difference. The Watcher wondered if Mrs Johansen had ever suspected that she was not really alone as she sat there playing her part in this tragedy.

The Subject yet again raised her wineglass to the empty place on the other side of the table and made a toast. Then she took a few small sips of the white wine, a Sancerre. His favourite.

'How dare you?' she said bitterly. 'How dare you die and ruin this? Dinners together as husband and wife. You and I. Together. Forever.'

Lonely people did that. Talked to themselves. Or to their dogs, fish or TVs. To anything that, with a little imagination, felt like company. Once he had watched a woman hold a long conversation with her toaster. Humanity was a lonely creature. Social animals with a tendency to spend too much time in solitude.

Chapter 12

'The eyes see only what the mind is prepared to comprehend.'
– Henri Bergson

This time it was Adam who had suggested they get together again for coffee. The same Starbucks as usual. Alex and Adam had met several times over the past few days and Alex found it valuable to be able to discuss her ideas with someone who was an expert on children, and with someone who was not from school. Especially as she did not want to go to Patrick for advice any more. That awkward dinner a week earlier was finally just an annoying memory. Adam was just much easier to talk to than Patrick. Alex found the meetings with Adam interesting. She found him interesting.

Adam arrived first and texted Alex to see what she wanted so he could order for her too. When it was his turn to pay, the man behind him burst out, 'Hey man, you glow in the dark, or what?'

Some adults could just not help poking fun of his albinism. Most often it was children who teased him, but that he could tolerate. He had been young and ignorant too. It was the reactions of adults—usually men—that he found hard to accept. Adam really wanted to reply with a sarcastic remark, but he braced himself and ignored him.

He paid and found himself a free table.

Adam wore sunglasses as an easy way to signal to people that he was visually impaired. But partly also as a shield.

But when Alex arrived, he took his sunglasses off and let her look into his eyes for the very first time. They were bluer than any other eyes she had ever seen. Framed by his pale skin, they reminded her of sapphires. Perhaps they were not perfect at seeing, but they were perfect to look at. She was so attracted by his gaze that, at first, she did not hear what he was saying.

'Let's play a game,' Adam repeated. 'I'll think of something and you have to guess what it is by asking questions.'

'Like Twenty Questions?'

He nodded. Alex found this a bit strange, but played along.

'Is it a thing?' she asked.

'No.'

'Something living?'

'Yes.'

'So, an animal. A kind of living organism?'

'Yes.'

'That last question doesn't count. It wasn't a question; it was a clarification.'

'Sure. You have eighteen questions left.'

'Is this living thing still alive? I mean—it isn't a historical animal or person?'

'Yes, it's still alive.'

'Is it big?'

'No, it's very, very small. Tiny.'

'Can it be found in this country?'

'Yes.'

'In this town?'

'Yes.'

'In this room?'

'Yes. Now you're getting hot . . .'

Alex hesitated.

'Is it bigger than my hand?'

'Yes.'

'But wait a minute. You said it was a living organism that can be found in this room and can be seen with the naked eye. It's bigger than my hand, yet you said it's very, very small! The only living things in this room that are bigger than my hand are people . . .'

'Yes.'

'So it's me? The right answer is myself?'

Adam smiled.

'But I'm not small!'

'You are very, very small. In the context of the universe, humans are tiny and insignificant. Humanity's biggest problem is that it overestimates its own significance.'

Alex looked at him sceptically.

'What do you know about nature?' He surprised her once again.

'What kind of question is that? It's like asking, "What do you know about global politics?" You wouldn't make a very good journalist,' she said with a smile.

'And you would be an awful kindergarten teacher . . .'

Alex's smile faded when she thought about what he had said. 'Are you talking to me as if I were a little child?'

Adam sighed. 'Why are you always so defensive?'

She relaxed. 'Maybe because I grew up with a very anxious mother, a dominant father and an overly ambitious brother, who was always snapping at my heels?'

'What I meant was: when you think of nature, what do you think of?'

'I think of flowers, trees, birds . . . fish . . . Is that what you mean?'

'So you don't think of bluebells and orchids? Maples and oaks? Canadian geese and cormorants? Perch and bream?'

He continued. 'Do you know that the average ten-year-old nowadays knows the names of a thousand different brands but no more than ten names of plants and animals in his or her own environment?'

'When I have a child, then I'll study all of that so I can answer my child's questions.'

'So you choose to be blind to the beauty of nature until you become a mother?'

'Well, that's a pretty depressing way of looking at it, don't you think?'

'Or just an honest way of describing someone's pretty depressing way of looking at the world?'

Alex opened her mouth to answer, but stopped herself. How many flowers did she know the names of? How many birds could she identify? How many insects? If you can only divide your world into rough categories, then how well can you understand the world you live in? When the word 'fish' makes us think of a fish fillet lying on a plate rather than an animal swimming in water, then how far from the natural cycle of life are we?

Was it possible that children, with their curiosity and willingness to learn, were better at grasping nature than we thought? Once again, he had got her thinking so deeply that she was lost in her own thoughts. She felt the need to take control over the direction the discussion was heading. She shot out, 'I thought we were here to discuss my project?'

'Well, isn't that exactly what we have just been doing?' he suggested.

He got up and reached for his cane. That's it? He just came here to play a game of Twenty Questions? And now he is leaving again? Alex was confused. She looked up at him without really knowing what to say next. She was also tired. Exhausted. All she wanted to do was to drink her tea. That would have to do as her next line. 'I'll just stay and finish my tea . . .' she stated as composed as she could.

As soon as the Watcher was sure the woman was asleep, he sat down at her computer. The Subject had clearly been unproductive all evening, mainly sitting and staring at the screen. Even though the Watcher knew the Primary Queen would not like it, he could not stop himself from helping the woman out a little. As quietly as he could, he corrected the misspellings the Subject had failed to correct herself. If the woman later would wonder how those corrections had been made, she would probably come up with an explanation involving being too tired to remember what she had done.

The Watcher liked doing small, secret services around the house. However, the corrections took longer than he expected and he still had some left when the clock struck one and a very faint knocking could be heard. The Watcher got up and opened the door cautiously.

One of the Wise entered quietly and the Watcher stayed guard by the door to give space to the Wise to complete his assignment. It was the duty of the Wise to give insights into how the Yangyang saw the world.

On the Primary Queen's orders, Alex was going to be invited to sleep on it.

It was the responsibility of the Wise to get the Subject to think more about what it meant to be alive. The Wise did that by describing how beautiful the world could be in a series of monologues. The purpose of these sessions was to make sure that a Subject was as prepared as possible the day he or she finally realized that the Yangyang were real.

They knew from experience that fewer Subjects would share their insights if they were let into the secret gently. And if there was something the Primary Queen disliked, it was Yinyins who felt the urge to share what they knew with others.

If all went according to plan, the woman would not even understand that she had been exposed to their teachings. A great speaker was one that made people believe in the message without even thinking about how good the talk was. A skilled waiter was a person who managed to help the dinner guests enjoy their meal by offering services they did not even notice. In much the same way, the Wise succeeded if they managed to convey their message without the students finding out about their teacher.

Now the Wise sat on the edge of the woman's bed. He had left the bedroom door open and left a light on in the hall outside, so that he could see her face more easily. The light would also make her less afraid if she were to wake up.

In a crisp voice, he whispered in her ear:

'In everything you do—learn.

With everything you learn—do.'

He carefully ran his fingertips over her forehead. He knew from experience that his touch would make her body produce oxytocin, which would make it easier for the woman to remember what he taught her. She would feel better too. Single women in their thirties often suffered from a chronic lack of oxytocin. If they just had the resources, the Wise could have worked full-time giving healing body massages to single women. But that was not why he was here. He was on a greater mission.

He repeated his message.

'In everything you do—learn.

With everything you learn—do.'

Reading out short words of wisdom could—from an outsider's perspective—seem a simplistic way of teaching, but the brain worked differently when a person was asleep. In the same way an extremely tired brain could only take in the simplest of instructions, and often interpreted them incorrectly, so too could an extremely rested brain take in deep, complex messages when they came in a condensed form. And when a person was asleep and the alpha waves were at their peak, then the body was most open to new ideas. And the mind best primed to learn profound things. The Wise should not show the whole path; just light it up.

As with so many other things, humans had lost this basic knowledge about the nature of Nature. In certain Asian countries, a fragment of this knowledge still remained when parents encouraged their children to put a book under their pillows to help with the understanding of what they had studied. But this was of course mostly symbolic and didn't actually work.

The Wise continued his routine.

'Not later. Not recently.
Not earlier. Not soon.
Just now. Practice nowfulness.'

He stroked her hair with his hand.

'Not here. Not there.
Be unaware of where.
Practise herefulness.'

The student jerked in the bed. Her entire body arched back for a fraction of a second and then relaxed again. It was the body's way of saying the message had been received; that the information had gone straight to the superconscious without getting stuck in the judgemental clarity of the consciousness.

When the superconscious made her body tense up, it was as if it wanted to show the consciousness how unconscious it was of what was going on. As if saying, 'Look! I made your body kick but you have no idea why your leg twitched.'

Waking up briefly and wondering why she had had a spasm, the student went back to a deep sleep where the superconscious ruled. She was ready to learn some more.

Calling the part of the brain that was not conscious the subconscious was typical of the way humans saw the world. As if everything humans were not conscious of was beneath them. The subconscious was, of course, really the superconscious—the part of the consciousness that was above what people were conscious of.

It was time for the Wise to start the third lesson.

'Everything passes.

Nothing remains.

Never deviate.

Always appreciate.'

This was yet another message people had distorted until its basic meaning was lost. The Buddhists claimed that everything was in a state of suffering because it was impermanent. No possession was valuable because it could be lost. No person was to be loved because sooner or later she would die.

The lesson, of course, was the direct opposite. By always appreciating the most beautiful things you had at the moment, you always had something to be grateful for.

This point of view alleviated the suffering. Lessened the sorrow. Decreased the greed. They called it The Beautiful Life. It was not the meaning of life—but it was what life was meant to be.

It was time for the last part of the session. He leaned over stroked the woman's cheek and whispered:

'Listen carefully. See everything.'

Chapter 13

'To most of us nothing is so invisible as an unpleasant truth. Though it is held before our eyes, pushed under our noses, rammed down our throats—we know it not.'
– Eric Hoffer

'How the hell do you lose a diamond ring?'

Daniel looked at his wife with a mixture of contempt and astonishment.

'I know I put it back right here. I'm sure of it.'

Laura combed through the jewellery in her drawer one more time.

'That's right. Small elves must have come and taken it while we were asleep . . .'

'But I know I did! Maybe someone stole it?' Laura suggested. She did not really believe that, but she wanted to find a logical explanation. Wanted to understand how the ring she had received from her husband on their two-year anniversary could suddenly disappear.

'Do you honestly think that thieves could break into an apartment on the ninth floor without us noticing?'

Daniel continued to raise his voice as it dawned on him that the ring that had cost him three weekends of overtime seemed to be gone. Laura's voice had become softer as she too had to accept that the ring was nowhere to be found.

'Please lower your voice. You'll wake up Junior,' she begged as she approached him.

'So now I'm a bad father too? You lose a fortune and that somehow makes me a terrible dad?'

Laura put a hand on her husband's shoulder.

'Don't touch me!'

As he broke free, he gave her a hard push. She fell headlong into the dressing table. Rings and necklaces clattered to the floor. Laura curled up into a ball. She tried to silence her sobs but failed. The commotion woke up Junior who began screaming in his room.

Daniel shouted at them to shut up.

He exploded with an aggression that he just could not control. He knew it was wrong, yet at the same time, it felt right. How could her mistake be his fault? They had both made a mistake so now they were even. How would she learn to keep things in order if he never disciplined her for her errors? And he had not really hit her—just pushed her a little.

The doorbell rang.

'It must be Alex.' Daniel realized her sister had arrived early.

'I am sorry, Honey,' he said to calm his wife down. 'I know how much you love that ring, and I got frustrated when we couldn't find it. We'll look for it later. I'm sure we will find it then. Now let's go and welcome my sister.'

He was still angry, but it was important to present a good facade, especially when the family came to visit.

The Watcher had wondered how the family would react when they discovered the diamond was gone. It was worse than he had anticipated. He almost regretted taking it, but he could not help himself; he had a very special relationship to diamonds. Amazed by how Nature could create something so exquisite. The fact that black, soft coal under pressure could be transformed into something clear, transparent and hard was visible proof of the magic of Nature. Just as he was. He had just borrowed the shining stone to study it more closely.

He would put it back in a few days, probably into the very same drawer he had taken it from. The woman of the house would wonder how she could have missed it when it must have been right in front of her all the time. She would probably curse herself for—once again—making her husband angry for no reason.

People really were hopeless at trusting what they had seen. And incredibly skilled at making up stories to support their own narrative.

Chapter 14

'We are more closely connected to the invisible than to the visible.'
– Novalis

Daniel opened the door and let in his sister. 'Come in. Laura is still getting ready. You know what women are like! Want a drink? It's Friday after all, and you look like you could use one.'

'You know what? Give me a Vodka Red Bull,' Alex replied. 'It's my last weekend before I have to go back to work, so I might as well drink when I can.'

Laura came out of the bedroom with a big smile on her face. 'So nice to see you again!' she exclaimed. 'Now let's have a nice dinner together.'

Nice, thought Alex. What an irritating little word. Especially when it was repeated.

After dinner, Laura excused herself and said she was going to take care of the dishes so that Daniel could answer Alex's questions. After a few minutes of brother-sister banter Alex asked if it was okay to begin the interview and if he was OK with having it recorded. When Daniel confirmed, she pressed the Record button and got started.

Alex had decided to do an interview with Daniel; partly, because his son had imaginary friends, and partly because he knew a lot about biology and zoology. Daniel had actually wanted to be a veterinarian instead of a doctor and would probably have become one too if it had not been for their father's obvious contempt for vets. Many years ago, their father had killed Daniel's dreams with the words, 'People who become vets are people who want to become doctors but are so afraid of hurting their patients that they choose patients that can't talk and therefore can't sue them.'

Daniel had fallen back into his father's footsteps and become a doctor, but he had retained his interest in nature. Not that he loved being outdoors, or had a great love of animals. No, Daniel's interest in nature was more about the need to understand a system. He wanted to create order and structure in the world he lived in.

'Can nature create things that can't be seen? Do invisible animals exist?' she asked.

'If you're asking if there are animals we can't see, the answer is, of course, yes. There are thousands of species we can't see because they are too small to be seen with the naked eye. But I think you're really asking if there are animals big enough for us to see that we don't see anyway? My answer would still be yes. Most people can walk around in a forest full of animals without seeing a single one. I know you didn't mean this—but it's an interesting observation. Modern man is so unaccustomed to being outdoors in nature that when we are there, we don't see it.'

A lot of animals have mastered the art of camouflage to perfection. Like the chameleon that can change colour to blend into the background. There's even an octopus that can change colour according to its surroundings so that it's basically invisible to us.'

'Why aren't you answering my question? Do invisible animals exist?' Alex asked with a smile. She quite liked sibling bantering with her brother.

'Yes, it's possible there are animals people can't see as our senses are pretty underdeveloped. Let me give you an example: a person can hear up to 20,000 Hz while a rat can perceive sounds up to 100,000 Hz. Pigeons are aware of sound as low as 0.1 Hz while humans can't hear anything below 20 Hz. In a nutshell, our hearing is pretty bad. So is our sense of smell. We train dogs to sniff out and pinpoint everything from truffles to drugs because their sense of smell is so much better than our own. We can hardly pick up the aroma of a chanterelle until it's right under our noses.

'If you spread out the olfactory cells in our noses, they cover the area of a stamp. Do the same thing for a dog, and they would be as big as a football pitch.'

He leaned back in his chair, clasping his hands behind his neck.

'The sad reality is that our ability to observe the world is highly limited. We can only see a very small range of light waves, for example. Yet there are scorpions with twelve eyes, bees with more than 5,000 lenses in their eyes and penguins that can perceive ultraviolet light. Thanks to the microscope, humanity has discovered the billions of animals and organisms that have always been here on earth without us knowing anything about them.

'An aborigine in Papua New Guinea who hasn't seen a microscope still lives in a world where large quantities of animals don't exist because he can't see them.'

Alex interrupted. 'So there is a possibility that animals we haven't yet seen exist?'

'Not a possibility. It's a fact that we'll keep on discovering new species for many years to come.'

Daniel fell silent, mulling over his words.

Alex took this to mean she could make a comment. 'Let me summarize what you've just said. It's likely, even highly probable, that there are numerous animals—even large ones—whose existence we humans aren't aware of yet. And that we can't see, hear or notice them because of our underdeveloped senses.'

'You could say that. But how are you going to use this? What does all this have to do with your assignment on kids with imaginary friends?'

'I want to put forward the theory that it's actually biologically possible that children can see animals—let's call them creatures—that we can't.'

Daniel became hostile. 'You're joking?' Alex had the feeling that he was afraid of being quoted in an academic paper as someone claiming that invisible animals really existed.

'Relax!' she laughed, trying to make it sound as if she had just been making a joke. 'But one of the children asked me a question I couldn't answer at first—and that always annoys me. I'm sorry, but as an aspiring reporter, I can't help wanting to follow up loose ends.'

'What was the question?' Daniel asked in a voice that was calm again.

'If a person can see an animal that no one else can see, does this mean the person is crazy? Or does it mean the animal doesn't exist?'

'What was your answer?'

'I said, "It just means that person has a little secret. A bit like a girl who hides a treasure but doesn't tell anyone. The treasure still exists, even if no one else knows about it. Because the girl still knows".'

Laura stuck her head out of the kitchen door, still trying to be the perfect hostess while wearing rubber gloves. It did not really work.

'Are you nearly done? Then why don't you give Alex a ride home, so she doesn't have to take the bus?'

Daniel chipped in, 'Yes, of course I will drive you home, Alex. That's what brothers with cars are for.'

Alex could not get out of Laura's well-meaning suggestion, so she reluctantly accepted the offer of a ride, packed up her things and thanked Laura for the 'nice' dinner.

When they came down to the garage they walked in silence until they got to his car.

Three Watchers sat on the hoods of the parked cars. One of them was the Watcher assigned to Alex. The other two used the garage as a resting place while waiting for their Subjects to come home in the evening.

The Watchers observed the man and woman arriving. When they were close to the man's car, the Watcher silently slid off the hood and positioned himself behind one of the back doors, ready to jump in when the door opened. This was one of the most critical moments for a Watcher but also one that they had practiced extensively. It only took him a split second to sneak into the car without the passengers noticing.

Normally, he would not hitch a ride in a car, but the Watcher in the apartment on the ninth floor had sent a message and it was urgent. The message had to be relayed to the Queen. It was very likely that the Queen would decide someone had to be taught a lesson.

Chapter 15

'While we look not at the things which are seen, but at the things which are not seen: for the things which are seen are temporal; but the things which are not seen are eternal.'

– 2 Corinthians 4:18

Alex was stunned when she looked through the peephole and saw who had just knocked on her door. It was her mother. Outside her apartment. On a Sunday. To be clear: Alex's mother did not visit Alex. It was Alex who would visit her mum. Alex could only remember her mother coming to her apartment once and that was when she had just moved in. She had said something about the place being small, whatever that was supposed to mean.

Alex opened the door and then just stood in the doorway looking perplexed at her mother.

'Aren't you going to let your dear mother in? Junior needs to eat.'

Alex was so surprised to see her mother that she had not even noticed that she had brought Junior. She picked up the baby carrier and said, 'Of course, let's give this kid a drink. Come on in!'

When they got into the living room, Alex's mother hesitated.

'I was just about to tidy up,' reassured Alex, as she put Junior down and freed him from his carrier.

'I see,' her mother said and started to pick up some freshly-washed underwear that Alex had hung over the back of a chair to dry.

Alex took the pile of clothes from her mother, and then spent the next few minutes frantically tidying up the apartment while trying to look calm and composed until she felt her mother could relax, at least a little bit. Alex then tried to steer the conversation away from how messy her home was. 'So, to what do I owe the honour of your visit?'

'We were out for a walk and just happened to be in the neighborhood.'

Alex went to prepare beverages for the adults and when she came back and apologized for not having anything suitable for Junior to eat, her mother just replied: 'Oh, I figured, but I brought something for him.'

After a few minutes of chit-chat about Junior, Alex's mother put down her tea cup and cautioned her daughter, 'I heard you're writing an essay about imaginary friends. I think you should choose a different topic.'

The look that accompanied her words warned of an incoming uncomfortable conversation.

'And why is that?'

'I don't think it's appropriate.'

'Not appropriate?'

Alex had to drag the answer out of her mother. It was obvious that this was the true reason for her visit, and just as obvious that she rather not have this talk at all.

'Considering your background, I don't think it's healthy for you to study imaginary friends.'

'My background? Mother, what are you talking about?'

'Elizabeth. I'm talking about Elizabeth!'

Her mother burst out crying. Alex did not understand a thing. After a few minutes of uncontrolled sobbing, where the only thing Alex could really do was to gently hold her mother as she cried, her mother finally started to talk.

Elizabeth was the name of Alex's sister, the second child to be born into the Johansen family. A baby who had never grown up. Elizabeth had died after only a few months when Alex was three. Her mother said they never talked about Elizabeth. 'No need to spread the grief.'

Alex squeezed her mother's hand and tried to understand. 'I'm sorry, mother. It must have been difficult. But what does this have to do with my essay?'

Alex's question triggered another explosion of emotions. Her mother burst into tears again.

The more Alex picked up from her mother, the more the memories started to come back. It was as if the floodgates had opened after a long and snowy winter. Memories she had suppressed for years rushed over her. Her memories merged with her mother's revelations. Everything flowed together into one story. A story that had been hidden too deep, for too many years.

It turned out that Alex had also had imaginary friends. She had called them The Secret Ones and her parents had laughed at her crazy stories about invisible friends that helped her go to sleep at night.

Alex had forgotten all about that, but now she got a picture in her head of her lying down and stroking the family dog while she could see a secret person stroking another dog. The harmless fantasies of a child. But the death of Elizabeth had made those stories anything but innocent.

Her mother told her how Alex, at Elizabet's funeral no less, had confessed to her parents that it was The Secret Ones who had killed her little sister. That they were forced to let her sister die, but that they had told her that death was nothing to be sad about.

This was the only time Alex had been slapped as a child—to teach her that funerals were absolutely not the right time to make up stories about death.

Alex had always known that her father had hit her once—the humiliation of your own parent abusing you gets carved into every child who gets beaten up—but now Alex also remembered the feeling of surprise and disappointment she had felt over being hit for doing nothing wrong. That feeling she had carefully tucked away for decades.

Elizabeth had apparently got tangled up in the bedclothes and slowly suffocated to death. When her mother came into the room to feed the baby, Alex was sitting quietly next to her baby sister and said that her sister 'was sleeping forever'.

'I could never understand why you hadn't saved her, instead of just sitting there watching. But you were only three,' her mother consoled.

Alex looked at her mother. 'Are you blaming me for the death of my sister?'

'No, no. You were only a child. What could you have done?'

'I obviously didn't have anything to do with her death!'

'Let's not talk about it. I just wish you would write about something else instead of rubbing salt into that dreadful wound after all these years. Please write about something else . . .'

'I didn't even know there was a wound!'

'There are some things you just do not talk about . . .'

Alex was just about to bombard her mother with a new round of questions about what had really happened when she was interrupted by Junior's wailing.

Alex could see that her mother was too emotionally drained to look after Junior at this point, so to help she picked the child up. She rocked him gently in her lap to make him stop crying. It did not work. After what felt like an eternity, grandma came over and took her grandchild from her daughter. The child stopped crying immediately.

Her mother abruptly gathered her things and walked towards the door as if she felt she was rescuing a child from a dangerous witch. When she walked by her daughter she gave Alex a look that seemed to say 'some people really should not be close to small children'.

'Good Bye, Alexandra.'

And they were gone.

Her mother leaving mutilated Alex's heart. Finding out that her own mother seemed to blame her—the three-year-old version of her (!)—for the death of her sister for something she did—or did not do (!) hurt Alex like no other words had ever hurt her. They burnt like acid.

The silence after her mother left was brutal. Alex's head exploded with questions. She had been in the room when Elizabeth had died? Could she had done something to save her? Did her mum have a point? She had had imaginary friends as a child? Was that why she had subconsciously chosen to write about it now? Was losing her sister the reason she always felt so alone? As if she had lost a soul mate? A never-ending river of questions. A desert of answers. It was going to be a very long night.

The Watcher picked up the feather he had used to tickle the baby. Tickling babies under the chin was a good technique for making them feel less frightened, but it was also a dangerous method as it meant that he was forced to get very close to the other people in the room.

It was risky, but necessary. A baby's scream was a cry for help and it would not be long before his cries made the adults nervous. And nothing good came out of nervousness.

'The more they worry, the more we have to worry about them,' as the Primary Queen used to say.

Chapter 16

'The crux . . . is that the vast majority of the mass of the universe seems to be missing.'
– William J. Broad

The Carte Blanche Association held its meeting on Tuesday evenings in the auditorium of an old school building that was built as the monuments of knowledge that schools used to be built like.

Even if the building was not used as a school anymore—it was absolutely grand, but not very suitable for modern education—it was still called 'The School' by everyone. The names of buildings tended to stick. Alex was reminded of the directions she had once received: 'turn left at the Old Old Post Office'. Even though the Post Office had moved premises, not once, but twice, the locals still called the original building the Old Old Post Office. And the School would be called The School for many years to come. The only teaching that went on there currently were a few evening study groups. The building was mostly used as a meeting place for the local community.

The Carte Blanche Association was a group interested in historical symbolism. At least, that is what was written on the attendance list Alex signed. The list was sent to the local authority so that the association received funding. In actual fact, Carte Blanche was an association for people interested in The Unvisible. Trying to get funding for a group studying invisible people had been difficult, so they had tweaked the group's purpose slightly when applying for their grant.

This evening's meeting was in the school's auditorium. Luckily for Alex the meeting was in the evening. While classes and school work took up most of her days, she had recently seen her work around her assignment eat up a lot of her evening time; time that she previously had set aside for quality time for herself, for activities like reading novels. She could not remember the last time she had sat down to read a book for fun.

A small group of people, a mix of quirky personalities, had gathered in the large hall. 'Originals.' This was the best word Alex could come up with to describe them. 'Nerds' was also an apt description. Most of the people there looked slightly antisocial. Nearly all wore glasses. Apart from a quiet, younger woman with raven hair and matching black clothes, Alex was the only woman attending.

Mr Williams had been able to persuade Alex to attend the meeting. The first time he had called, she had not even bothered to answer. But he persisted. And when he sent her a bouquet of white roses and a card that read, 'Give an old man a second chance. Admit that I've awakened your curiosity,' she had given in. Partly because she could not remember ever having been sent white roses before, by any man. And partly because he was right. The meeting with Mr Williams had piqued her curiosity. After throwing him out of her home, she had thought a lot about what drives seemingly reasonable adults to start believing in things like UFOs or that the world was flat. And why did these people, often men, so often meet in secret clubs to discuss their odd interests with like-minded people just as odd as themselves?

Even though she was annoyed by Mr Williams, she had to admit his gesture had won her over. And who knew? Perhaps she could learn something about people's and their weird imagination that she could use in her project.

Mr Williams was chairman of the meeting. He looked very comfortable in the role. There were no signs of the insecurity he had shown last time Alex had met him. This was most likely the one place he did not have to drink in order to relax. This was his family.

Mr Williams sat behind a desk. Next to him was a timer to make sure the speakers kept to their allotted time slot. 'Today's first speaker is Shadow,' he said as he looked at the timer, clicked up her first slide and gave her the clicker.

The young woman in black got up. Alex tried to guess what she did for a living but could not imagine any place that might suit the woman. Perhaps she was a student at some obscure community college, or if she had a job, it must be in a nightclub or a record store. Did record stores still exist?

Shadows' voice was mellow, yet sharp. Captivating. She did not look the audience in the eye when she spoke, but they kept their eyes on her anyway. The contrast between her black hair and pale skin gave her a distinctive look. Alex wondered if she used a lightening cream or if it was make-up that made her look deathly pale. People like Shadow scared Alex. They always seemed to walk around carrying some big, dark, secret that made them take life too seriously. As if everyone else should feel bad for not taking life as gravely as they did.

The next slide in the young woman's presentation was of a Japanese rock garden. Alex perked up. The picture showed a number of irregular large gray stones that seemed to have been placed randomly on a bed of white gravel. The gravel was carefully raked in circles that radiated from the large rocks, like waves on an ocean. Alex counted seven big rocks. What was it about Japanese rock gardens that made them so beautiful to look at? From an aesthetic perspective, gray stones were, perhaps, the most boring things you could think of. There was nothing there to attract the eye. Maybe that was exactly why she could not stop looking at the picture.

'This is a picture of the rock garden at the Ryoan-Ji Temple in Kyoto, which is probably one of the most famous rock gardens in Japan. It's thirty metres long and ten metres wide and consists of fifteen different rocks standing in a 'sea' of white gravel that is raked every day. Isn't it beautiful?'

There was an affirmative silence.

'As I'm sure you all know, these Zen rock gardens are also known as Gardens of Nothingness. One of the basic principles when creating a rock garden is to use Yugen. This is a technique where you never let the viewers see the entire garden. For example, you can hide a tree behind a wall or only let the viewers see the garden through a small window so that they can't see everything at once.'

'You mean that rock gardens are created by people as a homage to the interaction between visible humans and The Unvisible?' Mr Williams interrupted the woman's presentation.

'Something like that,' she answered. She carried on.

'This rock garden is especially interesting because it was built by the forefather of Zen rock gardens, Muso Soseki.

Soseki San was born in 1275 and died in 1351. The stones in the rock garden at Ryoan-Ji are placed in such a way that no matter where you stand in the garden, you always see fourteen of the fifteen stones. Legend has it that only people who have achieved enlightenment through Zen can see the last invisible stone within themselves.

I believe that this garden was created by the Yangyang as a hidden homage to the Knowers. As a reminder to Yinyins to learn the method that makes it possible to see all of nature again.

In conclusion, I think that Muso Soseki was a Knower and that the rock garden is one of the most beautiful guides to the road to awareness about the Yangyang that has ever been made.'

Alex had to admit it was a beautiful theory.

The room was flooded with comments and questions. Someone suggested the garden was built together with Yangyang and the idea of seeing the fifteenth stone was a metaphor for seeing one of them. Or perhaps a Yangyang used to jump between the different stones. Then the phrase 'see the fifteenth stone' could have been a homage to the people who were able to see the Yangyang. That it was a ritual, almost like a dance, between one Unvisible and one observer.

Others in the group started a discussion about whether this ritual was still carried out in the temple's Zen garden. Someone pointed out that the ritual probably was not active any longer and that the original garden could not have had well-raked gravel as this would have made it harder for the Yangyang to move from rock to rock. Someone else pointed out that perhaps they were just really good at walking on gravel, or walked very slowly.

'We should go there! To find out!'

The man who had burst out the order was sitting in the back corner of the room. The place where trouble makers and non-conformists always sat. Alex had once read some advice on public speaking about never taking questions from the people in the back corners of the room because people who choose to sit there were almost always people who liked going against the grain. Alex had remembered that because she too liked to sit in the back corner of a room full of people. The only reason she was not sitting there tonight was because both back corner seats had already been taken when she arrived. By Shadow and by this man who had just spoken.

'Ola, no we should not,' said Mr Williams in a voice of someone who's been telling someone off too many times.

'Ola.' Alex decided to remember his name.

Ola, was a sullen man. He was fiddling with an electronic device as he was speaking.

'Why not? I'll say we go there. Jump on the stones together with them.'

'We should not,' Mr Williams repeated himself. 'I know you like to push limits and be provocative sometimes, but this is another one of these "bad-Ola-ideas" that we do not need.'

Shadow stepped in to answer the objection Ola was bound to fire back. 'Because if the Ryoan-Ji garden is one of the most sacred examples of interactions between Yangyang and Yinyin we should do everything we can not to draw attention to it. The more we want to go there, the more we should convince ourselves that we should not.'

Ola hunkered down in his seat, like a dog that had been beaten up to know its place.

The second speaker of the evening was Mr Williams himself and he showed his first slide right away. It was a close-up of a baby. Was it his own child? Or a grandchild? It struck Alex how little she knew about him.

'I'd like to talk about the relationship between Yangyang and children,' he said.

Had he chosen this topic because Alex was there? Most likely. This presentation was not for the rest of the group, it was for her. Mr Williams started by observing that even though people's noses and ears never stopped growing, our ability to use our senses got worse as we age. When he wistfully noted that he could no longer hear the chirping of the crickets, it made Alex think of the special ring tones for phones with high-pitched tones that had been invented for students. Schoolkids could hear these high-pitched sounds, but their teachers had already lost that ability. What Mr Williams wanted to highlight was the fact that a person's ability to fully use their senses was dramatically reduced as humans aged.

'We go from being able to hear all sounds to hearing almost nothing. The older we get, the more difficult it is to learn a new language while children can learn the sounds of all languages when they are young. We go from being able to speak all languages to forgetting almost all.'

Mr Williams explained that a baby can swallow and breathe at the same time for the first few months of its life and that they are more comfortable under the water than adults. In his third example about breathing, he also pointed out how all children know how to breathe from the abdomen while most adults breathe from their chests. How we have to relearn to breathe again by taking yoga or breathing courses.

'We go from instinctively knowing how to breathe to forgetting how to do it.'

Mr Williams then presented his theory that since we know that people lose their ability to see, hear and speak, it should be totally plausible that very young people, infants, can see things that we adults cannot. And if this happens before the child can talk, then there is no way the child can tell others, like their parents, what it saw.

During the discussions that followed, it was clear that Mr Williams' theory was not new to the others in the group. His aim was to convince Alex. In the group discussion, Mr Williams claimed that new technologies designed to help our senses actually made them dull. He gave the example of how the humble calculator had made us lose our ability to do mental arithmetic and how the use of mobile phones meant we had forgotten people's phone numbers.

'These technological wonders are practical, but how much of our natural ability to understand nature have we lost because of them? We invent things to do what the brain used to do—and the brain is just like a muscle, it shrinks if we do not use it. The brain of a dog is twenty-five per cent smaller than the brain of a wolf, as dogs are not as dependent on having well-developed senses to find food.'

To round off the evening, Mr Williams invited Alex to talk about her project. She presented it as an essay on children's myths, but she noticed that the group interpreted her in the same way as Mr Williams. They heard something other than what she thought she had said. She felt that it was best not to go into a deeper discussion about what she really thought about the evening's lectures. It was not meaningful to argue against people who believed in conspiracy theories; they just cherry-picked the facts that supported their thesis.

When the CIA did not release images from the surveillance cameras that filmed the plane flying into the Pentagon on September 11, it was interpreted as evidence that the CIA itself had crashed the plane in order to get support to go to war with Iraq. And when the CIA then released the film and it did not show anything sensational, this, in turn, was 'proof' that the CIA must have tampered with the film to hide a secret.

The meeting was coming to a close. Alex thanked Mr Williams for inviting her and explained that, unfortunately, she had to go home to study. She was the first to leave the auditorium.

When she opened the door, three boys jumped out at her. One tried to throw a white sheet over her head, but she managed to grab it. The other two boys took out huge water blasters and tried spraying Alex with water. Most of it missed. All three shouted, 'Ghostbusters!' Then they burst out laughing.

Alex became more perplexed, than annoyed, and before she could say anything to the boys, Mr Williams came out shouting, 'Hey! Stop that!'

The three youths quickly ran away, waving their water blasters above their heads. Their laughter echoed down the old school walls. They disappeared down a long, broad, staircase made of marble.

Suddenly, their laughter stopped.

'One day I'm going to get those bastards and teach them what real fear is,' he said.

Alex put her hand on his shoulder. 'It's OK. They're just kids. Let them be. And we got a trophy.' She held up the white sheet.

Mr Williams glanced at the staircase and said, 'You're right. And I think we've already got our revenge.'

He turned and went back into the hall. Alex folded the sheet, put it on one of the benches, and walked down the big corridor.

Manda stood at the top of the stairs and watched the boys come running towards her. She knew that it was actually a good thing when people ridiculed the Knowers. It reduced the risk of the secret spreading. But the boys' contempt for her race had displeased her.

When the first boy came dashing out, she carefully placed her spear in front of his feet as he was about to go down the first step. The spear pushed his one leg behind the other and, from his friends' point of view, it looked as if he tripped himself. He tumbled helplessly down the hard, marble steps, banging against the ledge at the bottom.

His two friends stopped and gave a perplexed look at their friend lying in a strange position below them. They turned around to see if anyone was following them. Then they ran down the steps and picked him up. He must at least have twisted his ankle or maybe even broken it. Together they managed to help their injured companion out of the place. Their prank was not funny anymore.

Manda remained on the top step, watching them. She enjoyed the fact that the humans had such inferior control over their own bodies that they thought it more likely that they had tripped themselves than that an invisible force had caused them to stumble. Even though the boys may not have understood it, she had taught them a lesson. The Yangyang—and Yangyin—deserved respect.

Chapter 17

'Those who see what others do not, see more.'
– Destiny Playback

The prime duty of a parent is to protect her child. But how does a mother protect her child if the threat comes from its father? Mary had been sitting in front of the computer in her home office for several hours. Her eyes were red and swollen. The Internet was not a friendly place for a mother wanting to find useful information about whether or not a man was sexually abusing his daughter. No matter what keywords she used on Google to find relevant and sensible information about having a paedophile in the family, all the links she found had repulsive content.

The most unpleasant search results were the hits that seemed normal in the search list, but that turned out to be porn sites once you clicked on the link. She closed them as soon as she saw what they were, but it was impossible not to get a glimpse of the revolting content. And now she could not get those disturbing pictures out of her head. She had cried more today than in the last five years.

The day had started out so well. Saga had come running out of her room and thrown her arms around her neck to give her a big hug. The hug had been extra-long as Mary had been away for two nights on yet another of her business trips and this time she had not arrived home until Saga had already gone to sleep. They were both so happy to see each other again.

Mary and Thomas had a modern relationship in which she earned the money and he was a stay-at-home dad. Sure, Thomas called himself a 'freelance book designer', but that was mostly to stroke his male ego. It was more than three months since he last had a paying assignment, so in practice, he stayed at home to look after Saga, while Mary concentrated on her career. It had worked well, even if he had been a bit distant lately and Mary sometimes felt she was away from her family a little too much.

But today was Saturday and Mary was spending the whole day with her daughter. Thomas was going on a fishing trip all weekend with his old gang of friends and Mary and Saga had decided to have a 'home spa experience' complete with bubble bath and manicure.

It was as Saga was sitting in the bathtub that she first started to feel worried. Her daughter asked her mother why 'men had spears' and then said something about not sleeping alone in her room anymore.

When Mary asked what she meant, Saga quickly hid her face in her hands and said that she had promised not to tell. Mary had dragged her daughter out of the bath, dried her and sat her down in front of the TV. While the sounds of a children's TV program flooded out of the other room, she had manically looked for information on the Net. She lost track of how long she sat there, but when Saga came back to tell her that she did not want to watch TV any more, she knew it must have been a very long time. Mary decided it was time to talk to her daughter. She tried her best to ask in a non-judgmental and friendly way:

'Tell mummy again what happens in your room in the evenings.'

'I don't know if they'll let me . . .'

'Of course they will. This is our home. Who's said you can't tell?'

'The person in my room.'

'Daddy?'

'Not daddy! The invisible! He told me not to say anything.'

Mary thumped her fist on the keyboard so hard that the mouse fell to the floor.

'Saga! Stop talking about men that don't exist. Has daddy been sleeping in your room at nights?'

'No, but . . .'

Saga avoided her mother's eyes.

'So no one sleeps with you at night?'

'Yes, they do.'

'But you aren't allowed to say who it is because the invisible people have told you not to?'

Had her mother finally understood what she was trying to say?

'And what happens if you talk about the invisible?'

'Then you will die.'

Mary kneeled down and hugged her daughter so hard that the girl had to ask her to stop. The anger and frustration that Mary had felt that morning was replaced by fear and hate.

Looking for information about how you could tell if a father was sexually abusing a child, she had learnt that the children often tried to tell their mothers, and that they often disguised their stories by saying nameless men came to visit. The children described the men in these stories as imaginary figures because the truth was too hard to share. Apparently, it was common for the father to threaten the child by saying that the mother would die if the child ever told. The stories were usually told by the children while taking a bath, or while being naked in one situation or another.

Almost everything applied to what Saga had said today. But it was probably the fear in the little girls' eyes that scared Mary the most.

Even if everything indicated that the unthinkable really had happened, Mary hesitated to confront her husband. If her suspicions turned out to be wrong, he would never forgive her. And even though he had been stressed and moody recently, he was still her husband and the father of her child. She hoped her suspicions would prove to be wrong.

She decided to get more proof. In a court of law, it was the child's word against the perpetrator's and, if it came to that, she needed more than just Saga's confession.

The shock she had been feeling gave way to decisiveness. A plan started to take shape. A search for surveillance cameras came up with some interesting hits, and within the space of an hour, she had ordered three wireless, motion-activated, web cameras that automatically connected to the Web and sent video clips as files to a web site that only she could access. To be on the safe side, she ordered the equipment to be delivered to her work so that Thomas would not find it by mistake.

Telling his own daughter that he would have her mother killed? How detestable could a man become?

The Watcher assigned to Saga and her family was lying on his back on the lawn in front of the house.

People were often more afraid of the unexplainable at night. That really did not make much sense. Yes, the dark made it harder to see a threat, but it also made it easier to hide. For most threats the victim tended not to see the attacker, regardless if it was day or night. For a threat from an invisible creature night or day obviously did not matter at all.

The Watchers did spend some nights at their Subjects' houses, but not every night. After all, Watchers wanted to sleep with their own families too. They tried to be in the Subjects' homes in the evenings so that they could find out as much as possible from the Subjects' chatter about their day, but then they usually tried to get home to their Vimanas before their own children went to bed, which for many reasons usually were slightly later than the bedtimes of the children of the Yinyin's.

Watchers did not watch more when it was dark; they watched all the time. People who worried about visitors they could not see should not be afraid of the dark, they should be afraid of going out, because although they spent a lot of time watching people in their homes, they spent an inordinate amount of time watching them outdoors.

Like all animals, including humans, Watchers were made to be in Nature, though humanity seemed to have forgotten this in recent years. For example, there was only one third as many people spending time in forests now as there were twenty years ago. Perhaps it was because they regarded forests as warehouses for unprocessed lumber. And who wants to spend time in a warehouse?

However, for the Yangyang the idea of looking at Nature as a storage place was ludicrous. They instead looked at human cities and saw huge human warehouses.

So when the Watcher realized that the girl and her mother were going to be at home alone all day, he had decided to go out into the garden so that he could watch the front door from the lawn while studying how the cherry tree leaves danced in the wind, how the blades of grass stretched towards the sun and how the seagulls played high up in the breeze.

Life was beautiful. And everything seemed to be under control.

Chapter 18

'Develop your senses—especially learn how to see. Realize that everything connects to everything else.'
– Leonardo da Vinci

Alex sat down on the last unoccupied bench in the university park. A number of people had walked past without sitting down. She was happy about that. How would she react if someone sat down next to her? She would probably nod her head slightly to acknowledge that she had detected the intruder, or perhaps get out her mobile phone to have a reason not to acknowledge the other person at all.

Alex liked to be by herself. But at times she hated to be alone. Or she specifically hated it when people pointed out that she was alone—for example, in a restaurant when the waiter would look at her pityingly and ask, 'You're alone?' Why not ask, 'A table for one?' Alex did not mind sitting by herself. That she did not enjoy making contact with random strangers or that she preferred to spend time with herself did not make her weird. Alex thought it made her normal. She might not have that many friends, but surely it was quality, and not quantity, that counted when it came to friendships?

Two women out walking their dogs met just in front of Alex. The women were as different as their dogs. The older woman wore a strange short brown cape and a red hat. She was walking a white poodle on a short, white leather lead. The other dog owner was a tall, lean woman, about thirty-five, in a sweaty jogging outfit and she was letting her black Labrador have a breather after their training session. Both dogs pulled on their leads to greet the other. Their tails wagged cheerfully in the air. As the dogs full-heartedly and quite literally jumped at each other to say hello, their owners exchanged short, meaningless phrases about the gender and age of the dogs. And about the weather.

As excited as the dogs were meeting a fellow canine, as uncomfortable were their owners meeting a specimen from their own breed.

Alex was naturally reserved when it came to interacting with strangers, but there were times she hoped that someone would come along and start talking to her. But when strangers, on occasion, actually would come up and talk to her, she would often either become too friendly, or too reserved.

From a social perspective, her paradoxical behaviour of wanting to be by herself and hating to be alone was a disaster. She sent out mixed signals that resulted in her at times feeling as if she was being seen as either a moody loner or as an annoying, overly social chatterbox. Neither one was an asset when it came to getting men interested in her.

She had thought a lot about that. Was she unhappy because she was antisocial, or was she antisocial because she was unhappy? She had come to the conclusion that she was not happy because she was antisocial. And that bothered her.

Dusk had fallen and with the dark came the cold. Without her noticing, the park had slowly emptied. Now all the other benches were unoccupied.

Alex was irritated by how a species like the humans—who were obviously pack animals—had created social rituals that made it so hard to interact with other people. After tens of thousands of years of civilization building, shouldn't we have developed better structures for effective social behaviour? If we were programmed to care about our own little groups—and be on our guard against strangers from competing flocks—then how smart was it to create a world in which people spent so much of their time away from their flock, surrounded by people they did not know?

As for Alex, she did not have a flock. She did not even have a family. She had relatives, but not family.

Behind her, with their backs resting against a tree, sat two Watchers. They were sitting with their shoulders and arms touching. One of them had the job of watching Alex, but as she was sitting on her own, the assignment was not exactly demanding.

The Watcher looked at her. The more urban a society, the more lonely it seemed to become. City people had forgotten how to weave strong social fabrics and instead focused on building thin and temporary threads. The further away from Nature humans lived, the more fragile those threads became, and the harder it was for people to see how damaging their artificial alternative to reality really was.

When artificial sweetener was seen as better than sugar. When people thought air conditioning in cars was healthier than rolling down the window to let some fresh air in. How could fake air be fresher than fresh air? It could be cleaner, but fresher? And why had people created social networks where they would sit alone and watch pictures of their friends hanging out with other people?

The Unvisible had taken the thought of a social net a step further by dividing their society into 'hives'. These separated societies consisted of up to a thousand members who all knew they belonged to the same group and were expected to work together. The Yangyang had created a world with a good balance between the need to meet new, interesting faces and the need to have a protective, private sphere where most people felt familiar and many people knew your name.

The Watcher assigned to be watching Alex allowed himself to gaze around the park. Two Watchers lay in the grass and compared the maple leaves above them. Others sat in pairs on the other four benches with their arms around each other's shoulders. Apart from Alex, there were no humans left in the little clearing where the five benches had been put up. And yet there were more than ten individuals there.

Alex was anything but alone—she just did not know it.

Chapter 19

'Some things have to be believed to be seen.'
– Ralph Hodgson

'It's true. Everything is true!'

Alex sat up in her bed. Wide-awake and yet still inside the dream that had just woken her up.

Completely calm and in a mental chaos. Confused and insightful at the same time. She tried to stay in that limbo between dream and reality. She must not wake up and forget what she had just come to comprehend. That was a delicate tug-of-war between the conscious and the subconscious. She managed to hover in this no-mans-land where she could think clearly without thinking at all.

The puzzle pieces continued to put themselves into place as Alex let the stream of insights rush by, terrified that the smallest movement would scare them away. It was as she was getting a peek into nature's master plan.

Babies who cry . . .

What had Daniel said? 'We can't understand what babies cry about.'

Her thoughts raced from Daniel at her mother's house to Mr Williams at the club. To her own childhood.

'The senses of infants are much more sensitive.'

'Children can hear high-frequency sounds that adults can't.'

Her mind was racing.

She saw dogs on their backs being scratched by white people. A snake. A bird. All white.

All the children with their secret friends.

'They don't want us to know they exist. But they do. Because I've seen them.'

The seriousness in Saga's eyes when she explained how her parents dismissed her stories about invisible people who slept under her bed.

Suddenly the pictures in Alex's head came more irregularly.

Even quicker . . .

The children's drawings. The snakes again. The drawings Mr Williams gave her.

The pyramids . . .

Faster than the clips in a music video, the images flew by her and she noticed all the connections.

It could not be a coincidence!

She was floating. Became one with the universe. Saw The Truth. She felt reality pushing back, like the light creeping into a dark room—a powerful force. Soon she would be fully awake. But that did not matter. She knew she would remember everything. Because this was no ordinary dream. This was the Revelation. The revelation that it was all true.

People are going to think I am crazy, she thought.

Alex stumbled to the bathroom, switched on the ceiling light as well as the light on the bathroom cabinet and threw water on her face as if to test whether her insight could survive out in the cold, logical light of reality. It could.

Her reflection in the mirror showed a face at peace. As peaceful and kind as the faces of born-again Christians who claim to have seen the light.

Except she had not met God.

She had met Nature.

For some reason Alex's mind located a memory of an article she had read about a woman who had survived two terrorist attacks in London in the space of a few hours. The woman's entire worldview had been transformed by these close calls with death. 'It feels as if I have been given a gift, a second chance to understand what life is all about,' she had said. Now finally Alex understood what the woman had meant. A gift—that was exactly what it felt like.

She left the bathroom to get her phone. After grabbing the phone from the bedside table, she sat down on the floor and started to randomly scroll though the contact list. She had to call someone. But who?

Her mother? She quickly dismissed that thought. Jade? She would just laugh. Patrick? No, that just felt wrong. In the midst of this glorious intoxication Alex had a sobering insight. Like a cloud in a clear blue sky that covers the sun for a few seconds, she now knew for sure that things would never get serious with Patrick.

If she did not want to contact him to share the single most significant and private event she had ever experienced, then she was forced to see that, in all honesty, he was not worth pursuing. A heart cannot be convinced. A heart can only open itself unconditionally to invite another soul. And it did not matter how much she wanted a man, Alex now knew Patrick was not going to be the one.

Alex felt like a little girl holding the most stunning butterfly in her hand, knowing that if she opened her hand to show it to someone the butterfly would fly away and vanish.

She had been given the gift of seeing the world, but she had no one to share it with. And even if she did, no one would believe her. A wave of loneliness crushed down on her.

Alex stood up and went over to the bed and saw her black notebook lying open on top of the sheets. She looked at the page. Apparently, without her noticing, she had picked up the notebook while experiencing the whirlwind of images in her head to write something down. She looked at what she had written.

'Listen carefully. See everything.'

Alex smiled. It was true. All of it.

She put back the notebook on the bed, took a pillow from the bed, and lay down on the floor with her chin resting on the pillow. She reached out to the lamp on the bedside table and turned it off. Her eyes were blinded by the darkness. She could not see anything yet she continued to look under the bed.

Alex could have sworn that somcone was looking back at her.

The Watcher lay motionless under the bed looking straight into the woman's eyes, fully aware there was no way she could see him, yet instinctively sensing that she had become one of the enlightened ones. He would have to report this tomorrow. Sending in the Wise had been the correct decision.

The Primary Queen had made it very clear to the Watchers that they must not destroy the moment when someone became a Knower. 'Understand that as soon as a person becomes a Knower she can never go back to not knowing. At that point we have to treat them as the fragile souls that they are. Help them with the transition. Do as much as we can to guide. And if all else fails there is always the final solution. A Knower can never become unknowing. But she can become unliving.'

The Watcher kept looking into the woman's wide-open eyes. At this point his main job was to create a safe mental environment by spreading calmness. But he could not avoid entertaining the thought that the woman in front of him would not live for much longer. A Killer would most likely be paying her a visit.

Chapter 20

'I am seeking for the bridge which leans from the visible to the invisible through reality. It may sound paradoxical, but it is in fact reality which forms the mystery of our existence.'

– Max Beckman

Alex was woken up by sunshine beaming into her bedroom. Her back hurting. Still dazed, she glanced at her watch: 9:06 a.m. Then she saw her notebook and everything came flooding back to her.

It was true.

'Listen carefully. See everything.'

She had to speak to someone, but who? Mr Williams! Alex picked up her phone, and while it was ringing, the purpose of Carte Blanche hit her. Just like Alcoholics Anonymous, the members of Carte Blanche had to have a club where they could vent freely. A place where they could share, without having to explain. A safe environment where they did not have to feel embarrassed. Her train of thought was interrupted by Mr Williams picking up with a, 'Hello?'

'It's true! Everything you've said about The Unvisible is true!'

There was a long silence on the other end, then Mr Williams answered in an almost theatrical voice. 'So you have seen them?'

'No, but . . .'

'So, you had a dream?'

After Alex described all the magical moments of that night—from the quick images in her head to the writing in her notebook and how she had looked into the darkness under the bed—Mr Williams explained that there were basically only two ways for a person to finally realize that The Unvisible existed. One way was to see them with your own eyes, and the other was that the truth came in a vivid dream.

They decided to meet in the afternoon the very same day, so that Alex could unburden herself, as Mr Williams put it. He suggested a café close to her university so that Alex would not have to miss any classes, but when Alex objected that the food there was terrible, he explained that that was precisely why they should meet there. They should be able to talk undisturbed.

Alex had attended all her classes that day, but not registered a single thing that any of her teachers had said. It had been a wasted Thursday from an academic perspective, but her mind could not care less about school. Finally the time had come for her meeting with Mr Williams and she headed over to the café.

Sure enough, the place was more or less empty when Alex arrived. A single man sat by the window, drinking beer. He looked unhappy. Two teenage girls sat at another table and compared ring tones—perhaps it was that noise that was making the man grumpy.

A woman was cleaning tables that looked as if they did not need another cleaning. Alex guessed she was the owner of the café. She looked like someone who had lost her job in a bank and decided to use her severance pay to make her dream of owning a café come true. A woman who loved going to cafés but had no idea how to run one. She looked so tired. As if she had recently woken up to the truth that making one's dream come true can be the worst nightmare ever.

The café had bland chairs and tables. Worse: there were fluorescent lights in the ceiling, giving the whole place a cold and sterile feel. The owner obviously did not have much taste when it came to design. She also did not look like someone who could cook. Strange how you seemed to be able to see that by just looking at someone.

Alex saw Mr Williams waving from his table. *I probably would have seen you even if you hadn't waved*, Alex thought.

Over the next half hour, Alex told him all about her dream, her insights and how everything was connected. Initially Mr Williams just sat there and listened. Alex talked incoherently, jumping between her interviews with the children, her dreams and the theories she had heard at the Carte Blanche meeting. Sometimes she sounded convinced that everything was true. Other times she was doubtful and argued against what she had just said. And sometimes, she even argued against her counterargument. In her head she was fighting a battle between mind and reason, between intuition and logic. Mr Williams had seen it before. He knew the stages Alex would be forced to go through.

'Alex—have you heard how Gandhi described the process of getting others to accept your idea? Gandhi said, "First they ignore you. Then they laugh at you. Then they fight you. Then you win".'

'Actually, that's a myth. Gandhi never said that,' Alex butted in.

'Oh, interesting,' replied Mr Williams. 'I was convinced that was a genuine quote. Thanks for correcting me.' He looked almost joyful for having been corrected on an error.

But then he continued. 'My point, Alex, is that to accept the Yangyang and go from being an Unknower to a Knower, you have to go through seven stages. First ignorance, then rejection, followed by self-ridicule. After that comes doubt. Then conviction and doubt once again. And finally, either suppression or tranquillity. Right now, you're in one of the two doubting phases.'

Mr Williams knew that the best way to help Alex was to first sit quietly and only explain what was absolutely necessary, and then, when the time was right, start to share more about the world she had just opened the door to. But first listen. His interest in Yangyang had made him a better listener.

Mr Williams wondered if his own marriage might have survived if he had learnt the art of listening earlier in his life. But it probably would not have mattered. His ex-wife had claimed that she could accept the bottle, but his 'obsession' with invisible people had been too much. When his wife confronted him about his drinking, he had initially denied having a problem. It was only now, several years later, that he could use the words 'I am' and 'alcoholic' in the same sentence.

He still thought of himself as an Alcoholic Light: as if he drank alcohol the way others smoked light cigarettes. He was not a 'real' alcoholic . . . But looking back, he was grateful she had made him try to tame the dragon.

However, he had never gotten over how his wife despised his dedication for The Unvisible. And what was worse, she had turned their children against him. His family had been custodians of the secret for generations, but his wife had somehow managed to create a deep rift between his children and himself. So deep that Mr Williams had lost all hope of ever turning his off-spring into Knowers.

While the children were growing up, he had decided not to show them the yangsee until they were mature enough to understand the responsibility that came with it. When the children were old enough to understand, his wife had already convinced them he was a deranged alcoholic that they should avoid at any cost. Several years had passed since they last had contact. This sorrow had created a black hole in his heart. A hole that sometimes made him give up on life. But the thunder cloud had a silver lining. Now he had a new meaning in his life—to stop people like Alex from rejecting the truth and to help them become insightful Knowers.

Few were the men lucky enough to find a greater purpose with their lives. Knowing he was one of those men who had, made it easier to survive the dark times.

'Mr Williams, why do you sometimes call them The Unvisible and sometimes Yangyang?'

'The Unvisible is more of a description of how they look. Just as we carelessly might call Caucasians White. "The Unvisible" is, quite simply, the name people call them, our invisible cousins. They call themselves Yangyang, in much the same way a white European from Sweden will call himself Swedish. It's getting more and more common for Knowers to call The Unvisible Yangyang too, but there is a danger to that. If a little child starts talking about The Unvisible, then its parents will just dismiss these tales as stories about imaginary friends. However, if a child starts talking about Yangyang, then there's a risk the parents will Google the word and find similar stories from other parents—and that's something we want to avoid. So, Yangyang is a term we try not to use too much, especially not around children.'

'Why is it such a problem if more people find out about The Unvisible?'

'The Yangyang and humans, whom they call Yinyin, lived in harmony for thousands of years up until about 3,000 years ago. We lived side by side and, more importantly, we all lived close to nature. We really used our senses. Back then, we could see Yangyang as well as experience so many other beautiful things in nature that we no longer can comprehend.'

Mr Williams looked saddened. He continued in a subdued tone. 'But as human civilization developed, the two human families got further and further apart. We people gradually began to build cities, come up with inventions and used technology more and more. We started seeing ourselves less and less as a part of nature and more and more as a species that stood above nature. Or as a species that stood on top of nature. And then we started to look at ourselves as superior also to Yangyang.'

'The ultimate ethnic conflict,' Alex said philosophically.

'I've never thought about it like that, but it's a very good description. When the people in, what is now, Egypt started to use the Yangyang as slaves in their wars, the Yangyang had enough. It's a betrayal that The Unvisible still can't forget. The leaders, or their Queens as they are called, got together and decided to disappear from the lives of the Yinyin. They avoided us for seven hundred years and, during this time, most people lost the ability to see them.

'The human brain is very good at remembering things it has a use for, but it's also really good at forgetting things it doesn't need. So, the Yangyang disappeared from our worldview and were forgotten. When the Yangyang slowly and methodically got closer to us again, they killed everyone who could still identify them. It was a long and bloody war. Hundreds of thousands of people died. Many Yangyang too. But they achieved their goal: after more than five hundred years of guerrilla warfare, the only people left were the ones who could no longer see the Yangyang. And then they could start to live more closely with humans again and once more work on creating harmony in the world.'

'But why did they move closer to us again?'

'It has something to do with harmony, that's the best way I can explain it.'

'Do Yangyang and Yinyin have anything to do with yin and yang, the Asian symbols for how everything is connected?'

'Yes, for a long time the yin and yang symbols symbolized how the two human families lived in harmony with each other. Yin is the black figure and it stands for shade, cloudiness or darkness. Yang means sunny, sunshine and light. Yang stands for peace and calmness. Yin means confusion and chaos. We people are yin because we're darker and cloudier in the sense that we can be seen just like the clouds in the sky. The Yangyang are yang: lighter and brighter. Just like the sky—it's there but you can't really see it.

'The two circles in the classic yin and yang symbol used to represent how we people were a part of the Yangyang's world and how they were part of ours.

'Yin and yang isn't about opposites, but about creating harmony. One can't exist without the other. If yang is too strong, then yin is too weak and vice versa. We need each other. Need to be close to each other. When we are, we feel a harmony that both we and the Yangyang want and that makes us feel good.

'Like the dark force we are, humans are constantly drawn to make selfish decisions. One of the most beneficial, but also most depressing, things about being a Knower is that you get the ability to look at humankind from the outside. And it's not a pretty sight. Man is a pitiful creature. In spite of the power of the human brain and the potential of our hearts, we still don't have what it takes to create a world in which we can live happily together with our closest relatives. After 80,000 years of human development and 5,000 of human civilization, we still haven't managed to create a world of happy people.'

Alex interrupted Mr Williams' monologue and objected, 'Well, I am sure we're happier now than we were a few hundred years ago. And healthier.'

Mr Williams continued on his path, 'But are we as happy or as healthy as we could be? When one of the most common prescribed medicines in developed countries today is anti-depressants. When we live in a world where more people die of diseases related to obesity than starvation. How well have we really succeeded in building a harmonious world?'

Alex wasn't going to let him win the argument so easily, 'How happy and harmonious are the Yangyang then?'

'They don't live in any Nirvana, they live here on earth just like us. They have the full spectrum of human emotions, from happiness and joy to sadness and hatred, just like us. But compared to most of us they are, how should I put it . . . More mentally advanced. More aware. But you also have to remember that they are afraid. Afraid of being exposed, and that creates a lot of stress. Because of their invisibility, they are currently superior to us, but if the wrong people got their hands on the technology that makes it possible for us to see them, then they know they would be wiped out.'

'What do you mean?'

'History is full of indigenous people that have been superior in hiding in nature, but that have still lost against a more technically advanced enemy. From the Native Americans to the Aboriginal Australians. Or the tribes in today's rainforests that are driven out of their homes by hi-tech logging companies. The Unvisible are very aware of this. They live in constant fear of being eradicated. But this seems to make them enjoy life more. People who know they can die at any moment appreciate the beauty of life. The majority of "civilized" humans aren't afraid of anything and so we're jaded with life's grandeur.'

Mr Williams rummaged around in his briefcase. 'I want to show you something.' After a while, he found what he was looking for. He reached across the table. 'Hold out your hands.'

He cupped his hands over hers and gave her something that felt fairly heavy. And cold. It was definitely made from metal.

When he removed his hands again she looked down at the secret item. In her palm lay a circular enamel plate in black and white. She immediately recognized it. It was the yin and yang symbol. But something was not quite right. Were the symbols the other way around? Perhaps. She did not know if the black figure was supposed to be on the left or the right, or if it even mattered.

Then she saw it. In the yin and yang symbols that we are used to seeing, there is a little black dot in the white part and a white dot in the black. But the medallion she was holding in her hands was missing the black dot in the white part.

'What is this?'

'It's The Unvisible's symbol. They call it yang and yin. The larger white part symbolizes the Yangyang and their world while the little white dot shows they have a small part of their lives interwoven with ours. The large black part of the symbol symbolizes the Yinyin—in other words, us humans—and the way the two parts are curved around each other shows how we should all strive to live harmonious lives close to each other. But as you can see, there's no black dot in the white part because we have lost our ability to see and be a part of Yangyang's world.'

She looked at the symbol. The missing dot meant that it was not in perfect balance, but that was why Alex liked it. Perhaps because she herself did not like it when everything was perfect. It reminded her too much of her mother.

'If we're going to live peacefully together then I don't understand why they can't just tell us they exist. Why is a conflict that happened several thousand years ago stopping them from contacting us now?'

'Well, history is full of conflicts that go on for thousands of years.'

Alex thought of all the news reports she had seen about the conflicts in and around Jerusalem. She nodded for him to continue.

'There are examples of The Unvisible and humans who tried to live openly together, but they always ended in disaster.'

'But I still don't get it. If they are to be kept secret, why have you worked so hard to get me to believe in their existence?'

'Because you've been chosen by me. Chosen to be one of our new members. Carte Blanche is an organization that works on creating mutual understanding between humans and The

Unvisible without revealing their secret to the general public. We want to make sure the Yangyang are not exposed; we're on their side in this. However, we also want to do everything we can to limit the number of Knowers the Yangyang decide to kill.'

'Are you telling me my life is in danger?'

'Anyone who knows about The Unvisible has a potential death sentence hanging over them, but Knowers are much less likely to be killed as they are more informed about what you can and cannot do.'

'Is this supposed to make me feel relieved?'

'I hope so. We want to help the people who already know about the Yangyang to understand them better. The better you understand the secret, the easier it is to keep it. As you know, fear feeds on ignorance. And since the ignorance around The Unvisible is monumental, there's a huge risk of massive fear. We want to learn as much as we can about them to better understand the sensitive situation we're all in. As we're a selective group, we're very careful about the people we recruit and now . . .'

Mr Williams paused theatrically.

'And now you want to recruit me?'

Alex looked at him with disbelief.

Only a few days ago, the mere thought of one human kind spying on another would have made her laugh, but so many unexpected things had happened recently that she preferred to keep a cautious and open mind rather than always confronting herself with contradictory evidence.

She thought of countries like North Korea and former East Germany. Societies where large numbers of the population spied on each other. Countries where children betrayed their parents and brothers fought on different sides. And where it was possible to live an apparently rather normal life while under surveillance.

'I need to think about this,' she said, trying to sound more interested than she really was.

'Promise me one thing. Don't talk about this to anyone. I hope you understand just how important it is that this doesn't become public knowledge.'

'Don't worry. No one would believe me if I did.'

'I'm serious. Don't tell a soul. Not one. Promise me that.'

She nodded.

Mr Williams left and Alex sat alone in the almost empty café.

Left alone with her thoughts Alex felt surprisingly sane. She had the same feeling as when you solve a really hard problem and you finally see the solution. Like when you are working on a big jigsaw puzzle and get to the point where you can see what the finished puzzle is supposed to be, even if you have not yet put the last few pieces into place. She was now looking forward to putting the remaining pieces down.

She looked around the deserted café and wondered how many people were really there. It was quite likely more crowded than it looked.

She smiled.

There was only one other guest left in the café: the grumpy old man in the corner. It seemed as if he thought that Alex had smiled at him, and he gave her a bewildered look in return.

But Alex had not been smiling at him. She had been smiling at someone else.

The Yinyin had a new recruit. Was it wise, or even right, to ask a journalist to join the group? Wasn't it the Primary Queen's opinion that all contact with the media should be kept to a minimum? The Queen would not be happy—that was certain. But how would she react? Would she send in a Killer? The Watcher who left the café a few minutes after his Subject almost hoped that the recent developments would lead to some kind of action. It had been far too quiet in this part of the world for too long. A little disorder to create order was never wrong. It looked like it would be an interesting month. A month in which several people would most certainly die.

Chapter 21

'I am an invisible man. I am a man of substance, of flesh and bone, fibre and liquids—and I might even be said to possess a mind. I am invisible, understand, simply because people refuse to see me.'
– Ralph Ellison

Thursdays were Daniel's running day. He was alone in the gym—there was usually never anyone else in the gym in the afternoons—and he liked having the place to himself. He thanked his lucky star that society still believed doctors were professionals who deserved so many benefits and perks. Being paid while exercising—not bad. But this place could use some freshening up. The hospital management had not exactly prioritized the gym in their budgets the last few years and the equipment in the small, damp windowless room was probably more than ten years old.

According to the treadmill, he had already run two kilometres. The monitor on his arm told him that his heart rate was up. He could not help looking at himself in the mirror as he ran. He liked what he saw.

But seventeen straight hours on duty had left their mark. His body got a kick out of the running, but his eyes still looked exhausted. It was not tiredness from running, but from too much work and not enough sleep. To advance in your career at the hospital, you just had to put up with it. That's just how it was. Always take on as many shifts as possible. You could sleep when you made it to Chief Physician.

He slapped his cheek to wake himself up. Eight kilometres left. Then a cold shower and perhaps he could even sneak in a power nap.

But why was it so hot?!

He looked over at the air con and, to his surprise, saw that it was turned off. Hadn't he switched it on when he came in?

Daniel jumped off the treadmill, ran over to the unit and turned it up to max. It was a big, old, floor mounted unit on wheels, that once must have been white, but now looked more yellowish. The fan coughed into life and cold air started pouring out. He jumped back onto the treadmill. But after only a few minutes, it was hot again. He looked at the air con and saw that it was off again.

'What the hell!?'

He ran over to the unit and gave it a whack. It came back to life. At the same time, there was a strange silence in the room. Daniel saw that the treadmill had stopped. The wiring in the gym was clearly done by an amateur. Perhaps you could not have the air con and the treadmill on at the same time? He pulled out the plug to the air con and the treadmill restarted.

Typical! All his running statistics had disappeared.

After a few minutes, he was sweating copiously. The combination of fast running, a warm gym and a tired body made him feel dizzy. He would have to cut the session short.

Five kilometres today, instead of the usual ten. Time to increase the speed.

When he touched the button that controlled the speed of the treadmill, he heard a sound behind him and looked up into the mirror. The air con had started again. But how was that possible? Then the lights went out and the room was plunged into total darkness. At the same time the treadmill came to an abrupt stop.

Daniel fell helplessly in the dark. He did not know which way was up and he hit both his back and head before he found himself lying next to the treadmill. He swore. He was not seriously injured but his back hurt like hell. A sliver of light came from what must have been the door and he started to crawl towards it. On the way, he bumped into something sharp and swore again. He finally made it to the door, fumbled his way to the handle and opened it to let in some light.

He went to the air con and kicked it. Damned low-budget hospital that could not buy proper equipment. But how could the unit have started on its own? He was 100% sure he had pulled out the plug. Or had he taken out the wrong cord?

That was enough training for one day. No point in using machines that had a life of their own.

The three Watchers in the room had worked in unison. One stood next to the light switch, one by the air con and the third next to the treadmill. The universe had a way of evening out injustices. Water ran from one vessel to another until balance was achieved. Air was sucked into a vacuum. Harmony.

People saw balance as something static. They said they 'would have' balance. But balance was not something you 'had'. Absolute balance did not exist, just temporary states that seemed to be in balance. Balance was not a stone that lay still. It was a constant motion—like a tightrope dancer who always has to shift weight in order not to fall. Balance was not peace. It was a continuous evasion of situations to achieve equilibrium. And now the Yangyang had corrected the balance.

It was not part of Yangyangs' assignment to meddle in the affairs of others. Yinyin had their lives and the Yangyang had theirs. But sometimes the two worlds would touch—and that was what had happened tonight.

The Watcher watching Eric was upset that Laura had been blamed for the disappearance of the diamond ring. The Yangyang could not be a part of Yinyins' world, but small intrusions were forgiven. So, together with some colleagues, the Watcher had decided to teach the man a lesson.

At a given signal, the air con was switched on, the light in the gym turned off and the treadmill stopped—causing the doctor to tumble as planned. The Watcher nearest Daniel could not help giving him another push when he was crawling towards the door.

It was a symbolic way of teaching him to respect his fellow human beings.

The Watchers knew that the Yinyin would manage to come up with a plausible explanation for what had just happened. They always did.

Chapter 22

'The poet ranks far below the painter in the representation of visible things, and far below the musician in that of invisible things.'
– Leonardo da Vinci

The instructor stood at the front of the room demonstrating the next position. Alex stood at the back trying to keep up. The yoga studio was really a gym and not particularly well suited for creating a harmonious atmosphere, but it was the cheapest yoga course she could find.

A few months earlier Laura had bugged Alex to go with her to a free introductory yoga class. Alex had desperately tried to get out of it. When she had finally succumbed and agreed to give it a try, Alex had—much to her own surprise—rather enjoyed it. Yoga made her feel good, both physically and mentally.

Alex could easily understand that all that stretching and bending she did in Yoga would have a positive effect on her body. How it also, somehow, had a positive effect on her brain she found harder to explain. But work it did—she was noticeably less stressed after every Yoga class. So regardless how it worked, she was thankful that it did.

She tried to go once a week and now that one hour at yoga had become something she looked forward to. A moment of calm in a turbulent life. She needed something to balance all the stress she had been feeling lately. At yoga she could focus on one thing: getting her body into approximately the same position as her instructor. A refuge. A brief moment of no Unvisible in her mind.

A Yangyang stood just behind Alex, only a few centimetres away. The trick was to position his body as close to his Yinyin partner as possible without her becoming aware that he was there. In the same way the visible and Unvisible birds danced together, so too did Yinyin and Yangyang.

Behind every participant in the yoga class, stood a Yangyang who performed a move that complemented the one the Yinyin did. This choreography had been refined into an elaborate ritual over hundreds of years.

Nature was a stage on which brutal spectacles of survival were performed every day. But Nature was also full of gentle scenes where different species had forged beautiful symbiotic partnerships. Like the way bees help flowers spread their pollen while also getting the material they needed to make honey. Or how the oxpecker eat the insects on the backs of hippopotamuses and the hippos tolerate this in order to get rid of those irritating parasites.

Partnerships that created harmony. Harmony from working together. But like all of Nature's creations, they were fragile. Bees could not just decide to stop pollinating flowers as this would mean the end of both of them. In much the same way, the Yangyang knew that they had to live as close to the Yinyin as possible. The world was more beautiful when they did. No one knows why, but then the universe is full of answers that we do not know the questions to. Why are sunsets romantic? Why does a quiet rain make you feel peaceful and melancholy? Why does looking at a beautiful flower calm the human heart? No one could really explain how harmony was created when

Yinyin and Yangyang lived in close proximity to each other, but the Yangyang knew that this intimacy was vital.

That was the reason they had chosen to move back to live next to humans a long time ago, even when they knew they would have to kill tens of thousands of Yinyins who could still see them. It had been the price that had to be paid in order to create a world where Yinyin and Yangyang could live in close proximity to each other, without Yinyin being aware of the fact that they did. The harmony that this proximity created was crucial.

Yoga and tai chi classes were perfect opportunities for nearness as people moved slowly, and were following set patterns. That meant that the Yangyang could be really close without being detected.

Chapter 23

'Sometimes the heart sees what is invisible to the eye.'
– Jackson Brown, Jr.

As Alex left the gym, she was struck by how light it was. She looked up and saw the most beautiful full moon she had ever seen. It shone so brightly that she found it difficult to comprehend how all this light could come from just a simple reflection of light. As she was admiring the moon some other students from her class came out of the door and followed her gaze. They too saw the moon, smiled a little and commented on how beautiful it was, before excusing themselves to move on with their lives. But Alex stayed and let the cold moonbeams slowly warm her face.

What compels so many eleven-year-olds to lie and watch the night sky and count the stars in amazement, when almost no adults do so, unless they are in love or drunk?

What makes a four-year-old go to a park, pick up an ant and then study it so closely that the world just disappears? What makes us lose this ability when we grow up? Why do we stop being delighted by nature's astonishing ability to create life in countless different forms?

Most people who do have a close connection to nature are humbled by its greatness, while most people living in cities seem to look down on nature. It was a naïve, ignorant and very dangerous way of looking at the world. Hadn't she recently read that humanity had now passed the point in history where the majority of us lived in cities? Perhaps we should flip that and instead say we had now passed the point where a minority of people lived close to nature.

It was getting cold and she had to get home, but the very thought of getting on a bus made her feel claustrophobic. Alex started walking home to get her thoughts into some kind of order. Walking with the light of the moon as her guide felt like the right thing to do.

Mr Williams had told her not to talk about The Unvisible with anyone, but surely she must be allowed to share it with someone she really trusted? How else was she expected to keep such a gigantic secret safe? Wasn't there a bigger chance of keeping a secret if you had like a safety valve? Alex felt as if she would explode. Her heart raced. The calming effect of the yoga was already gone. The stress was back.

She could not tell her friends, classmates or teachers. Especially not Patrick. She could not tell Adam. But she had to tell someone. Daniel? After all, as a doctor he was used to hearing things in confidence. Knowing him, he would not even tell Laura.

Growing up, Alex had not really had a best friend to share everything with. Books had been her substitute for friends and her diary had been the one to listen to her innermost thoughts. But to write about The Unvisible in a diary felt pathetic. No, it would have to be Daniel. Her mother would have a heart attack if she told her, but Daniel would probably be all right. After all, he was her brother and now he would just have to listen to his big sister or she would go crazy.

No Watcher was watching Alex. They were not watching anyone. Whenever there was a full moon, the Yangyang celebrated Poya Day. Under the light of the moon, they all danced until dawn—everyone from the Carers to the Queens. Everyone, except the Killers. They retreated to the most remote places in the woods to bellow their anguish towards the sky; the sky that during a full moon was so paradoxically dark and light at the same time. Just like they were.

The myths about werewolves and wolves howling at the moon were mere pretexts to protect the truth about the Killers seizing the chance to release their frustrations.

Chapter 24

'Some look at things that are and ask why. I dream of things that never were and ask why not?'
– George Bernard Shaw

Alex had booked a small room in a café where they could sit and talk in private. The place was unusual in that the venue was actually a series of small rooms. The decoration was also quite quirky: second hand chairs and sofas, lots of stuffed animals everywhere, and colourful plastic flowers. Alex had not picked it for its quirkiness, but for the fact that they allowed guests to reserve exclusive access to one of the rooms.

It cost a little extra but it was worth it as Alex knew they would not be interrupted and she would hopefully have his full attention. Alex had nicknamed her brother The Dictator when they were young, as Daniel often dictated how things should be done. It had been annoying at times, but she had secretly admired that ability of his of being able to get what he wanted by convincing others and by taking charge. It was one of the things that made him a good doctor.

'Are you out of your mind?'

Alex's brother did not even try to pretend that he took her seriously.

'I said you wouldn't believe me.' Alex looked at him with disappointment.

Daniel laughed. 'Invisible people who live among us and talk to kids? That's ridiculous!'

'Just forget I said anything.'

Alex wished she had kept quiet. In retrospect, she knew that her decision to talk to Daniel was a bad idea. That she might have broken her promise to Mr Williams by revealing the secret to someone—someone who did not even believe her—made it even worse.

Now The Dictator sat there and humiliated her—and that after promising to listen to her problems. Wasn't the whole point of having siblings that you had someone you could talk to about anything? Her brother sat there looking at her with that authoritative doctor's look. And he did not look happy.

'You don't actually believe something you've dreamt? Dreams are dreams! The definition of a dream is that it isn't real!'

'Dreams can also be a way for our sub-conscious to work through complicated issues. Many truths have been revealed in dreams as have a lot of great ideas. The story of Frankenstein came in a dream. So did the idea for Dr Jekyll and Mr Hyde. Even Nobel Prize laureates got their winning ideas through dreams. The most common answer to the question 'Where do you get your best ideas?' is 'In my dreams.'

'It's also the answer to the question: 'Where do you get your craziest, most bizarre thoughts?'

'I didn't say I believed my dream. I just told you what I dreamt.'

'I think the message from your sub-conscious is that you should stop working with psychos. I think you've been infected by someone at that hospital.'

Alex felt her energy draining. She had had enough of his behaviour. Alex and Daniel had jokingly called their frequent, back-and-forth arguing 'sibling bantering', but now Alex realized it could just as well have been called 'her brother bullying her.'

Enough of this, she thought. She replied, 'You know what? Just forget about it.'

'Come on! I'm just kidding! How can you even get involved in such an improbable theory! Can you give me one good reason why any normal person would believe in stories about invisible creatures?'

Amused, Daniel looked at Alex. She did not know what his look meant. She decided to try another tactic.

'Do you know what kills most people in the world?'

Daniel hesitated, taken aback by her direct question. 'Traffic accidents? Wait, Heart Attacks?'

'No. Smoke inhalation. Millions of people in developing countries spend hours in poorly ventilated huts with wood fires or oil lamps as their only means of getting light and warmth. However, they do not understand that the smoke-filled air they breathe every day is killing them. The fire means survival, so instead they curse some evil spirits, misfortune or the weakness of the sick.'

Daniel just sighed.

'Let me give you another example that might resonate better,' Alex said almost desperately.

'Before the discovery of the atom, people thought that matter was something solid and indivisible. But then they realized that water, for example, was made up of two hydrogen atoms and one oxygen atom. This discovery meant we had found the smallest building blocks of the universe. The word atom means 'indivisible'. The fact that later on we discovered the atom itself consisted of smaller particles is an ironic reminder of people's ability to believe they have reached the ultimate answer in a world where no such thing exists.

'The most exciting part of the discovery was that the spaces between the neutrons, protons and electrons are empty and that even the most seemingly impenetrable lead wall isn't as solid as you might think. We think that things function one way only to find out they don't. Appearances deceive us again and again.'

'That doesn't necessarily mean that there are loads of other invisible things that we don't know about, does it?' Daniel replied.

'But the interesting thing is that many of the people who discovered new truths have found it very hard to get them accepted. Doctor Semmelweiss was put into a mental institution after criticizing doctors for not washing their hands. They thought he was crazy because he talked about germs that existed but couldn't be seen.'

'Sure, Alex, but it sounds as if you really do believe that these invisible people exist for real?'

Alex had not really thought about how to present all this to Daniel. And instead of choosing just one argument, she had jumped around describing her theory about The Unvisible sometimes as fact and other times as myth. She heard how illogical and disconnected her arguments were and decided to distance herself from it all.

'But it's a weird coincidence that the same story pops up with five-year-olds around the world, with the mentally ill and in documents from different periods in history—and that they all say the same thing. I'm just saying that it's interesting.'

They sat in silence for a few minutes to get rid of that uneasy atmosphere that appears when two people with completely different viewpoints try to meet without actually getting closer to each other.

Just as Alex took a deep breath to start talking again, Daniel interrupted her. 'Shit!' he burst out. His voice showed a completely different level of commitment when he swore. Alex realized how uninterested he had been during their talk. 'I think I forgot to switch off the iron this morning! Shit—it's probably been on all day. Shit, shit, shit . . .'

'Calm down. If it hasn't already started a fire, then it probably won't.'

'But Laura isn't home today! I really have to go. Can you pay? We'll finish this another day. Or perhaps we were already done?'

Daniel got up and, without waiting for an answer, put his papers into his briefcase. 'Catch you later!' he shouted and then he left. Alex could hear him running through the café.

She remained sitting on the sofa for a while.

The Watcher sat on the window ledge, looking out at the squirrels chasing each other up and down a tree. When the owner of the apartment came home, the Watcher tore himself away from the squirrels and went to meet the man. The Watcher wanted to see the Subject's reaction. Sure enough, the first thing the man did, before even taking off his coat, was to run into the room to check on the iron. It was unplugged.

When the Subject had left the apartment earlier that day without switching off the iron, the Watcher had at first just kept an eye on it to make sure no accident happened. After twenty minutes, the Watcher knew that the man would start doubting his own memory. Had he unplugged the iron or not? So, the Watcher could then safely pull out the cord so he did not have to watch the iron any more.

The Watcher could see the confusion in the face of the man who came running in. For some reason people who thought they had left an iron on had a tendency to pick up the end of the cord, and hold it in their hands, as if that would help reassure them that the iron really wasn't plugged in.

When Daniel grabbed the cord to do just that, the Watcher could not help smiling.

Chapter 25

'We don't see things as they are, we see things as we are.'
– Anaïs Nin

'How come you can't hear them breathe? Or cough?'

When Daniel called her the next day, she was surprised. Her brother was not the kind of person who voluntarily reached out to family. It was always someone else who had to remind him about their mother's birthday—or that Christmas was coming. If anyone from his family called, it was Laura, the woman who had taken it upon herself to nurture the Johansen family unit even though she had only married into it. It was Laura who made sure everyone had a 'nice' time.

Resigned, Alex noted that Daniel did not waste any time on pleasantries but came straight to the point.

'When was the last time you heard a breath?' Alex answered. 'And I guess the explanation is that we aren't suspicious about those noises because we don't know who is making them. So, even if they did make a sound, we interpret it as a twig breaking, or a gust of wind or whatever. But now

I am just guessing. I'm going to a meeting tonight where there will be some real experts. If you're really interested, I can ask them. But my guess is you're only asking me this to bug me.'

'You're going to meet a gang of experts on invisibility? Why?'

'To see if I can pick up something I could use for my school project.'

'So, you're going to gossip about death?'

Daniel was so nonchalant when he quoted their father that she could not be angry with him. Why did he have to make such unnecessary comments sometimes?

She sighed.

'I want to come too,' her brother said. 'I want to see what a group of lunatics looks like.'

'I don't think . . .'

'Are you saying no to your own brother? Are you backing out? What time does it start?'

'Seven o'clock, but I . . .'

'I'll pick you up so you don't have to take the bus.'

Her brother finished their call as abruptly as he had started it.

Alex decided to call Mr Williams and make sure it was okay to bring him along.

'I will bring someone tonight,' Alex said when Mr Williams answered.

'What?'

'I invited my brother. Or should I say, he invited himself.'

Mr Williams words shot back, 'The Carte Blanche meetings are not meant for just anyone. You're invited, but your brother was not. Call him back and tell him he isn't welcome. You haven't told him anything specific, have you?'

Alex was silent as she scrambled for what to say.

'Alex? Have you told your brother?'

'Well, yes . . . No, not directly, but . . .'

'So you've told him?

'A little bit. It just sort of happened.'

'Alex, listen to me very carefully. I do not think you understand the magnitude of what you have been told. The Yangyang are a secret. It's a remarkable privilege to be a Knower—but it's also a huge responsibility. Under no circumstances are you allowed to tell another living soul who isn't already a Knower. I thought I made that very clear. Have you told anyone else?'

'No. Definitely not. I give you my word.'

'Okay. Now that your brother knows, we have to change the strategy. This is what we'll do. Bring your brother to the meeting. We'll stage a pretend meeting where only theories that can be easily dismissed as myths are presented. The aim of this evening's meeting will be to convince Daniel that the stories about The Unvisible are just myths and nothing else. It will all be an act to get your brother to lose interest.'

'So, I'm supposed to lie to my own brother and play a role so that he doesn't believe anything that I've just realized to be true?'

'That's right. I understand that it's a tough situation to be in. But that's the way it has to be.'

'But telling someone more about a topic you want them to know less about sounds very counter-productive . . . Can't I just call him and tell him the meeting was cancelled or that he wasn't invited?'

'Sorry, I should have explained. Here's an interesting thing with human behaviour: The more you tell someone they cannot have something, the more they tend to want it. Tell a child that they cannot pick apples from a tree and they will come back and pick from that tree. There is a reason why teenage girls are advised to play 'hard-to-get' with the boys they are interested in. It makes them more desirable. The more secret the US government tried to make Area 51 the more conspiracy theories flourished around the highly classified military base. When the FBI publicly acknowledged the existence of the base for the first time in 2013 by detailing its history and purpose, the magic pull of the place was actually drastically reduced.'

'Adam and Eve had to eat from the forbidden fruit . . .' interjected Alex.

'Precisely. If we tell your brother he cannot come, now that he has already invited himself, there is a big chance he gets more curious than ever. Curious in a way we neither can control, nor predict. Trust me on this Alex. I know it sounds counter-intuitive, but we have done this many times and it always works. As long as everyone plays their part. It would of course be much, much better if we did not have to do this. If your brother did not know. But now you've told him . . . I thought you understood that keeping the secret was more important than anything else.'

'Even family?'

'Even family . . . Even family . . . Especially family . . .' The pauses between the words were even sadder than the way Mr Williams repeated the words.

The Watcher who had just been monitoring Mr Williams listened to his Queen. She had asked him to sit at the front and explained that the day's meeting would be about what he had just reported. The room was filled with Watchers.

The Primary Queen spoke. 'One journey into the unknown creates no trail. Walking the same track twice makes a path.'

The Watcher thought about what she said. The woman Mr Williams spoke to had told her brother—a man whose son was already a Knower. Two family members had now mentioned the Yangyang to him. And all the Watchers knew that one of the surest ways for a person to realize that The Unvisible existed was through hearing it from a family member. If the same message came from two different family members, then the risk was even greater that the Unknower would start to wonder if it was all really true. That was why the Watchers would spend most of their time watching the Subject when he or she was with family.

Modern day humans' definition of family was laughably narrow, at least to the Yangyangs. It was most often a relatively easy assignment to watch a defined family of a mother, father and child, sometimes including the grandparents too.

It was as if people had forgotten the meaning of the word 'together'. As if family no longer meant 'all of us' but 'only us'. As they wanted to be pack animals without actually belonging to a pack.

In many small villages, especially in Africa and South America and even in certain places in Asia, the old idea of family lived on. There people said that it took a whole village to raise a child—and they meant it. The African expression 'ubuntu' meant 'I'm only a human because you're a human'. It was all about learning to see how the collective was greater than the individuals in it.

The idea of the extended family still exists in many Arab countries too. Instead of borrowing money from a bank, you go to your cousin's father-in-law. If an acquaintance of some distant relative is in town, then you invite him in. In these countries a family's survival can depend on having close connections. But the more developed a society became, the easier it was for people to do without an extended family. And the richer the society, the smaller the families and the looser the relations got. When a country became richer, it became connectionally poorer.

The Primary Queen stood up and declared, 'Every person is an island. All islands are connected. We are all together on an island.'

The Watcher reached out to hold the hand of the Watcher sitting next to him. They all did. When their fingers connected and their eyes met, a social band was formed between the two. They were both a part of the same family. Then they looked to the other side and connected to that person. Everyone in the room was a part of the same family. A very large family in the sense of seeing others as a part of yourself and yourself as a part of others.

Chapter 26

'The true mystery of the world is the visible, not the invisible.'
– Oscar Wilde

'I'd like to start this evening's meeting by welcoming our guests.' Mr Williams smiled at the group from behind the old teacher desk that he sat behind. The others turned in their chairs and looked at Alex and Daniel, who sat by themselves in the back of the room. Daniel had his arms crossed tightly and nodded briefly in response. Their curious glances made him feel a little uncomfortable.

'Freaks,' he whispered to Alex when the others had turned back.

Mr Williams got up and started his presentation. His first slide read: 'Indications of man's tribute to the white ones'.

'The African Yaka people have their dwellings along the Wamba River and they use a lot of masks and adornments. Their masks are painted white with black rings around the eyes. They're used for frightening the younger men of the tribe.

'Another African tribe are the Murzu, a small, nomadic people in the border regions between Ethiopia and Sudan. As you can see on the slide, it's their tradition to paint their faces white when going out to war. And for thousands of years, the stately Maasai of Kenya have whitened their faces to look stronger, holier and more masculine. This doesn't only apply to the indigenous people of Africa. In Australia, for example, the Tiwi tribe paint themselves white as a tribute to life. This is also common for many Native American tribes.'

The discussions at this meeting were much shorter. Alex guessed it was because the participants wanted to give Daniel the impression that they were just a group of people who spent their time studying strange, historical theories that they didn't want to discuss with strangers.

Alex noticed a couple of new faces in the group, two men in their thirties who just had to be brothers. They looked so alike that Alex wondered if they were twins. Mr Williams introduced them as Ibrahim and Abraham.

The two brothers stood up. 'We believe that the old Pharaohs achieved their divine status by using a partnership between the Yangyang and Yinyin.'

The brothers had a theory that the Egyptian hieroglyphs were based on the sign language of the Yangyang and that they had given written language to the Pharaohs as a gift. One of the brothers held up a little, plastic souvenir pyramid and put it on the table in front of him. The other brother held up a similar pyramid, which had clearly been painted white.

'We believe The Unvisible taught them how to transport heavy objects in the sky, so the Pharaohs built the pyramids as a tribute to thank them.

'We even think that the construction of the pyramids has a deeper meaning. That humans and Yangyang built common structures, called Vimanas, that were connected to each other.'

Abraham turned the white pyramid upside down and placed it on top of the other pyramid. He did his best to place the pyramids so that their tops just touched. For a second, it looked as if he had managed to get the upper pyramid to balance on the lower one. But then he was forced to use his hands to keep the pyramids on top of each other.

Alex saw that he still had white paint on his hands.

Ibrahim picked up an hourglass that looked really old. He turned it upside down and let the sand run down. When he put the hourglass next to the two pyramids with their tops touching, you could immediately see the resemblance.

'We think that the hourglass got its shape from the double pyramids. An hourglass isn't just a way of keeping track of time. It's also a symbol on a more existential level about the passing of time. It symbolizes the mortality of all living things and the endless flow of time. It's a symbol of life and death. Of yin and yang.'

'Hang on a minute.'

It was Daniel butting in. Mr Williams looked quickly at Daniel, then at the brothers and finally at Alex. It was a good time to let Daniel into the conversation.

'If I understand it correctly, these floating pyramids are made of solid matter but we can't see them and they have also managed to invent some sort of technology to get heavy matter to float?'

'Exactly,' the brothers answered in unison. Then one of them continued, with the other nodding along in approval, 'We think—well, we're pretty convinced—that the structures are held up using the same principle as helium balloons: in other words, they are light but strong structures that are kept afloat with some kind of substance that is lighter than air. A gas perhaps, but one that is mixed with air so that you can still breathe. Like the balloons you get at McDonald's, but probably without sounding like Donald Duck.'

'So, if the floating pyramids are physical structures and you say they're built on top of the pyramids in Egypt, then I guess all you have to do is to fly a helicopter over the pyramids. If it crashes, you're right. If not, you're wrong. Simple deductive reasoning.' Daniel was trying to put the brothers on the spot.

While the brothers looked at each other to decide who was going to answer, Ola turned around and glared at Daniel.

'The Yangyangs' pyramids are, of course, no longer on top of the Giza pyramids,' said Ibrahim.

'Of course not,' Daniel muttered ironically.

'It's our belief that the Yangyang have moved their pyramids, but that there are still several thousand floating pyramids around the world. The Unvisible must have developed a system for moving them whenever a plane or helicopter comes near.'

Abraham continued. 'When the pyramids were moved from their harmonious positions, it was a sign to the Yangyang that harmony between the two races was impossible at the time. The pyramids will be put back together when Yinyin and Yangyang live together in peace again.'

There was no stopping Daniel. He did not care if he made an enemy of everyone in the group. They would have to come up with a better argument if they believed in what they were saying. And if Alex had understood the strategy correctly, that was the scenario the group wanted. To get Daniel to feel as if he was winning an argument which would in turn make him permanently convince himself about how nonsensical the whole idea of an invisible species truly was. But if they let him win too easily he might get suspicious so the group had to offer just the right amount of push-back to his opinions.

'Very interesting . . . But why don't we see them on radar?' asked Daniel next.

'Radar?'

'Yes, RADAR. You do know it stands for "radio detecting and ranging". It's literally a technology for detecting things.'

Once a besserwisser, always a besserwisser, thought Alex.

Now it was Ola's turn to explain. 'Firstly, we have a rule that we don't take questions until the presentation is over. And secondly, I think you ought to watch your tone. You're a guest here and should behave like one.'

Daniel rolled his eyes and gave a lopsided smile. 'I am so very sorry. As you say, I'm a guest and I don't know all the rules you have in your little club. And, by the way, haven't you just broken the rule yourself?'

Ola's eyes flashed, but he did not manage to come up with a smart reply before the two brothers spoke in unison again. 'We were finished . . .'

'Let's start off by answering your question about radar . . .' Ola said.

Ola enjoyed this opportunity to finally put the arrogant guest in his place. 'Now, radar isn't the world's most advanced technology. If people have managed to build a stealth plane that can't be detected by radar, then isn't it plausible that a technology The Unvisible have been fine-tuning for over five thousand years can avoid being detected by a simple radar? Oh—you do know what a stealth plane is, right?'

Daniel did not answer, but gave Alex a 'who-does-this-guy-think-he-is?' look. Instead he said. 'Can I ask you something else? If all these people exist like you say, then why can't we see their footprints?'

Now it was Ola's turn to roll his eyes. 'Aren't you going to ask why they can't be seen with heat-seeking cameras too?'

'That's actually a very good question. Let's add that to the list.'

'I think we have a sceptic in our midst . . .'

It was Mr Williams who had joined the discussion. The whole point of the evening's presentation was to get Daniel to think the group was wrong. Daniel had to feel he had won the argument.

Daniel ignored Mr Williams but turned his attention to Ola's last question. 'So, why don't we see them with heat-seeking cameras?'

'Let's start with your first question. Their footprints are visible—just like those of every creature that walks in sand, or snow for that matter. Why don't we see their tracks in the sand? For the same reason we don't see the tracks of Navy Seals or other Special Forces. They simply avoid walking in sand, snow or rain. And if they do leave a footprint, it's not usually a problem; they just have to make sure there's no one around at the very moment a print is made. In certain cases, they use special shoes that leave the print of a rabbit or dog. But the most important question you should be asking yourself is perhaps "How many footprints do I leave every year?" This is a minor problem in modern societies today.'

Daniel jumped to the more technical question. 'But why don't they show up on thermal cameras? After all, thermal cameras record the temperature of whatever they film, so unless they have no body temperature, they should still show up when using thermography.'

Ola replied, 'Thermal cameras detect temperature by recognizing and capturing different levels of infrared light. But just as the cell structure of The Unvisible distort the visible light, so also does it distort the infrared light. We've made our devices to measure ourselves and not The Unvisible.'

Ibrahim explained further. 'Even with a radio you can miss stations just because you're on FM and not AM. The radio is working but it's on the wrong wavelength.'

Ola continued. 'It would probably be relatively easy to program a heat-seeking camera to look for the Yangyang. But a thing does not need to be very well hidden in order to never be found, as long as no-one is looking for that thing.'

'And you expect me to believe all this?'

Ola: 'Do you believe that dinosaurs existed?'

'Um . . . yes. I think they existed. And no, I don't think that a spaceship killed them or an army of invisible blondes slaughtered them but that a meteorite crashed into the Earth and changed the climate . . .'

'No one has ever seen a living dinosaur. We've only dug up bits of bones that we think make up the skeleton of huge animals. So you believe in something that no human has ever seen because there's evidence that indirectly indicates they might have lived. But you don't believe in the existence of the Yangyang despite the many people living around the globe have solid proof they exist—many having seen them with their own eyes?'

Mr Williams raised his hands to the ceiling and declared. 'Let's pray for the visitors to see the truth!'

Everyone stood up.

Throwing in some religious references at the end was a brilliant way of getting a science buff like Daniel to lose interest. Alex now understood how smart the strategy for the evening had been. There was no way Daniel was going to leave here believing anything about The Unvisible was true when he would leave the meeting feeling that he had won all the arguments of the night. It was mental Judo, using the rhetorical power of Daniel against him.

'This is ridiculous! No one can argue with you. You've decided you're right and everyone else is wrong. The more someone attacks you, the more convinced you are that you're right. You're as fanatic as Hare Krishna followers. You can believe what you want, but I know you're wrong.'

'So, if you could see them, would you believe they are real?'

Ola looked at Daniel like a poker player who has just realized he has the winning hand. He knew he had Daniel's full attention.

'But I thought your theory was that they are invisible?'

The atmosphere in the room shifted. It got tenser. Something had changed in much the same way an audience can stop talking in unison to let the band know that now it was time to start playing, or the way dinner guests know when the party is over. A collective silence fell; a common decision was taken.

Mr Williams tried to prevent it. 'Let him go,' he said.

In the silence, Alex could hear the minute hand on the big clock move.

Ola fidgeted and could not control his annoyance. 'I'm fed up with people like him. People who think that their logical, square view of the world is the truth. Who have stopped learning. Who are like full bottles that are impossible to get any new liquid into.'

Mr Williams walked up and stood right between the two men arguing.

'Ola, look at me. This is one of those "bad-Ola-ideas". Just stop it.'

Alex was not really sure what was going on, but it seemed like Mr Williams had stepped out of the role he had been playing to convince Daniel, and now was desperately trying to get through to Ola.

Ola could not care less. He was obviously a loose cannon. Ola looked at Daniel again. 'So . . . Do you want to see them or not? Let's make a bet. If you haven't seen a Yangyang within thirty minutes, I'll give you my mobile phone. If you do see one, then you have to give me your phone and a new laptop. Deal?'

'That's not a very fair bet.'

'Well, it is, considering I'm betting you'll get your picture of the world turned upside down. So, what do you say?'

'All right. But when I win, you really have to give me your phone.'

'Ola! Stop it!' Mr Williams was furious.

Alex felt an urge to put a stop to her brother's inappropriate behaviour. 'Daniel . . .' She put a hand on his arm, but he pulled away and walked up to Ola. The two men stared at each other.

'You're all crazy. Completely crazy. Alex, stay if you want, but I don't want to waste my time on these nutcases. You can have your little club to yourself. I am out of here.'

Daniel turned on his heel and left the room. But Alex thought she saw Daniel wink at Ola and smile. As soon as Daniel had left, the mood lightened considerably. Mr Williams went and sat at his chairman's spot again, and order was restored.

The tension in the room decreased. When Ola mumbled a 'Sorry' to the rest of the group things quickly went back to normal. They were a well gelled group who knew not to let tension linger.

Mr Williams restarted the meeting to do the formal closing procedure and the announcing of the dates for their next meeting. At the same time Ola casually picked up his little bag, stood up, and excused himself with a short 'Guys, please excuse me. Got to take a leak.'

The Watcher standing in the corridor saw two men leave the auditorium in quick concession. The first man gestured to the second man to follow him and they ran into a smaller classroom next to the auditorium. He decided not to follow them.

Chapter 27

'What delights us in visible beauty is the invisible.'
– Marie von Ebner-Eschenbach

The meeting was formally over but everyone lingered in the room. Like no-one had anywhere better to be.

Mr Williams called Alex and they discussed how the meeting had gone. The consensus was that overall it had gone according to plan. Apart from the hiccup with Ola everyone had helped to convince Daniel that The Unvisible was an uninteresting thing to dig deeper into. He would most likely not come back to the subject as long as Alex did not bring it up again. Mission Accomplished.

Mr Williams took Alex's hands in his and looked her in the eyes.

'Now that the threat is out of the way, let's focus on the true purpose of tonight's meeting?'

'Which was?'

'To let you see them.' His eyes sparkled like a child on Christmas when he said it.

The feeling of Christmas was amplified when Mr Williams carefully lifted a pair of glasses out of a small box that had been in front of him all evening. He treated it as a precious gift.

He even sounded a bit like Santa Claus when he started to speak, or at least like what Alex imagined Santa Clause would sound like.

'These glasses are three hundred years old and once belonged to Isaac Newton. They have been handed down from generation to generation in my family ever since.'

'You are related to Isaac Newton?' Alex looked intriguingly at Mr Williams.

'I'm an almost direct descendant from him. Newton not only discovered gravity, which was an invisible force that existed before people understood what it was, but he was also very interested in the refraction of light. He was the first to understand that light was not indivisible. Before Newton, scientists going all the way back to Aristotle believed that you couldn't divide light up into smaller parts or affect it. But by directing light through a prism, Newton succeeded in showing that white light was, in fact, made up of a number of different colours.'

Mr Williams had captured Alex's attention just as he had when he told her about The Unvisible for the first time. And just like that time he took the time to go into details. 'Nowadays, we're convinced that Newton was a Knower. With his ground-breaking work on optics, he managed to see and understand things about the properties of light that no one had before. And while carrying out this work, he must have built an instrument by chance that could refract light in such a way that The Unvisible became visible. Others claim the opposite is true: that it was The Unvisible who taught

Newton about the properties of light. No matter which theory is true, most people in the know agree that knowledge of The Unvisible, and especially the realization of what it would mean if this knowledge became more widespread, was the reason why Isaac Newton at forty years of age—and in a time when he was one of the most respected scientists in the world—suddenly turned his back on science and went into a deep depression. It was as though he thought the increased advances in science would result in new technologies that could reveal the existence of The Unvisible to everyone.'

'Fascinating. What's that text on the box?' Alex had noticed an inscription. It looked very old.

'This,' Mr Williams said and held up the box that had contained the glasses, 'is a text written by Isaac Newton himself. A text that was also published in his famous work Opticks. It's a text that quite plainly shows he was a Knower. A text in which he describes the existence of The Unvisible, but cleverly wrapped up in reasoning about God's ability to create different kinds of matter.'

Mr Williams put on his reading glasses and started to read. 'And since space is divisible in infinitum and matter is not necessarily in all places, it may be allowed that God is able to create particles of matter of several sizes and figures, and in several proportions to space, and perhaps of different densities and forces, and thereby to vary the laws of nature, and make worlds of several sorts in several parts of the universe. At least, I see nothing of contradiction in all this.'

Mr Williams had emphasized the passage 'and thereby to vary the laws of nature, and make worlds of several sorts'.

He paused briefly and put the box down.

'We think that Newton wrote the text on the box as a clue for other Knowers to explain the glasses' function without letting other people understand what he meant.'

Mr Williams ran his fingers over the glasses. It looked as if he was stroking them. 'Just as 3D glasses give you a three-dimensional feeling when watching a film filmed with two cameras, these glasses make it possible for people to perceive light in a way we normally can't.'

'You mean that these glasses will let me see them? The Unvisible? How?'

'It's easier to explain if we use a rainbow as an example. We don't normally perceive light as a cascade of colours but as something without colour, or to put it another way, as white light. But when a rainbow is formed, the light in the water drops in the air is refracted at an angle of forty-two degrees, which means light is emitted with a slight variation. And we see a beautiful colourful bow of light.'

'What most people aren't aware of is that sometimes it's possible to see a second rainbow above the normal one. The second rainbow is visible when the light is refracted at a 50-degree angle and it's not as visible; often we can't see it at all. The second bow shows the different colours in the reverse order of the more visible primary rainbow. Between the two rainbows there is a band called the Alexander's band. This band is perceived as being a darker patch of sky, but that's because we can only see a limited spectrum of light.'

Mr Williams was in lecturing mode, and Alex let him run with it. She also had nowhere better to be. She was not very convinced that she was actually going to see some Unvisible at the end of the night, but she found the information he was sharing quite interesting.

He continued, 'There's also something called multiple supernumerary bows that only appear on certain special occasions. They're small, thin green or purple bows that can be found inside the inner blue side of a primary rainbow.

People say these bows are an insult to today's knowledge of geometric optics as they break all existing theories about how light works. And yet—there they are. As you can imagine, they annoy a large majority of the scientific establishment that study light refraction.'

Alex could feel that his monologue was coming to an end.

'Just as a rainbow lets us see all the lovely colours that exist in normal invisible light, so can a pair of glasses like these break down light into smaller parts. Using these glasses, we can see invisible light with the naked eye. In simple terms, you can call it a reverse rainbow.'

Mr Williams held up the glasses and pointed them at the ceiling light so that Alex could look at them.

'As you can see, they are made of different coloured glass lenses. There are a total of seven lenses for each eye, one for each colour in a rainbow. By letting the light refract several times through the different colours, we can create the illusion of real light.'

'Real light?'

'That's right. Light that spans across its entire spectrum. With these glasses, a person can see a complete rainbow for the first time, including the Alexander's band—and not just the outer edges that we see today. But more importantly . . .'

Mr Williams stretched and made a theatrical pause while holding up the little device in both hands.

' . . . but more importantly, this makes it possible for a Yinyin to see a Yangyang. It makes an Unvisible visible to people like you and me. We call it a yangsee.'

His gaze was so intense that Alex instinctively took a few steps back.

Mr Williams took the glasses and approached her. He put the device on Alex's head while he explained, 'Turn this lever on the side if you want to see the world the normal way. Switch it back to see everything again.'

Then he cautioned her. 'I do not want to scare you—what you will experience will be nothing short of amazing and your world will forever change—but there are a few rules you need to be aware of.'

Alex listened very carefully. She had started to pick up when Mr Williams was not kidding around.

To be honest she was nervous. Nervous in a way she had not been since she tried bungee jumping many, many years ago. Thrilled and scared to death at the same time. Or how she had been feeling when she travelled abroad by herself for the first time in her life as a teenager. A whole world to discover, and yet so very alone.

She was happy Mr Williams started to talk again to interrupt her inner dialogue.

'Rule number one is: no body contact. People who experience body contact with a Yangyang tend to want to share that experience with someone else. And remember, The Yangyang kill all humans who find out they exist, and who cannot keep it a secret . . . Most often, they kill them through "accidents". Once upon a time, they made people fall off horses; nowadays it's often traffic accidents. Or fake suicides. Sometimes they will infect those they want to eliminate, especially if it's a large number of people.

'Rule number two: you can be totally captivated by what you see, but don't let them know you can see them. The Yangyang don't understand what a yangsee is, so it's usually quite safe to wear it—as long as they don't feel you are watching them. But please understand that if they found out we had the technology to see them, then they would definitely kill us all, so the second rule is very important!

'Rule number three: if you see a Killer, hide or, at the very least, stay away.'

'A Killer?' asked Alex.

'Yangyang communities work similarly to an ant colony or a hive of bees. In the nest, there's a queen who rules over the people in her community. She is called the Primary Queen, or sometimes just referred to as "the Queen". To her help she has two Secondary Queens. In her entourage there are a large number of Carers who take care of the Queens, the children and the home they live in.'

'That's the floating pyramids we described,' said one of the twins.

'The Watchers and the Killers work outside. The Watchers' job is to observe us humans. There are nearly as many Watchers in a city as there are families. The Watchers monitor, collect information and report incidents between the Yinyin and Yangyang, but they don't interfere. If the Queen decides that someone has found out too much, or cannot keep the secret, she sends out her Killers to eliminate—that is, to kill—the person in question. The Killers' job is—just as it sounds—to kill people. Something they are frighteningly good at.'

'I understand. No body contact. Don't reveal that I can see them. And avoid the Killers. How do I know which are the Killers?'

Ola replied, 'Oh, you will know.'

'Ready?' Mr Williams took Alex's hand in his and led her out of the classroom, then he let her go with a soft 'Brace yourself for the beauty of life.'

Alex walked out of the School and began to wander around the neighborhood. It was a normal day. The sky was a little gray. Perhaps it would rain soon. And yet the world was more beautiful than she had ever seen it. Wherever she looked, there they were. A young, female Yangyang sat with her back to a post box and looked up into the sky.

The woman's short blonde hair shone in the sunlight. She sat with her feet sticking out into the road, and every time a car came along, she pulled in her legs to let the car pass without taking her eyes off the sky. She smiled every time and Alex looked up to see what the woman was gazing at.

About fifty snow-white doves, and as many black birds, were circling in the sky thirty metres above the ground. They did not fly like other birds Alex had seen; they flew in formation, as if dancing. They soared in pairs in a complex pattern where they criss-crossed their paths, swerving at the last minute to avoid colliding with each other, and then they rose up to the sky, swooped right down, flew out to the sides, turned around and flew into the middle. It was a spectacle. A completely astounding and silent spectacle. Alex just stood there open-mouthed. Were the birds also invisible?

She moved the control on the goggles and saw the world as she was used to seeing it. All the Yangyang were invisible again. As were the white birds. Only the black ones remained. Without their pale partners, the flight of the dark birds looked chaotic and like an uncoordinated muddle, just as big flocks of birds usually did. She moved the knob back and saw once again how beautiful and synchronized the birds' choreography was when she saw it in its entirety. It was clear that the normal birds from her world had not lost their ability to see The Unvisible birds. A moment of sadness came over her as she realized that she did not even know what kind of birds she was looking at. Where they jackdaws? Ravens? Here they were giving her the most amazing dance and all she could call them was 'black birds'.

Two birds broke away from the flock and flew, as if on command, directly to two Unvisibles that had come out of a house. The two men sneaked out of a door that a courier had been too lazy to close after himself.

They must be Watchers, Alex thought. The men walked with straight backs and looked as if nothing could harm them, and they knew it. When the two birds flew to them and sat on their shoulders, it looked completely natural. Only a few days ago she would have laughed at the thought that there were invisible animals, not to mention invisible people, living among us. Now she stood admiring two invisible birds that had landed on a couple of Yangyang and thought it was the most beautiful and natural thing she had ever seen.

The whole experience made her feel unique—and alone. Alex stopped for a moment and quietly admired the world.

She completely ignored the fact that the people she met probably wondered what kind of weird glasses she was wearing. An old Unvisible man sat on a bench by a bus stop. He got up gracefully when a businessman sat down on what he thought was an empty bench to tie his shoelace. When the businessman moved on, the old man sat back down. On one side street alone, she saw a group of five Unvisibles. They seemed to be everywhere. What was it Mr Williams had said? That there were nearly as many Unvisibles as there were families in a town? She looked up. On the roofs of several houses, young Unvisibles stood, watching the street below.

Alex walked around the neighborhood and, even though she knew the area very well, it was as if she was seeing it for the very first time. Everything was the same and yet it was so different. She felt she had been living in two dimensions all her life and had just experienced the third. As if she was seeing the world for the very first time.

She could be walking around like this for hours, but it was time to go back to Mr Williams. She reluctantly started to walk back to the School.

She thought to herself: *Is this what a deaf person feels like when she gets a hearing aid and hears the sounds of the world for the very first time?*

The old Yangyang who jumped up from the bus stop looked at the woman walking by him. He marvelled at the strange contraption she was wearing on her head.

These people have the weirdest sense of fashion and the most peculiar addiction to technology, he thought to himself.

Chapter 28

'In how many lives there lurks a hidden romance or a hidden terror.'
– Anna Leonowens

A few minutes earlier.

As soon as Daniel saw Ola come out of the auditorium Daniel signalled to Ola to follow him. Together they tried a few of the doors in the hallway until they found one that was not locked.

They quickly went inside.

When Ola had locked the door, he turned towards Daniel.

'So, did I read you right? The bet is still on?'

'It is.' Daniel could not wait to at least get something out of this evening.

When Daniel had excused himself from the main meeting earlier Ola had noticed how Daniel had given him a subtle nod and a smile. Ola had, correctly, interpreted that as Daniel signalling that he wanted to go through with the bet in a more secluded place where no annoying opinionated people would disturb them.

Now it was just the two of them. Time to do some business.

Out of his little bag Ola ceremoniously took out a metal box that housed a pair of bizarre looking glasses. It had two five-centimetre-long lenses which dominated the front of the goggles. On the side were some knobs and buttons as well as a couple of electronic sockets. The contraption looked too heavy for the head, but it was clear that was where it was supposed to sit. Two ends stuck out at the sides holding it in place behind the ears. In addition, there was a thin metal frame that started between the two lenses and went around the back to bear some of the weight. The goggles were not pretty and were, quite obviously, homemade. But they were well built and, with a little adjustment, could pass off as an advanced prototype, or some kind of military instrument.

'Stand still,' Ola instructed Daniel as he stood behind him helping him put the device on Daniel's head. When Ola was happy with how it fit he took a step back.

'Look, before I turn it on, please know that I am not doing this because I like you. I am doing this because I think you are an asshole who needs to be put in his place.'

'Whatever works for you.' Daniel just wanted the bet to be over with.

'I hope this will make you a better man. And I hope, for your own sake, that you will know how to keep The Unvisible a secret . . .'

Daniel decided to humour the guy, 'I'd like to remind you that I'm a doctor and as such I am used to dealing with sensitive information. No need to worry, buddy.'

Ola bit his lip. The two men behaved like two lone wolves who had accidentally wandered into each other's paths and now tried to look cool and composed—and intimidating—

at the same time. Two alpha males mentally fighting for domination.

Ola flicked a switch on the device and told Daniel, 'We usually talk about the two worlds, the normal world and the real world. The normal world is the one everyone sees without the yangsee. The real world is the one we can only see when we're wearing the yangsee glasses.' Ola explained that the real world had a weak light gray-blue tinge to it, and that this was due to the limitations of the glasses.

When the yangsee was in place, Ola asked Daniel if he could see properly and Daniel gave the thumbs-up sign, like a diver under water. 'You can still talk, you know,' Ola laughed.

'I know,' Daniel replied, irritated. 'So, where are all these invisibles then? I can't see any.'

Ola answered. 'Hold your horses. We cannot go out there now, what if we run into the rest of Carte Blanche?'

'I don't care.'

'Well, I do.' Ola blocked the way.

Daniel conceded. No reason to risk for the bet to be called off.

The two men grabbed a couple of chairs, sat down, and let their mobile phones distract them from being bored from waiting.

After a while Daniel stood up and stated, 'OK, enough. Let's do this, OK?'

'Sure, just go out into the corridor. I wouldn't be surprised if you can see one outside the door.' Ola too was eager to win the bet and teach Daniel a lesson.

Before Ola could finish his sentence Daniel was already at the door unlocking it.

'Banzai!' Daniel shouted before tearing open the door and jumping out into the corridor. As quickly as he had jumped out, he took a step back.

Then it was quiet for a few seconds.

Daniel stood completely still in the doorway, with one hand on each door frame. He slowly placed his hand on the control and switched between the two positions several times.

'Holy shit! How did you do that?' he whispered to the room.

'What can you see?' Ola wondered.

'A man at the end of the corridor. He's completely white. So . . . beautiful.' Daniel sounded as if he were in another world.

'A Watcher,' explained Ola

'I have to get closer.'

Daniel started to walk down the corridor. Ola followed a few steps behind.

'Just so you know, he'll disappear before you get there,' whispered Ola.

'Shit!' murmured Daniel.

'He disappeared? OK, that's enough. You got to see them,' said Ola.

But Daniel was not listening. He crept forwards like a hunter that has caught sight of a deer and does not want to scare it away while trying to get closer for a better shot.

Daniel had forgotten all about Ola. He had forgotten all about everything. The only thing he could see was that white figure at the end of the hallway. The only thing that went through his mind was the thought 'What is this?' combined with an intense urge to catch it. Somehow the experience had connected him to his primal brain. He was a hunter.

When Daniel came to the staircase he gasped. There, only a few metres in front of him, sat a completely white man on the floor, fiddling with something on his shoes. It was a Watcher, but Daniel did not know that yet. The Watcher jumped to his feet before Daniel really understood what he was seeing. Without thinking, Daniel threw himself onto the man's legs. Just then, Ola came running down the corridor and jumped onto Daniel and the Watcher.

Daniel still had his arms around the Watcher's legs and held him down. The Watcher tore himself free in less than a second, but it was already too late. Ola, of course, could not see the Watcher, but he had been able to feel the Watcher's body and work out where his throat was. When he found it, he squeezed as hard as he could.

'What the hell are you doing?' Daniel yelled. 'Stop!'

At that very moment Alex came walking up the stairs. She saw her brother lying on the floor with a pair of yangsee on his head, and she saw Ola laying exhausted next to a dead Watcher.

'He killed him,' Daniel said to Alex in disbelief.

Ola's face was covered in sweat and he looked dead tired.

'What are you talking about? Who killed whom? What just happened!' Alex was shouting now.

The commotion had alerted Mr Williams who had waited for Alex in the auditorium when the rest of the meeting delegates had gone home.

'Be quiet!,' Mr Williams demanded of Alex and Daniel. To Ola he ordered, 'Put the body at the bottom of the stairs. If we're lucky it was the only Watcher inside here.'

Mr Williams took Alex by the hand and led her gently back to the hall. Daniel, mindlessly followed a few steps behind them. He was in shock and had, for the time being, lost the ability to speak. Ola came running after them.

'What the hell just happened?' Mr Williams looked furiously at Ola.

'He killed him,' Daniel said with a mixture of surprise and contempt in his voice.

'Be quiet. I'll deal with you later.' While Mr Williams addressed Daniel, he kept looking at Ola.

'Sorry, Mr Williams. I screwed up. I just wanted to shut up his smug face,' said Ola who looked at Daniel while he apologised to Mr Williams.

'And by doing that you put us all at risk.'

'I am sorry . . .'

Alex quietly reached out to Mr Williams, 'Can you please explain?'

Mr Williams calmed down a little.

'For some reason Ola decided to give his yangsee to Daniel, and Daniel then must have come too close to a Yangyang. Ola, let me guess, you did not inform Daniel about the rules?'

Ola's face turned white and Mr Williams continued without giving Ola another chance to apologize.

'When Daniel got to the staircase, he must have surprised him.'

'He was just sitting there on the floor. I think he was fixing something on his shoes,' Daniel shared.

Daniel sat looking at the yangsee in his hands. Alex had never seen him this vulnerable before.

'That explains a lot,' Ola said. 'When I came down the stairs, I managed to keep him there while I liquidated him.'

'But why did you have to kill him?' Alex asked, still confused.

'Listen to me now,' Ola explained. 'If The Unvisible were to find out that someone who hasn't been approved had come into close contact with a Yangyang that would automatically mean the person had to die. The Primary Queen doesn't take risks. It was a question of him or your brother. I guessed that both of you would prefer Daniel to be the one who kept on living.'

'Ola's right,' Mr Williams said. 'If a Yangyang is discovered by a Yinyin, then they don't take risks. They just get rid of all the evidence. If Ola hadn't come, then Daniel would be dead by now. We'll have to hope that the Yangyang who finds the Watcher that Ola killed thinks he fell down the stairs, landed awkwardly and broke his neck. It really was a close shave.'

'So, we're safe now?' Daniel had gotten his powers of speech back.

'Yes,' replied Mr Williams. 'We are no longer in danger. We were very lucky. But thanks to you, your ignorance and arrogance—and Ola's foolishness, all of us could just as well have been dead.'

Mr Williams told Ola to go home as he just could not stand seeing him. They would have to have a longer talk later. Then he apologised to Alex for not being able to listen to her share her initial experience of seeing the Yangyang. Right now nothing was more important than debriefing Daniel who had become a Knower, gotten to see the Yangyang and witness a liquidation all in just a few minutes. Being exposed to that much world altering information in a short period of time could make the strongest man crazy, if they did not get proper guidance. Guidance was crucial—as crazy men did crazy things.

The Primary Queen sat on her throne and listened carefully. 'You mean to say a Watcher fell and killed himself right outside the room where the Carte Blanche held their meeting?' The leader of the Watchers nodded. 'And you believe it was most likely an accident?' The leader nodded again. 'You're probably right, but we mustn't take any chances. Double the watch on them. From now on, you watch everyone in the group in pairs. We mustn't lose control. We will know; they will remain ignorant. We will see; they will live blindly. We will control; they will be controlled. If we need to send in a Killer we will do so promptly. Better to kill a few sometimes, than to kill many too late.'

Everyone nodded. The orders of the Primary Queen would be carried out. The Primary Queen's orders were always carried out.

Chapter 29

'Sometimes I think we're alone. Sometimes I think we're not. In either case, the thought is staggering.'
– Buckminster Fuller

Laura snuggled up to her husband and gave him a hug. 'I love you,' she said softly against his shoulder.

Daniel returned her hug, but instead of returning the affection he said, 'Hold me and let's fall asleep together.' His thoughts were somewhere else. His brain was frantically trying to make sense of what he experienced the night before.

The married couple lay in their king size bed. All the small, multicoloured, decorative bed pillows were neatly stacked on the lounge chair next to the bed. A night light that Laura had insisted they should keep on, in case the kids would sneak in during the night, glowed in a faint, orange light in the corner.

Why was it so hard to lie about saying that you love someone, when it was so easy to lie about almost everything else? Daniel found it difficult to express his love to another person. Or to be more precise, he had never truly loved anyone but himself.

Daniel was of the belief that only people who did not love themselves fell in love with others. He could see proof of this in the women who fell in love with him. They all had issues with their self-esteem: their parents had not loved them as children or they were women, often with fabulous bodies, who did not love the way they looked. These kinds of women lacked a sense of belonging as they were always searching for love externally. They had a desperate need to be loved. According to Daniel, this was because they had never learnt to love themselves.

He had given up trying to get others to accept his theory, but the more others, especially women, objected to his idea, the clearer it became to him that it was true. What was the point of loving someone else more than yourself? Could you even love another person totally and uninhibitedly if you did not first love yourself? And if you did fully love yourself, then how could you possibly love someone else more than your very own soul?

A woman, who had once been forced to listen to his argument, had given up her attempt to reason with him and finally replied, 'I just hope that, one day, you get the chance to become a father so that you too can experience what genuine unconditional love is.' Daniel had sniggered and said that if the unconditional love you learnt from becoming a parent was anything like the love he had got from his father, then there was not much to aspire to. Daniel still remembered that conversation with a sour taste in his mouth, and it had not changed his mind. Daniel Johansen would love Daniel Johansen. That did not stop him from loving his children; they were, after all, fifty per cent genetic copies of himself.

His eyelids felt heavy, but he did not want to sleep. He wanted to keep thinking. Wanted to keep lying in the darkness to try to create some order in this chaotic world he had crash landed into. To be able to do that, he needed some peace and quiet. He needed to stay awake while he got his wife to shut up and go to sleep. It meant nothing to him that Laura was lying next to him. As far as he was concerned, he lay alone in his bed. Always alone.

It's me against the rest of the world. Or perhaps it's the world against me. No one is on my side. But they'll see. Daniel Johansen has a plan. Daniel Johansen would finally get the recognition he deserved.

He was not aware of it, but whenever he gave himself a pep talk, he had a tendency to talk about himself in the third person.

'A penny for your thoughts?' Laura interrupted him again.

'I'm thinking about how beautiful life is.'

He really had been thinking this when Laura asked, but what he meant was something completely different to how she interpreted his words.

His train of thought was cut off again when the baby monitor broadcasted Junior's wailing into their bedroom.

Manda stood and watched the small child in the crib while she reflected on the beauty of taking a life. How she—being a Killer—could not help killing.

As a Killer, she really only had one task: to kill the people the Queen told her to eliminate. Her victims were often people who had found out about The Unvisible but who had not been able to keep the secret. The faster you discovered that someone threatened to reveal the secret, the fewer people you had to kill. It was just like cancer: discover it early, when the tumour has not grown too big, and it is easier to get rid of it.

The Killers walked through life in constant conflict between trying to live in harmony as a Yangyang while striving to dominate the world as a Yinyin. The only way for them to keep on living was to follow the Queen's orders and to kill as many people as they were told to. In this way, they could channel their human side—their hunger to kill and the need for influence—while also satisfying their Yangyang need for harmony.

All Killers had the same troubled family background: a human father and an Unvisible mother—a Mohini. Mohinis were female Watchers who had been attracted to their Subjects. Even though it was forbidden, they had sex with the men they were watching and became pregnant. These women for the most part would not reveal themselves to the men they had sex with. They knew that if they were caught the Queen would have the men killed. Often the men did not even understand what had happened. With their soft voices and their bodies, the Mohinis seduced them while they were still sleeping. When the men woke up, usually when they had an orgasm or just afterwards, they thought they had had an unusually realistic wet dream. But by then, the Mohini was already on her way out of the room. She had got what she came for, knowing full well she would never be able to go back to the man again.

The children who were the results of these nocturnal encounters got the invisible cell structure of their mothers but the blood cells of their fathers. They were called Yangyin—half Yangyang and half Yinyin.

When the umbilical cord was cut right after birth, the fetal heart of the baby stopped pumping low oxygen containing blood, back to the placenta which caused a toxic chemical reaction in the mother's womb. The mother's body rejected this new mixture and, simply speaking, the woman got blood poisoning from her own child and died in childbirth. The children grew up knowing that they had killed their own mother. They were raised to feel that they were born to kill, that it was their purpose in life to continue to kill and that they were Killers.

Sometimes there were not enough active assignments from the Primary Queen to satisfy the Killers' cravings. It was then that she sent them out to eliminate human babies. Since all infants could see the Yangyang, it was principally correct to have them killed since anyone who could see the Yangyang risked giving the secret away. It was important for the Queen to be consistent with the rules concerning her Killers. She only sent them to kill the Yinyin who could see The Unvisible. If that meant some babies had to die it was purely collateral damage.

Lately, Manda had been frustrated. She had had too little to do. The restlessness had begun to tear her apart. The infant she had suffocated at the hospital had made her feel better for a while, but that had been weeks ago now, and she needed to kill again soon. The Primary Queen had not granted her permission to kill any more infants, but there was no harm in going out to look for suitable candidates. And it was never wrong to practise the sensitive process of getting close to a baby without making it scream in fear. That's why she was here tonight.

When she stood over the little child and let her snake slide down onto the mattress, she leaned so close that her eyelashes touched the child's. The contact woke the boy and he opened his eyes only to find himself staring right into Manda's pitch-black eye sockets. The child instinctively started to scream, one of those heart-breaking, death-fearing screams that only babies can produce. Manda did not move. She just stood there and stared into the child's blue eyes. Without taking her eyes off him, she whispered, 'Death is never cancelled. Just postponed.'

Only when the child's mother approached the crib did Manda take a couple of steps back. Manda stared at the child for a few more minutes before moving away. As soon as she left the room, the child fell silent. The mother credited the newfound peace to her parenting skills.

Little did she know.

Chapter 30

Invisible
adjective

Impossible to see: ***Air is invisible.***
Out of sight or hidden: ***The tops of the mountains were made invisible by the mist.***

A week had passed and so far, no-one had tried to kill Alex, or anyone else in the group. That was the good news. The bad news was that Alex had been on an emotional roller-coaster. There had been times when she had seriously considered getting a gun, times when she just wanted to run away, and many moments when she just wanted to hide under the covers of her bed. She had basically had all the classic fight-flight-freeze responses that were the body's natural reaction to danger and crisis. Most of her recollections of the last few days were a blur, and she had really been looking forward to going to the Carte Blanche meeting again.

But early on Tuesday morning Daniel had sent a text message saying that the evening meeting with the Carte Blanche was cancelled as Mr Williams was sick. So instead, Alex had planned to meet up with Adam in a park. She needed some kind of stability.

They had just sat down on a bench when her phone rang. It was Mr Williams.

'Alex, I think we have a problem. Can you talk?'

'Yes. I heard you were sick.'

'That's the problem. I'm not.'

'Daniel said . . .'

'Daniel called me late last night. Said he wanted to come over to discuss some ideas. It was late and I was tired and I didn't . . . I didn't feel so well.'

Alex had an uneasy feeling that Mr Williams was not giving the full picture. His voice faltered when he said 'didn't feel so well'. She hid her urge to ask if his tiredness and sickness had anything to do with him drinking a little too much earlier in the evening. She had begun to worry about Mr William's drinking habits. She kept noticing that he smelt faintly of old wine. And weren't his words a bit slurred now as well?

Mr Williams voice came through the phone speaker again, 'Daniel said he had spoken to everyone in the group and most of them couldn't make it, so he suggested we cancel this evening's meeting. He offered to call everyone. That of course turned out to be a lie. He just did not want me to come.'

Adam looked at Alex with a small frown. She had forgotten he was there. She got up and whispered apologetically while holding up five fingers in the air, 'Five minutes.' She walked away and stood with her back to a tree.

'Just so you know, I've got this guy waiting for me on a bench right now. What were you saying about Daniel?'

'He tricked me into thinking we shouldn't have a meeting. Then he sent a text message to Shadow and to you too, apparently, saying I was sick. He knew you would think that meant that the meeting was cancelled.'

'He knows just how I work . . .' Alex thought to herself. ' . . . that I would interpret "Mr Williams is sick" as "Meeting is cancelled".'

'You mean it wasn't cancelled?'

'It was just a plan to make sure you, me and Shadow didn't turn up and to do it in a way that he couldn't be blamed for later. They just had the meeting without us. Apparently Daniel then nominated himself as the first speaker and used his fifteen minutes to argue that it was a crime to know about a technology that could threaten the country's security. He ended his speech by saying that if the group decided against informing the authorities, they all risked going to prison. He also said that if they wouldn't inform the military about the existence of the Yangyangs, then he would go there himself and report the others for withholding information that was harmful to the state.'

'But that's absurd!'

'Technically, he's probably right. Knowing what we know and not telling the authorities is arguably both immoral and illegal if you were to ask a lawyer or politician.'

'But knowing about the Yangyang is about the balance between people—and to stop a war between the two races. It's infinitely bigger than being about a certain country!'

'You know that, and I know that. But Daniel isn't us. He's someone who wants vindication and attention.'

'But doesn't he realize that if we tell the authorities about the yangsee, then they'd want to use the technology? And if that happens then more people will know that the Yangyang exist. And if more people find out about them, then there's a risk of setting off an attack from the Yangyang . . . Oh my God! If we let Daniel do this, they'll kill him and everyone he's told!'

'So you now see why we have a problem?'

'We have to stop him! I'll call him!' Alex hit her forehead in despair.

'I don't think it's quite that simple. He's got the backing of most people in the group and if we create a rift between different factions, then we run the risk of people breaking away—and that can be very dangerous. But I have an idea, and for it to work I need you on my side. Alex—can I trust you?'

'Of course. I'm sorry I brought Daniel to the Carte Blanche. If I knew this was going to happen, I'd never . . . I'm really very sorry and . . .'

'What's done is done. Now let's focus on how to fix it. First of all: Do not call him. I know you want to, but sometimes the right thing to do isn't what feels right. We have to dare to think one step further. I've been in similar situations before and I'm asking you to trust me. If you confront him, you might make things worse. If you just do what I ask you, then everything will be all right. Hopefully.'

Mr Williams went through his idea with Alex. She still thought it was less risky to get Daniel to change his mind, but Mr Williams explained that it had already gone too far for that. Instead, they had to focus on minimizing the damage.

'Is everything all right?' Adam asked when Alex sat down next to him.

'Yes, thanks. An old friend is sick and he had an emergency he needed help with.'

'If you need to leave right away I can give you a lift.'

She was about to say yes, but then changed her mind and burst out, 'Wait, you can't drive!?'

He laughed. He had an infectious laugh.

'No, of course not. But I have assisted transportation and I can accompany you where you want to go and then continue home.'

'Thanks, but that won't be necessary. It's not that urgent.'

Alex did not want to go into details. 'Come—let's walk by the lake.'

She wanted a few more minutes alone with him. Alex liked his calm manner and the fact that he really listened to what she said. She understood that she could no longer talk about the Yangyang to outsiders, but that did not stop her from talking to him in more general terms about life-changing situations. Because that is how it felt—like this situation had changed her life. Alex needed someone to talk to and Adam was the best person she could think of. She felt he had understood what she was talking about when she told him about the children's drawings on that day they first met.

Luckily for Alex, the summer break had just started which meant she would hopefully have more time to meet up with Adam going forward. It also meant that she would be less stressed about school—or about neglecting school. Her grades this semester would be terrible, but she honestly did not care. But she did want to finish her assignment for professor Gardener, and had gotten him to extend the deadline so that she could finish it during the summer break.

Alex took Adam's arm and led him to the little lake about a hundred metres away. She knew he did not really need the help, but she felt safe by his side. Alex led Adam, but the opposite was just as true.

At one end of the lake a stunning Vimana was floating in the air. With the structure hovering over the water there was less risk of someone stumbling into the thick cables that held the floating construction to the ground.

Today was washing day. At least once a week, usually on Saturdays, or whenever the Vimana got too dirty, all the Carers living in a Vimana were sent out to wash the outside. This washday was essential to ensure that dirt and dust would not stick to the outside and make its contours visible to the Yinyin. In some polluted places, the dwellings needed washing every evening.

Today an extra cleaning day had been ordered. A hose that released a very thin mist of water wet the outside walls that were then wiped clean very quickly by the hundreds of Carers hanging out of the small holes that could be found along the entire building. The Unvisible were also forced to make sure that they did not have any dust on themselves when they were out and about among people. To polish themselves and their uniforms all the time was a habit the Yangyang had copied from the birds, and something they had to learn since childhood. They might very well be invisible to people, but the smallest slip-up when it came to cleanliness could mean becoming visible.

Chapter 31

'To see what is in front of one's nose needs a constant struggle.'
– George Orwell

The two men who worked for the Department of External Ideas had just spent an hour listening to a woman who was convinced that her neighbour was a terrorist because she 'never saw him take out his trash'. It had been yet another meaningless task. But the men knew that their job of evaluating tips and ideas from the public consisted mainly of listening to nonsense. It was a job that needed to be done if they were to find anything of interest. Someone had compared it to panning for gold—you had to sift through a lot of sand to find the nuggets. Being a soldier was very seldom glamorous. It was mostly a lot of waiting, a lot of routine procedures, and a lot of time spent in bland looking barracks and offices. And yet their work was important. It was about protecting the nation.

'Who's up next?' the older man asked.

'Some kind of anti-camouflage technology, according to the description.'

The younger man glanced at a copy of the standard form all visitors had to submit. It had a short description of the invention, information or gadget that they wanted to present. The older man pressed a button and asked the secretary to let in the next group.

It had been decided that Mr Williams, Alex and Daniel would represent Carte Blanche at the meeting with the military. They had received their allotted slot for the meeting in three weeks. Mr Williams and Alex had been positively surprised by how fast a government entity had responded. Daniel had complained that it had taken so long. Because of the irregularity and uncertainty of his work their meeting ended up colliding with his schedule at the hospital. For the first time in his life Daniel had called in sick to work in order to make it to the appointment.

When they came into the room, Daniel was already wearing Ola's yangsee. Mr Williams had his with him but it was still packed in its box.

Daniel knew that the Yangsee was still Mr William's possession, but he regarded it more and more as his own. When the time was right, he was going to get Mr Williams to sell it to him. Daniel was convinced Mr Williams did not grasp the full value of the antique yangsee.

Mr Williams was an idealist. Everyone who spoke about things as being 'priceless' did not realize the true value of things. But all in good time. Daniel's plan was much bigger than a couple of yangsees and today's presentation was an important step in that plan. Nothing could go wrong.

Daniel took on the role as leader for the group and greeted the soldiers who sat behind a little desk. The two men were wearing name badges with their surnames and small stars on their epaulettes indicated their rank. The older one looked exactly like Clint Eastwood and the younger one could have been the little brother of Radar from the series Mash.

'Pencil pushers,' thought Daniel.

'Sorry about the equipment, but I have to scan the room to make sure it's clear.'

'Of course,' said one of the men behind the desk. 'Take all the time you need.'

When Daniel scanned the room with his yangsee, he immediately saw the Watcher sitting on the floor with his back to the wall. He seemed moderately interested in Daniel and focused instead on two doves dancing on the floor in front of him. As soon as Daniel saw the Watcher, he initiated Operation Diversion. It was important to entice the Watcher out of the room without him being aware of what was going on. The code word they had decided on was UFO.

Daniel addressed the two men, 'Was the last presentation here about UFOs? I can sense the presence of UFO rocket fuel, but it seems all the UFO's have left for another dimension.'

'We're not at liberty to disclose that information,' the younger soldier said.

Alex picked up on the code word and asked, 'Excuse me, can I use the bathroom before we start? I'd like to see what the feng shui is like there . . .'

Mr Williams had explained that, for some reason, Watchers must have orders to keep an extra close watch on people's interest in feng shui and that using this interest was an effective way to get a Watcher out of a room.

On hearing that, Alex thought that in one way the Yangyang were like crocodiles. By being optimally built for their function, both species had hardly developed over time. A crocodile was a perfected killing machine in almost all aspects, but if you hit it on the top of its head with a stick it would often abort the attack and walk away. In the same way the Yangyang were perfected 'human watchers' and yet in certain circumstances they could be surprisingly easily circumvented.

When the Yinyin, for example, found a new, successful way of luring a Watcher out of a room, that method could then often be used again and again for months until the Yangyang realized what was going on. Mr Williams had found out about the latest trick of referencing feng shui from another Carte Blanche group he was in contact with.

What was it about people that made them find the most absurd stories to explain the world? The Watcher never stopped being surprised. He usually sat at the very back of the room and listened to one strange story after another. It was interesting in a way but also so uninspiring.

Sitting indoors all day was killing him. So many people wanted to distance themselves from Nature instead of embracing it. The Yangyang could not understand how the Yinyin seemed to enjoy hiding from the sun or why they wanted to avoid the life-giving power of the rain. If he had not had his doves with him, he probably would not have been able to put up with it. As soon as he listened to what each person had to say and could establish it had nothing to do with the Yangyang, he usually studied his doves that played on the floor in front of him. He had special permission to have the two birds as companions as he was forced to sit inside every day. When he was immersed in the birds' play, the rest of the world disappeared and he felt harmonious again.

He perked up when the group started talking about feng shui. He got up, studied the group and weighed his options. On the one hand, he was supposed to watch the conference room but, on the other hand, one of the members was going to study feng shui in the room next door.

The Watcher decided to follow Alex.

Chapter 32

'Music is the harmonious voice of creation; an echo of the invisible world.'
– Giuseppe Mazzini

When Alex got to the toilets, she was met by the acrid smell of detergent. The lemon fragrance that was supposed to give a feeling of freshness only conveyed a sense of artificiality. She made a point of opening the toilet door widely and closing it slowly so the Watcher would have no issues sneaking in after her. Then she sat down on the toilet seat and pretended to meditate. The plan was that she would sit there during the entire presentation. The others would send her a text message when they were finished, and there was now no way the Watcher could leave the bathroom before she opened the door. She was glad she could shut her eyes while sitting there. The knowledge that a Watcher was only a few steps away from her made her feel warm inside, but also a bit nervous. If she had had her eyes open, she would not have been able to help staring at the point where he must be standing. She wondered how long she would have to sit there.

In the conference room, Mr Williams and Daniel took their places in front of the table where the two soldiers were sitting. 'Let me start off by apologizing for our rather unusual entrance. When our presentation is over, you will understand.'

'Perhaps we should wait for your friend,' the older man broke in.

'It's OK. We'll do the presentation without her,' Daniel said and cleared his throat. Daniel had hooked up his computer to the projector as Alex left the room. They had decided to use the first ten minutes of their fifteen-minute slot explaining the existence of the Yangyang before using the last five minutes to give the government representatives a chance to see the Yangyang for themselves through the yangsee.

Daniel had suggested they could just give the yangsee to the men and save ten minutes, but Mr Williams had successfully argued that people who had no knowledge of what they were about to experience could suppress the whole thing and—in some cases—the shock of having the world turned upside down so quickly could make them suffer a mental breakdown. Daniel had reluctantly let himself be persuaded as long as he was allowed to hold the presentation.

During the ten minutes, he went through things like how light is refracted, how the Yangyangs' pyramids work, what Watchers and the Killers do, and about historical scepticism to new ideas, and much more. It was a swift presentation that included eighteen pictures, but Daniel was sure his audience could manage such a large intake of information.

During the entire talk, the two officers made notes. Daniel could not tell if they were buying the whole story or not, but at least they did not look dismissive. When he got to the last picture that showed the yang yin symbol where he talked about the Yangyangs' need to be close to humans, he summed up what he had said.

He looked at the clock on the wall and noted that he had kept exactly to nine minutes as he had planned. The two men behind the desk seemed to show signs of interest. He decided to present the last part—a part he had not discussed with the others. He straightened up and tried to sound like a business man, 'That's the end of the first part of our presentation. I imagine that you have questions and feel a bit overwhelmed, but I'd like to ask you to save your questions until the end. Before we carry on with the more important part—that is, the demonstration—I'd like to ask you something.'

Daniel waited a second for an answer, but as it was silent, he continued, 'How does the remuneration system work?'

'The what?' the older man asked in a neutral tone.

'Remuneration. Money. Reward. This technology has enormous strategic benefits—not to mention commercial uses—and we will, of course, be applying for a patent and then license the technology to you. As long as you're ready to pay, that is . . .'

'Are you suggesting that you're considering selling your technology to a foreign power if they pay more?'

'I don't know what Dr Johansen is talking about.' Mr Williams had rushed up, and turned around and he now stood with his back to the other two men in the room. He gave Daniel a hard look. Daniel ignored him.

'Daniel—what's this all about? Since when did it become a question of money?'

'Of course we'd like a technology like this to help our own military, and that's why we've contacted you first. But we must also think about our own economic interests.

And we're interested in knowing what kind of financial payment is on offer if we license the technology to you. I hope you understand.'

The senior service man replied, 'Naturally. But in order for an invention to be patented, the inventor has to be the first person to think of the idea. And in this case, it appears to be a technology that these invisible people have developed and then handed over to humans over hundreds of years. I'm afraid that such an idea can't be protected and, therefore, is of no great commercial value either.'

Daniel became defensive. 'If you're not willing . . .'

The younger man looked through his papers and when he found the right section, he read out loud. 'Here. Let me see. In your application, you write: 'The technology we are going to show you could pose a considerable risk to the nation, our military power and our inhabitants if it fell into the wrong hands.' Are these your words?'

'Yes, we wrote that,' Daniel replied.

'Then I hope you also realize that if you decide to withhold such information from the Armed Forces, then you are guilty of a crime.'

'But . . .'

'And if you're trying to change your story now and claim that the technology you're here to demonstrate doesn't exist, then you're guilty of falsifying public documents and probably of racketeering too.'

The older man concluded, 'You now have fewer than four minutes left. I suggest you use them to demonstrate your technology instead of trying to negotiate payment at this stage. If it turns out that only a fraction of what you've told us is true, then you'll be rewarded beyond your wildest dreams. The Armed Forces is known for its generosity towards valuable inventions. You now have three and a half minutes left.'

Daniel put his yangsee on the table next to his computer and went up to the two men. He put his palms on the desk and leaned forward until his face was only a few centimetres from theirs. He looked the older man in the eyes and said, 'If, or should I say, when we come back and want to talk about money for the technology you're about to see, it's me you'll have to negotiate with. Me and no one else. Got it?'

The officer smiled and replied, 'Got it! And now I'm really looking forward to your little demonstration . . .'

'You seem to be in the zone so why don't you just keep going,' said Mr Williams to Daniel.

Daniel took Mr Williams' yangsee and explained how it worked to the two military men. Knowing how important it is with seniority he made sure that the older and higher-ranking officer got to put on the yangsee first. Daniel then put on Ola's yangsee on his own head, signalled to the rest of the group to follow him, and then slowly opened the door and went out into the reception area. A Watcher sat in one of the visitor's chairs, studying a flower arrangement on the little coffee table. Daniel discreetly nodded in the direction of the chairs and whispered, 'There—in the chair.'

The younger colleague, who was not wearing a yangsee, looked at his boss.

'I can't see anything,' the older man said.

'He's right there. On the chair to the left.'

'Sorry, but I don't see anything. Just a group of chairs.'

Annoyed, Daniel went up to the man and started pulling the lever on the glasses.

'Now?'

'Nothing except the glasses got a little less gray.'

Daniel moved the lever backwards and forwards. 'What about now?'

'Sorry.'

Daniel started to sweat. He was quite obviously stressed but tried to hide it to not create anxiety that might scare away the Watcher, who was still looking at the flowers. He tore off the yangsee and put it on the younger man.

'Can you see him?'

'See who?' It was obvious the other man had not seen anything to turn his world upside down.

'There!' Daniel shrieked. He took a few quick steps to get nearer, but his movements scared the Watcher, who jumped out of the chair and slipped into the stairwell.

'Here. He sat here. In this chair . . . Didn't you even see him jumping up and running out?'

'I understand . . .' the older man said.

Daniel was furious. He looked at Mr Williams who just threw out his arms. Daniel looked at the men and could not understand how they could fail at something as simple as seeing through a pair of glasses.

'Sorry, but your time is up.'

'Hang on a minute. You're just pretending not to see anything so you can make your own yangsee! I know how you people work! There's something very wrong here. Let's exchange glasses! try mine!'

'Sorry, we are very strict on assigned time slots. You should have spent less time negotiating about money . . .'

Daniel was fuming, but he could see that arguing for any more time was futile. He grabbed the yangsee and went to the toilets to get Alex.

Mr Williams remained in the reception and turned to the soldiers. 'I'm so sorry for my friend's behaviour. He can be a little aggressive when he gets emotional . . .'

He got a friendly, soothing smile in return.

When Alex and Daniel came back, the two soldiers accompanied the small group to the elevators. Then, when the doors had shut, they went back to the reception and one of them said, 'Yet another 'promising technology' that for some strange reason doesn't work when it's being demonstrated . . .'

'Something like that. I've had enough crazy ideas for one morning. What do you say about some lunch? What do you feel like? Fried invisible birds perhaps?'

Daniel, Mr Williams and Alex did not know it, but the Watcher that had spent the last fifteen minutes in the bathroom with Alex was in the elevator with them. He knew it was lunchtime and that meant no presentations for an hour. His two doves hovered in the air right under the ceiling. They were playing in the current created by the air conditioning.

The Watcher intended to use his own lunchtime to go to the park and let the birds fly free. He needed natural air. He needed to breathe.

Chapter 33

'Seeing ourselves as others see us would probably confirm our worst suspicions about them.'
– Franklin P. Adams

'Shit. Shit. Shit!'

Daniel banged his fist against the steering wheel. Since leaving the military area, he had constantly been driving a little bit too fast.

'What happened in there? Nothing worked!'

'Yes, very strange . . . Something must have gone wrong with the glasses . . .' came from Mr Williams in the backseat. He looked out of the side window when he answered.

'Wrong? But we saw them! I saw them!'

Mr Williams tried another explanation. 'Perhaps they were colour blind. The glasses don't work if you're colour blind. If you can't see red and green, then you don't see the rainbow spectrum when you look through them. And if you can't see all the colours, then you can't see the invisible light through the yangsee.'

'I don't think the military would have two colour blind people evaluating new technologies.' Alex did her best to play along.

'I should have given them mine!'

When Mr Williams had first suggested going with Daniel to the military and even bringing along a yangsee, Alex had been surprised. But Mr Williams then explained that it was better to get Daniel to go there and fail than to risk him going there alone. He had then shown Alex how easy it was to remove a pair of the coloured lenses in the yangsee Daniel was planning to lend to the military. With the lenses gone, the light did not reflect correctly and so, instead of seeing The Unvisible, you saw nothing unusual. Alex had initially expressed concern that the plan was too risky since Daniel could decide to lend his yangsee to the soldiers when their yangsee did not work, but she had relaxed when Mr Williams had informed her that Ola's yangsee had a hidden 'panic button', that Daniel did not know about. The panic button instantly rendered the glasses useless. It was a feature that Ola had added to his version and that Mr Williams could quickly and discreetly activate should the need arise.

Their plan had worked perfectly. Alex tried not to smile at how they had been able to trick Daniel and how he did not realize what they had done although the answer was—literally—right in front of his eyes. Sometimes the simplest ideas were the best.

'Something must have gone wrong with the technology ...' Mr Williams kept looking out of the window.

'Anyway ... Actually, maybe it was for the best. Did you hear their comment about patenting! Ridiculous! As if it were a useless invention? No, let's go to the corporates instead. Halliburton or Securitas. They'll see the potential.'

'Can you give me my yangsee?' Mr Williams asked. Daniel had it on his lap as he was driving.

'Why?'

'You're a little overenthusiastic at the moment. And it is an antique, after all. I'm honestly scared that you might damage something that is priceless.'

'I agree with Mr Williams. I think looking at this from a commercial perspective is frankly petty.' Alex cut in.

'Petty? Do you understand what we are talking about here?!'

They did not say much for the rest of the journey. Alex and Mr Williams sat in the backseat and felt sorry for Daniel; and Daniel sat in the front feeling sorry for himself, but for a completely different reason.

In the bright, white room, there were approximately forty young children. Some of the children were sitting, resting their backs against the wall. Others were lying down or leaning against a friend. They formed small groups and every child had physical contact with at least one other child.

The atmosphere was relaxed, but all of the children focused on the teacher sitting on the floor in front of them. A child was lying next to the teacher and resting his head on her knee. There was no furniture in the room except for soft cushions on the floor. Hundreds of flowers in all different shapes and sizes had been planted in grooves in the floor. The flower display formed a circle in the middle of the room, creating a stunning display.

Although all of the children were listening to what the teacher said, many of them were not looking at her. Instead they were studying how small ice-white butterflies and a few white bees were creating new life amongst the flowers.

The teacher looked at the children as she said:

'If we do not embrace life, we will always be alone.
As long as we are alone, we will never be happy.
As long as we are unhappy, we will never see life.
As long as we cannot see life, we will never embrace it.
If we embrace life, we will feel a sense of belonging.
When we feel a sense of belonging, we will be happy.
When we are happy, we will see the true life.
When we see the true life, we will embrace it.'

Chapter 34

'In the land of the blind, the one-eyed man is stoned to death.'
–Joan D. Vinge

The Carte Blanche had called an extra meeting. Two people stood up: Daniel and Shadow.

Shadow observed the group as she spoke. She had missed a few Carte Blanche meetings and now she was furious. 'What were you thinking?! Carte Blanche has protected the relationship between Yangyang and humans for centuries and then you suddenly think it's a good idea to go and tell the military?'

Ola sat at the back and avoided looking at Shadow when he answered, 'Daniel talked us into it. He somehow made it sound like a good idea.'

'A good idea?!'

'He's really good at persuading people, OK?!' Ola looked frustrated.

Alex glanced at Daniel to see his reaction. He seemed to take it as a compliment. Alex had grown up seeing her brother win arguments with his rhetoric. Many times she had started a discussion thinking he was wrong only to find herself changing her mind after hearing how he argued. *He was a master of rhetoric—and rhetoric is a powerful weapon*, she thought to herself.

Shadow was not as impressed.

'He's not even a member! You risk the lives of this entire group—not to mention the balance between the Yinyin and Yangyang because some guy—who wasn't even a Knower until recently—thinks it was "a good idea"? Seriously, how could you even let him into the group?'

Now it was Mr Williams' turn to avoid looking Shadow in the eyes. 'In hindsight, it probably wasn't such a great idea.'

'If I had been there that evening, you wouldn't even have been allowed to attend the meeting.' This last remark was aimed at Daniel.

'But now you weren't there. And now I am one of the Knowers. And now we happen to have laws in this country. And I, for one, am not going to risk spending the rest of my life in jail because some grumpy punk girl thinks her moral viewpoint is superior.'

He had no problems looking her in the eyes as he replied.

'This is going to end badly. Very, very badly.'

'Calm down, both of you.' Mr Williams had mustered up executive presence to take charge of the situation again. 'And sit down.'

Alex almost thought he was going to ask them to hug each other. Before sitting down, Daniel just had to get in the last word. 'Why is it such a bad idea to tell the military about The Unvisible?'

Mr Williams looked at Daniel and replied, 'The whole military apparatus is built upon a structure of climbing up the hierarchy. And you climb the ladder by telling your superior how good you are. When a soldier finds out about the Yangyang, he will realize what a great career opportunity this is and tell his commanding officer, who in his turn, sees the same opportunity and runs to his commanding officer. Before you know it, the entire chain of command will know all about this amazing strategic weapon—and that will create way too many Knowers.

'The result is that the Yangyang will decide to eliminate everyone who knows. The Yangyang understand that a small number of people will always know about them, but they have also learnt that it is when the group gets too big that it needs to be controlled. It's like gardening—you can accept a few weeds, but you use weed killer before they get out of hand.'

'That's ridiculous,' Daniel stated. 'Surely there is no organization as good at keeping secrets as the military?'

Shadow laughed out loud. 'Are you serious? There probably isn't an organization out there that has been more affected by leaks than the military. The list of soldiers that have revealed secrets to the wrong people is loooong. The old Soviet Union, for example, would train beautiful women, so-called "honey traps", to work as spies. The women became mistresses and pumped their lovers for information.'

Daniel just would not give up. 'Let's talk to the politicians then.'

Everyone in the room burst out laughing. Alex put words on what they all found so funny. 'The military might be bad at making good decisions, but politicians are arguably even worse!'

Daniel was starting to get pissed off. He turned to Ibrahim and Abraham. 'Are you willing to sit in prison for the rest of your lives?'

'If no one reveals what we know, then no one will go to prison,' Ibrahim said.

'Exactly,' agreed Abraham. 'No one needs to know.'

Daniel had lost his main allies. If he could not scare the Egyptians with the threat of jail, then there was no point in arguing further. In a group there are always strong and weak people, and as much as it annoyed him, he had to admit that in this group—at this time—there were some strong people who had been able to reverse his agenda. It was time to retreat and regroup.

He got up and said, 'I hear what you're saying. This whole Yangyang situation is out of hand. What's the point of knowing if we can't contact them, can't look at them, can't tell others about them or do nothing without their knowledge? Apparently the best that can happen is that you don't tell anyone so that they can let you live. The worst that can happen is that you are killed by The Unvisible or put in jail. Well, I'm sorry, but you can keep your little group to yourself from now on.'

As Daniel was leaving the room, Ola rushed forward and blocked his path. 'What?' Daniel asked.

Ola broke out into a malicious smile, held out his hand and said, 'Since I won I do believe you owe me a mobile phone and a laptop . . .'

Daniel sighed and took out his phone. 'You can have it next time we meet. I have to transfer my contacts to a new phone first. And you will also get the computer. Happy?'

'Very.'

'Glad someone is,' Daniel muttered as he pushed past Ola.

Alex called out after him, but he really did not want to listen to what his sister had to say. He knew it would be a long monologue about how sorry she was and how she wanted to apologize and so on. To get rid of her, he rushed out of the room.

The Unvisible had no classrooms. No schools. But a lot of teachers. Everyone with a skill had to put aside some time to teach others. The goal of all learning was to see the beauty in life.

In the hall outside the room where the group was meeting sat a few Watchers. They had not managed to get into the room, so instead they waited outside. To pass the time, the eldest Watcher was teaching two younger Watchers what a Wise one had once taught him.

'The more you see, the more invisible you become.' He signed to the others. 'How do you interpret that?'

'That it's hard to be egoistic when you study Nature?' one of the younger Watchers tried.

'That everything living is a part of what lives, and the more you focus on that, the bigger life becomes,' the other one said.

The older Watcher continued with his questions. He had been taught to teach by asking questions—not by simply giving answers.

'What is happiness?'

'Happiness is a life full of variety. Not necessarily always full of new experiences, but a life of wonder. Not always being taken by surprise, but surprising yourself.'

'Your answer is too complicated. Can you put it more simply?' the older one signed.

The young Yangyang thought a little before answering. 'Happiness is to feel "I'm alive".'

The two younger men looked at each other with mutual understanding. The older man nodded appreciatively and signed, 'Life is beautiful. Live a beautiful life.'

Chapter 35

'The world is filled with hidden love.'
– Daniella Kessler

Say what you like but her mother certainly knew how to bake. As Alex sat on the sofa in her childhood home and smelled the cinnamon wafting around the room, part of her became that little girl again helping her mother get the buns off the oven tray as a child. She remembered the taste of licking the last bit of dough from the spatula; the joy in her mother's face when she was young and happy. Even her father had laughed and given her a moustache kiss that tickled after he had eaten their masterpieces. Smell is perhaps our least developed sense—but it is also the sense that was best at bringing out memories.

Initially Alex had thought about bailing on the family dinner this Sunday. Today had been her last day at work and Alex could not bear the thought of seeing the disappointment in her mother's eyes when she would find out that her daughter had dropped her last connection to the medical field. But Alex could not do it anymore. Working with mentally challenged people when you went through huge emotional challenges yourself just did not work. She would soon look for a more relaxing job. Barista perhaps. In the end Alex had decided not to tell her mother that she had resigned and still go to the dinner.

Now she felt bad trying to get out of her mother's attempt at an all-girls' night. Her mother meant well when she tried to create a feeling of family among the Johansens. And she looked so happy when there was a bit of life in the house again. She had sacrificed a lot to create a happy family. Who was Alex to judge her mum for doing what she thought was best for her daughter?

The road to hell might be paved with good intentions—but to be honest, the road to heaven was probably cobblestoned with good intentions too. She looked at her mother, who had just come into the living room with a large platter of freshly peeled shrimps.

'I love you mum,' Alex said to her mother for the first time in many years.

'Oh, Alexandra—how sweet. I didn't know you liked shrimps that much,' her mother answered, as she put down the big plate on the table.

'That's not what I meant,' Alex said quietly.

'I know what you meant. But really, Alexandra. Shouldn't you be putting a little more energy into finding a man you can shower that affection on?'

'You can't hurry love . . .' Alex hummed in an attempt not to get dragged into a discussion she was doomed to lose.

'So now your life decisions are being decided by song lyrics? Seriously—are you seeing anyone?'

'Mum . . .'

'What happened to that teacher you talked so much about?'

'It's complicated.'

'You're over thirty and you are not getting any younger . . .'

'Mother, please!'

'How long has it been since you had a serious suitor?'

Alex rolled her eyes. Had her mother just called the potential men in her life suitors?

She might be annoying but Alex knew her mother had a point. The worst part of these discussions that her mother scheduled on a regular basis was that Alex had to try and explain why she had not managed to find a suitable man to marry. Her mother did not seem to understand that the younger generation of women were not satisfied with just finding someone to marry; they wanted a career too. And this meant finding a man who was smart enough to have his own career while also being open-minded enough to support his wife's. And there didn't seem to be too many men like that around.

The reality was, unfortunately, a little more complicated and it was the smart women who had drawn the short straw when it came to modern mating rituals. A handsome but not so smart man could get a beautiful but not so smart woman. A less good-looking man who was smart attracted a similar wife.

But then it became more complicated. It was socially acceptable for a handsome and intelligent man to marry a beautiful but less intelligent woman. And a nerdy guy became a 'geek', who was attractive for some unknown reason, even though he was not good-looking. But an intelligent girl had no advantages. Quite the opposite. In the worst case, she scared off men or gave them an inferiority complex.

There was nothing wrong with having a family—she wanted that too. But not if it meant giving up her own life. While she tried to balance this equation, the years had sped by. Meanwhile, her friends started to get pregnant. *Good for them*, she thought. But now some of her friends' children were having children of their own. She caught herself looking sourly at women who happily brought their strollers into cafés with them. It was as if every giggling, gurgling and crying baby was a reminder that her own high standards of what the world should look like had blocked her own life. The last thing she needed was advice from a woman who always thought she was right.

Alex gave her mother an angry look. 'Can't you give it a rest? When I find a man I want to marry, you'll be the first to know.'

Just as she said that, Eric strolled into the room from some adventure in the house. Alex quickly tried to wipe off her angry face. No need to drag the children into the family drama.

'I'm going to marry you, grandma, because your food is so yummy,' Eric said and ran to hug his grandmother's legs while throwing Alex a nervous look. Alex relaxed and grandma bent down to pick up her grandchild.

'You're so handsome you'll probably find someone much prettier than me. But you should probably wait a few years before getting married.' And to get in the last word, she added, 'Just don't wait too long . . .'

Laura had been allowed to bring Junior and Eric to the all-girls' night. *A brilliant decision*, Alex thought, because if the discussions between the women went sour, they could start talking about, or to, the children instead.

With her mother overwhelmed by the love from her grandchild, Alex took the chance to let the inflamed discussion about her marital status die a natural death.

Laura came out of the kitchen with a plate that had ten buns on it and two empty, round rings in one of the corners.

'Eric, we asked you to wait.'

'It wasn't me!' Eric cried and looked genuinely offended by the accusation.

'Hmm . . . Looks like a new case of the mystery of the disappearing buns,' Mrs Johansen said and smiled at her grandchild.

The buns were placed on the table and Eric ran over to try and pinch one. 'Eric! No more buns before dinner!'

'But, mummy, I've already told you I haven't eaten any . . .'

'Eric! You shouldn't tell lies,' said grandma Johansen sharply.

'Leave him alone, mum,' Alex said.

Alex had been passed over as Eric's godmother in favour of Laura's sister, something that hadn't bothered Alex at all. Alex had never really understood the role of a godmother. Instead she had assigned herself the role of being the cool aunt. And as the cool aunt, she had to stand up for her nephew when he got into trouble—like now, when too many adults were scolding him for taking a few buns.

'But Alexandra, you can't mean we should teach little Eric that it's okay to lie?'

'I just mean that all of us have pinched a bun or two when we were kids, right?'

'I see,' her mother said, as she got up to go back to the kitchen again.

That was how her mother won arguments. By mumbling a condescending 'I see' and leaving the room so that you got a bad conscience and came running after her to apologize for upsetting her. Feminists talked about Male Domination Techniques, but after observing her mother's way of manipulating people, Alex was convinced that there must be some corresponding technique in women. Call it Female Manipulation Techniques. The ability to prompt emotional guilt was one of the most effective tools in this discipline.

'But mum . . . that's not what I meant! I am sorry.'

Her mother remained stopped in the doorway, but she did not turn around. Alex made another attempt. 'Let's eat the yummy food you've cooked and have a nice time together.' She had put in that word, 'nice', to really try to get her mother on her side.

'Your generation is so funny. You come over for dinner and just assume that I've prepared everything so that you can have a good time. As if this were a restaurant.'

There it was: technique number two in the Female Manipulation handbook. Get the other party to think you have spent more time on your work than she has so that the other party, individually or collectively, are in your debt. Mrs Johansen had conveniently forgotten that she had insisted on doing the food herself and driven Laura out of the kitchen with the words, 'You don't want Eric to grow up feeling he had a distant mother, do you?' But now she was complaining that the young women had not helped.

'But . . .' Laura said. 'If you want help, we will help. Alex too, right?'

She looked meaningfully at Alex.

'Of course, mum. Of course. Just tell us what you want us to do and we'll do it,' Alex replied.

'No need . . . [Sob] . . . It's just that . . . [Sob] . . . since your father died . . . [Sob] . . . there's so much . . . [Sob] . . . around the house . . . with the shares, the authorities . . . I . . . [Sob] . . .' Mrs Johansen avoided eye contact with any of the others, instead she gazed towards the green armchair that had once been her late husband's favourite. The chair no adult in the family would even consider sitting in.

And that was technique number three: if nothing else works, cry. Her mother seemed to have a remote control to her tears that she could turn on and off at will. Very few people could argue with a crying woman. Someone had put it so well: 'Every woman is wrong until she cries—then she is instantly right.' Alex seldom cried. She guessed that she must have realized as a child that it would not matter how much she cried as her mother would always cry more.

Alex knew that the only thing left to do at this point was to admit that her mother was right. She went up to Eric, who had been trying to make himself invisible by pretending to read a book. She kneeled down so that her head was level with his and said, 'Eric, I know you say you haven't taken any buns, but sometimes we do things we can't remember . . .'

A lump of guilt began to form in Alex's stomach as she was trying to please her mother at her nephew's expense. The sparkles in Eric's eye were extinguished.

Enough. Alex felt that she had crossed a line. She did not have to put up with this any longer. She would be her mother's child all her life but she also had the right to live her own life—to speak out when she thought someone was wrong. Even if it was her own mother.

Alex stood up and looked at the woman who had raised her.

'I don't have a problem with you raising Eric, but I'd appreciate it if you would stop trying to parent me. I'm an adult woman now. I want you to start treating me like one—

and not like the child you think I still am. And can you please stop calling me Alexandra? You know that I prefer Alex.'

Alex tried to keep her voice calm, but wasn't quite able to do it.

'I call you Alexandra because that is your name! The name I gave to you! The name we gave to the priest who christened you. We—your father and I—your father who is no longer with us, your father who died . . . who no longer had the energy . . . who so very much wanted you to . . .'

Her mother left the room in tears. Powerless, Alex sat down. The all too familiar walls in the room seemed to cave in on her. The perfectly arranged, once modern, but now stuffy furniture enhanced her feeling of not being able to breathe. The room needed more lights, it was always too dark in there.

She knew it would be a long and painful retreat to get her mother's forgiveness. But she was honestly not sure if she could crawl back that road one more time. Alex could not remember the last time she had stood up to her mother. But the world had changed. What used to be big problems were no longer problems at all. Alex suddenly understood how profound the saying 'To see the world in a new light' really was. Seeing the world through the light of the yangsee had given her many new and profound perspectives on life.

The Yangyang were eataterians. They ate meat, but only meat from animals that ate meat themselves. Vegetarians do not eat meat. Omnivores eat vegetables and meat. But eataterians only ate meat from animals that ate other animals. It was based on the philosophy that only animals who themselves killed for food should be at risk of being eaten. If you are in the game, you are in the game, so to speak. Being an eatatarian was a moral standpoint; part of a palette of moral rules that The Unvisible had developed and fine-tuned over thousands of years.

Having a higher consciousness made it possible for The Unvisible—and humans—to know which animals killed their food. We are able to have a moral discussion about the ethics of eating only these animals.

To claim, like some vegetarians did, that people were morally superior to all other animals and therefore had a duty not to kill other animals was based on the incorrect assumption—according to The Unvisible—that killing is wrong. Killing to survive, and that included killing for food and energy, was not morally reprehensible. It was worse to claim that humans were superior to all other species.

According to The Unvisible, humans were not at the top of the food chain. People ate crocodiles, white sharks and lions sometimes, and people could also find themselves eaten by these very same animals at other times. People did not eat mosquitoes, ticks or gnats, but these insects lived off people. The Unvisible believed that all living things were part of the eternal cycle that was the universe. And no point on a circle is the beginning. A circle does not have a top.

In practice, it meant that eatatarians did not eat cows, lambs, horses or other herbivorous, non-killing, animals. Herbivores were a part of the cycle of life because other animals ate them, but they did not kill themselves. Therefore their lives should be respected, honoured and spared. There were plenty of carnivorous animals out there that humans could kill to get the meat that they needed.

The Unvisible might not eat herbivores, but they loved cinnamon buns. The Watcher had not been able to resist taking a couple of them as they came out of the oven. You could say it was the fault of the humans: The batch they had made was too small, and it did not look as if there would be any buns left for him to eat later. He knew this was a weak argument. But the buns had looked delicious and he could not resist. He was pretty sure that with the boy in the house, the adults would find a completely acceptable explanation for the disappearance.

The child would learn the important lesson that the truth was not always true enough to be true.

Chapter 36

'Reality is merely an illusion, albeit a very persistent one.'
– Albert Einstein

They were called 'man's best friend' for a reason: dogs were really good companions. But companionship had not been the criteria when Daniel bought Kirre. Only lonely people bought dogs for that reason. And no matter what other parents might say about buying a dog to 'teach the kids responsibility', Daniel knew that, basically, getting a dog was for most people just a way of bribing the children.

For the Johansen family it was different. They had not bought a dog for the kids, but to give the father of the house a reason to exercise. Daniel had chosen a Welsh terrier because they were so energetic. He knew he would not reach the ambitious goals he had set up in his life unless he worked hard. And to be able to work hard, his brain had to be in prime condition—and a good way of keeping the brain in good shape was to make sure that the body was fit.

Unfortunately, Daniel hated most sports; he found them nothing but silly games for grown-ups. Running was OK, but it was so incredibly boring that he only did it on paid time at the hospital gym. The solution had been to buy a highly energetic dog which needed long walks. Kirre was nothing more than a logical solution to a career problem.

A positive side effect of these forced evening walks was that they were great for thinking. On tonight's walk Daniel had been reflecting on why certain people decided that their actions were morally right even if they were illegal—or how others seemed to think that doing something illegal could be morally right.

He could not understand this kind of reasoning. Laws were not something society created to annoy its citizens. Laws were the collective rules that made the difference between us living in a civilized society and just being a bunch of cold and lonely, suspicious individuals. Civilization was the world when everyone respected our common rules.

People who called for civil disobedience were on the slippery slope to anarchy. Living in their suburban utopias, modern man had forgotten the true meaning of the word anarchy. It was not a word to indicate some moral high ground of the young; it was synonymous with a disintegrating society. If we let history be our judge we knew that Anarchy had created nothing but misery. Anarchy was when everyone took as much as possible from the same cake. It just did not work.

The dog's barking shook him out of his thoughts. Kirre looked up at his owner for guidance. The lights from the buildings were faint and formed a layer of shadows that danced in the wind. The clouds covered the moon and stars. There were few things darker than a forest at night. A twig snapped behind them. Daniel's body instinctively tensed and he quickly turned around on reflex. Kirre barked again, with more fear in the bark this time.

'Damn dog!' The dog's reaction had fuelled his imagination about what had created the noise. The forest insisted on making sounds that his brain could not interpret. He thought he heard footsteps, but told himself it was only the branches creaking. He could hear breathing, but convinced himself it was the wind. He saw movement among the leaves and explained it away by saying it must have been a bird. That was probably why the dog had barked. The bird.

It was annoying that he, a grown man, could still be frightened by some sound in the dark. Or rather, he was irritated by why he could not find a rational explanation for the sensations his brain was obviously misinterpreting. His body had chosen to physically listen to the terrifying pictures that his imagination had been painting in his head. He hated that.

If he could not even argue with himself in a believable way, then how could he convince others about things he wanted them to accept?

'I have been watching too many horror movies,' he said out loud to Kirre as they hurried home.

Dogs were not just man's best friends; they were also The Unvisible's best allies. If a dog was present when a Yangyang—or a Yangyin—accidentally made some noise they could call on the dog to create the illusion of a natural explanation. When they were too hungry to wait for the leftovers to be thrown out, they could easily eat the food and then use sign language to get the dog to jump onto the table before a human came into the kitchen so that the dog would get the blame. Dogs were great at taking the blame, so whenever there were dogs around, life became a little bit easier for the Yangyang.

In addition, dogs were much better at reading sign language than understanding verbal instructions. Yet humans insisted on trying to talk to their dogs. It was an unknown fact for most that all dogs could understand sign language. They had learnt it from the Watchers in their houses. A dog could often understand a Yangyang long before it understood its owner. And all dogs knew who their true masters were.

Manda was thankful for that now. She had come a little too close to her subject and the subject's dog had warned her. It was part of a Killer's training to practise getting close to a Yinyin without raising suspicions. When rehearsing it was advisable to perform these training sessions when a Yinyin had ventured into nature. It made it easier. Nature was the Yangyangs' home turf and modern man was so painfully bad at reading Nature's signals that it gave the Yangyangs an even better upper hand.

Manda had enjoyed making a sound just behind her subject while letting her snake caress the back of his neck giving the subject goosebumps. It was then the dog had reacted. Manda signed to the dog to be silent before she withdrew.

Chapter 37

'In a mad world, only the mad are sane.'
– Akira Kurosawa

The cold water embraced her like a protective layer. Alex had been in the pool for over an hour but she did not want to get out. The knowledge that someone was always watching her had started to make her feel dirty. Not knowing who was following her was getting under her skin. Recently she had started to imagine that someone kept touching her.

She would find herself throwing an arm or leg out when she was in bed just to make sure that there was no one leaning over the bed. Alex knew she could not see them, which is why she felt that she could feel them all the time. Just as the itch from a mosquito bite can make our whole bodies itch from imaginary mosquitos giving us imaginary bites, just in the same way the knowledge of The Unvisible made Alex feel as if she was constantly being observed. It was slowly driving her mad.

She found herself looking for places where the Watchers could not go, or where they would have difficulties getting in. One of her new favourite places was the local swimming pool. The puddles of water on the floor must make it tricky for The Unvisible to walk around the changing rooms without being noticed, so she guessed that their presence there was minimal. And she felt even safer in the water. An unexpected side effect of spending so much time in the pool was that, for more or less the first time in her life, she found herself doing something that could be called exercising.

Alex looked at the big clock on the wall. It read 4:23. She used it to keep track of her lap times. She was getting slower and slower for every lap, but she was not there to break any records. She was there to be left alone. It was not fair. Why couldn't The Unvisible just go somewhere where there were no humans? If there were no humans around, there was no one to reveal their secret to and no one they had to keep an eye on. No one to sneak up on at night or whose beds they had to sleep under. No one whose personal space got violated.

Mr Williams had said something about the Yangyang and Yinyin having to live close together to 'create harmony', but no matter how much she tried to understand what that meant, Alex felt far from harmonious right now. If it was possible for her to take a pill that made her forget everything, Alex would take it without blinking. She did not want to live with the knowledge that Watchers were observing her. Why couldn't the world go back to normal? Why had she had to find out? It was like she had been sentenced to carry around the secret as a heavy weight around her soul the rest of her life. Wherever she went, she was dragging the secret behind her. She wanted her freedom back!

'I don't care how invisible you are! If you step into the water, I'll see you,' she whispered with clenched teeth. Even invisible mass would repel water. Knowing that made her feel safe. The water was her refuge. She decided to swim a few more laps to delay having to get back to the complexity of reality.

Every time the Subject reached the edge of the pool, the Watcher put out a hand and patted her very carefully on the head. It was so gentle that she could not feel it, yet firm enough for her to almost sense it. People were so predictable. They went swimming. Or stood in the middle of a sandy beach or a pile of snow. These were, by far, the most common places people in the know went when they wanted a space where they thought the Yangyang could not follow them. And they were right: these were indeed some of the places where it was hard not to leave a trace, which is why the Yangyang avoided them. That meant that, for a while, they could only watch from a distance, but it did not mean that they did not watch. They always watched.

And by touching the woman on the forehead with a finger when she reached the edge of the pool, the Watcher wanted to send her a message. A message that she would not know she was receiving: 'You think you are clever. But you are not as clever as us.'

Chapter 38

> **'When men are doubtful of the true state of things, their wishes lead them to believe in what is most agreeable.'**
> – Arrianus

The best way to confront someone is to surprise her. His wife had just gotten out of the bath and was sitting on the toilet lid with her head between her legs, blow-drying her hair. She was naked and vulnerable. Daniel pulled the plug out and the sudden silence startled her.

'Why did you do that?' Laura gasped.

'I know you're cheating on me. What's his name?'

'Honey, what are you talking about?'

Daniel leaned over his wife. She shrank back. Was this a bad joke or a huge misunderstanding?

'Don't you lie to me!'

'You're not listening to me.'

'Shut up! How do you explain the fact that Eric says there's a guy at our house during the day and that he's told Eric he's not allowed to tell me about him? How do you explain the fact that Eric says he's here ALL THE TIME?!'

He showed her his notebook in which he had written, 'He's here. Everywhere. All the time.' As if the sentences were proof.

It had been weeks since Daniel had overheard Eric tell Alex about a man visiting their home. Daniel had given his wife plenty of time to come clean. The revenge was ready to be served.

'I really have no idea what you're talking about . . . It must be a misunderstanding. Let's talk to Eric—you know how he can make up these wild stories.'

'Don't you dare drag Eric into this!'

He threw the red hairdryer into the bath, where it burst into pieces.

Daniel left his wife sitting confused and perplexed—and scared—on the toilet. Hopefully, that would be enough to stop her escapades. Now that she knew he knew, she would stop. Not that he was really surprised she had a lover: their sex life after the birth of Junior was sporadic at best. He had solved this problem for himself in an excellent manner. The woman he met at a party a few months ago had been easy to chat up. She seemed fine with the concept of casual sex. And she lived conveniently close to the hospital.

It was a Tuesday, so she would be free. Perhaps he should call her and see if he could come over? The adrenaline had made him horny. He loved getting kicks like this out of life. He pulled out his phone and looked up her number, saved under the name 'student councillor' to avoid detection.

It was one thing for him to have a lover on the side, but quite another thing for Laura to do the same. She was his wife and should focus on being precisely that. And on being the mother of their children.

Outside the subject's front door, a Watcher was painting something on the doorpost with a small brush. Communicating with other Watchers by using symbols and pictures was something the Watchers had done for generations. It was a tradition they were proud of.

In the past, The Unvisible had carved their signs on the fence posts outside a house with visible paint so that even those in the know could get information about the people who lived there. But as The Unvisible became more and more cautious, they had started writing their messages with invisible paint that humans could not see.

The Watcher dried up some spilled paint from the ground and took a step back to evaluate his work. A ring with a line through it was painted on the door frame at eye level. The symbol meant: 'Here lives a dishonest man.'

Chapter 39

'The real voyage of discovery consists not in seeking new landscapes, but in having new eyes.'
– Marcel Proust

The experienced soldiers behind the old desk in the military's Department of External Ideas had just sat through yet another presentation from a hopeful inventor. This time, it was a weapon enthusiast who had high hopes for his innovation, but the response from the judges had been lukewarm.

The man Daniel had compared to Radar's little brother summed up his impressions. 'Scary, but I guess it's not illegal to weld together ten rifles like that. I just hope he doesn't try to use it.'

'I wouldn't call it scary,' said his partner. 'Something that heavy is more clumsy than scary. OK—who's next?'

Radar's little brother looked down at his papers. 'Some kind of technology for using film cameras to detect intruders. He'll be here in ten minutes.'

When Daniel came into the room fifteen minutes later, he was met by two frowns. 'What? You again?'

Daniel had not expected the two men to be overly excited to see him again as their last meeting had not ended well. That is why he had applied as Dr Johansen instead of Daniel Johansen so that they would not realize they were one and the same person. He had also described his invention as a sort of surveillance equipment instead of as invisibility glasses. He had decided to be humble and positive from the start and to avoid any mention of money until they had seen what the technology could do.

'Let me start by saying how sorry I am for my behaviour last time. And for twisting the truth a little to be able to come back. I see now that it was stupid to talk about money before proving to you that the technology works.'

'Don't count your chickens before they hatch,' said the older soldier.

'Exactly. And now I'm going to start hatching some serious eggs. This time, I'm going to skip the history lessons and philosophical mumbo-jumbo and go straight to the demonstration. I confess that I was just as sceptical as you when I first saw this technology. I now know that the best way to convince someone is to show them—and not talk about it.'

'So you're here to demonstrate the same technology as last time?'

'That's right. But before we start, I'm going to have to ask you both to leave the room.'

'We have rules, Dr Johansen, and one of those rules is that we get to decide how the demonstrations are carried out. Another rule is that we don't leave this room.'

Daniel was not discouraged.

'I find it difficult to believe that you don't leave the room if someone wants to show you, say, a jet fighter or a Batmobile. So there must be some exceptions to that rule. And, of course, I'm not questioning the fact that you are in charge. All I'm asking is that you wait outside for a few minutes while I prepare my presentation. You can observe me through the glass doors to make sure I am behaving if you like.'

The officers sighed heavily, but got up and went out to the waiting area.

Last time he was there, Daniel had noticed that there were a couple of doors between the waiting area and demonstration room that could be locked and, this time, he was not about to let The Unvisible get away.

Daniel put a large plastic container on the desk. Two plastic pipes went from the container to a smaller one made of glass. Daniel was very pleased with his handiwork and knew that it would most likely not make the Watcher in the room suspicious. He took out a little green watering can and pretended to have an idea. Then he said out loud into what looked like thin air, 'Water—I'll get some from the bathroom.' He took the watering can and the box with the yangsee and left the room. As soon as he came into the waiting area, he locked the door and whispered to the two men sitting on the sofa, 'Quick—follow me into the toilet.'

One of the men was about to object. There were limits to what they could tolerate, but when they realized that Daniel only meant the small corridor where the toilets were located, they relented.

Daniel took out the yangsee and helped the older officer put it on. 'Quick, look through the demonstration room door. Then tell me if you think I'm crazy.'

'Well, we do not consider anyone to be . . .'

'It's OK. I know what you think of me,' Daniel interrupted the well-rehearsed phrase that the officer had started to say without thinking about it. 'But that doesn't matter. Go to the door, but whatever you do—don't unlock it.'

The man peered into the room and his jaw dropped, 'What the hell?!'

'What the hell—what?' his colleague asked.

But he did not get an answer. The older man took off the yangsee and looked around the room again.

'What the hell!' He put the glasses back on. Then he froze, looking at something in one corner of the room until he finally burst out and said, 'Bloody hell!'

The younger officer could not remember the last time he heard his colleague swear so much in such a short period of time. He gave Daniel a look that said 'isn't it my turn soon?' Daniel got the point. He had to get both of them to see the same thing to be sure that they really understood what he was showing them. Daniel yanked the yangsee off the first man and quickly put it on his colleague.

'Do you see that man in the corner?' yelled the officer who had just put on the yangsee. 'Who is that?'

'That's what I've been trying to explain. It's an Unvisible—another human species with a cell structure that . . .'

Daniel was interrupted when the officer wearing the glasses knocked on the glass pane on the door.

'What are you doing?!' Daniel said as loud as he dared. 'He's going to realize that you can see him!'

Daniel could not see what was happening in the room, but by studying the man who had just knocked on the glass, he had a pretty good idea.

The Watcher heard knocking on the glass door and looked up. He initially thought that it was Daniel returning with the water, but when he saw three men on the other side of the glass door looking into what—for them—should have been an empty room, he knew something was wrong. He got up and walked across the room while he observed the faces of the people on the other side of the door. Two of the men did not react, but the youngest man in the group seemed very excited and his head followed the Watcher as he moved.

To see if he really had been detected, the Watcher went right up to the door and stood in front of the men on the other side. When he suddenly lunged towards the door, the man wearing the glasses shrank back. It was clear that one of them was somehow able to see him.

He had to minimize the damage. First he tried to pull the door open. But it was locked. He turned back and went to the window. It was locked too. Or to be more accurate, there was no way of opening it. He was cornered. Cornered and exposed.

While turning towards the door, he saw that the older man was wearing the glasses again. He was talking on his mobile phone while gesticulating furiously. The third man was filming the room with his phone. Time was running out. He had to make a decision. More people would very likely be coming soon. If they caught him, he was dead. Or even worse, he would be caught.

There was only one thing he could do. The Watcher picked up a chair and threw it at the window. The glass shattered into a thousand pieces. It was not the best solution, but all of the other solutions were even worse. The

Watcher climbed out of the window and gestured to his two doves to fly and get help.

Within a few seconds, they returned with fifteen other birds that grabbed his clothes with their beaks and claws in a well-rehearsed ritual. The birds struggled frantically against gravity as they plummeted swiftly towards the ground. Fifteen birds were not enough and they could not manage to hold him up properly. He fell dangerously fast. The landing was too hard and forced an unfortunate and unintentional groan from his mouth as he broke both his feet. But he was out of danger. That was all that mattered.

Chapter 40

'The more original a discovery, the more obvious it seems afterwards.'
– Arthur Koestler

When Daniel saw the window shattering, he was confused. Why had the Watcher fled? Weren't they always supposed to be watching? He took the glasses, rushed into the room, over to the window and looked down.

The Watcher was sitting on the ground, holding his feet, and pointing up to the window where Daniel was standing. Next to the Watcher were two Unvisibles looking up at where the Watcher was pointing. The expressions on their faces made Daniel take a step back. When they started to run towards the entrance, Daniel instinctively knew his life was in imminent danger.

His spontaneous reaction was to run away, but if The Unvisibles got hold of his two officers Daniel would be back to square one. That could not happen. He had already invested too much time and effort. Daniel turned around and screamed at the two soldiers who had now also entered the room, 'Follow me! Now! If you ever want to see your children again, follow me!'

The seriousness in Daniel's voice was convincing. This was not the time to ask for an explanation. Daniel was wearing the magic glasses and could still see those invisible people. They could not. That made them feel very exposed. Following a civilian's orders might not be the correct procedure, but right now procedure could go screw itself.

They quickly followed Daniel.

After a while, Daniel turned around and asked, 'Is there a garage in the building?'

'Yes.'

'Do you have your cars there?'

The men nodded.

Daniel turned to the younger man and ordered, 'Give me the keys. What kind of car do you have?'

'An old Toyota Corolla. Gray.' The man fished the keys out of his pocket and threw them to Daniel.

Daniel looked at the older, higher-ranking man. 'Follow me in your car. Ignore all the traffic regulations and don't stop for anything. Our lives are in danger. I hope you understand just how serious our situation is.'

Both men nodded again.

When they came to the garage, Daniel jumped into the light-gray Corolla, put on the seatbelt and started the engine. In the rear-view mirror, he saw a red Volvo driving towards him. He waited a few seconds for it to come closer. 'I hope they taught you high-speed driving in military school,' he thought to himself.

As soon as he came out of the garage, Daniel accelerated and put the yangsee over his head. It had been a close call.

Now he had to make sure he continued to keep the upper hand.

Suddenly a muffled bang and then the sharp sound of broken glass. Looking in the rear-view mirror, Daniel saw the red Volvo ricochet off a lamppost and slide over to the other side of the road. The oncoming truck did not have a chance to swerve away. It looked as if the car had been sliced in the middle and the two men must have died the same second the car was crushed under the front end of the truck.

Daniel swore.

When he looked in the mirror again, he was met by a pair of dark, dark eyes in the back seat. The world outside—everything else—just disappeared. The sorrowful eyes of the Killer were hypnotizing.

For a second, he saw three approaching cars. He aimed for the smallest one and accelerated. A second before the two cars crashed, he closed his eyes and covered his face with his hands—partly because he did not want to see what would happen next; and partly to protect the yangsee. If he were to survive this, then he was going to do whatever he could to take advantage of what he knew. Me against the world. The world against me.

The last thought he remembered was how dry and soft snakeskin was—not as wet and slimy as he had imagined it.

When you are in a crash, everything seems to happen in slow motion. The brain sees a million small details and manages to communicate this at a much slower tempo. As if life were a TV producer that wants the viewers to really enjoy every last second, especially if it might be the last seconds of your life.

When the Killer who had released his snake onto the driver's neck looked up, he saw that the pink car was way too close. He even saw the little, pink cloth elephant hanging from the rear-view mirror as it swung from side to side. Behind the ugly cloth creature, he saw the surprised face and shocked look of the woman who was driving. The two cars were on a collision course and he would not be able to escape in time.

He heard the sound of glass breaking, metal shrieking, airbags exploding. And he smelled old car mixing with newly torn plastic, leaking gas and something sweet that might be human blood. Or was he tasting his own blood? It did not matter how fast his reflexes as a Killer were, he would not be able to complete his mission. He might be able to curl up into a ball, prepare for the crash, protect his head from the windscreen—but he was still going to die. That did not bother him too much. What did disturb him was the fact that he would not be able to finish the assignment. He had waited too long. That had been a mistake. Watchers should be waiting; Killers should kill. And death should not be kept waiting. It was a beginner's mistake that he would never be able to rectify.

When he flew through the windscreen, he tried to focus on the beautiful. His eyes looked for the snake with its chalk-white skin and pale-yellow spotted head.

The snake's blood hit the dashboard in small, fragile drops as the serpent collided with the windscreen. Each drop that soared out of its body formed a pattern with the other drops. The drops splashed onto the plastic in a synchronized dance of chaos. A fraction of a second later, the Killer went through the windscreen and crushed his head against the side of the car. When the light went out in his brain, he felt peace for the first time in his distorted life. Dying was his final punishment for the crime of having killed his own mother by being born.

Chapter 41

'The greatest secrets are always hidden in the most unlikely of places.'
– Roald Dahl

The first thing that hit Daniel when he regained consciousness was the pain. His left shoulder was screaming in agony after being pinned by the seat belt. The face was throbbing after the impact of the airbag and his head must be bleeding, because he could feel blood running over his eyes. And there was something wrong with his right hand. The rest of his body just hurt. Was it possible to hurt in so many places at the same time?

He had no idea how long his blackout had lasted. Crash—nothing—pain. As if life had edited out a few clips that it thought he did not want to see. First, a lot of details and then no memories at all. And now, a firework of sensations. He kind of knew where he was, but not exactly when.

But he did know what he was: he was alive. He remembered seeing the snake and the Killer flying through the windscreen during the fraction of a second he had his eyes open. Luckily, Daniel had had the presence to notice that the Killer was not wearing his seatbelt. That insight had made him make a split decision to drive headlong into the little pink Volkswagen Beetle. He had followed a negotiation technique he had once read about. 'When faced with an unexpected situation—do the unexpected.' And it had worked.

He was alive.

But who was screaming?

Daniel carefully moved his arms, then his legs and finally his neck to make sure all his body parts were where they should be. It hurt, but not in a dangerous way. His body screamed of pain, but at the same time, it reported to him that it was in working order.

He pried open the door and crawled out of what had once been a car. Once out, he leaned back into the wreck again and scrambled to find the yangsee. When he found them he quickly examined them. They looked remarkably undamaged. Luckily, Ola had clearly chosen strong materials for his glasses. They might be bulky and ugly, but they were strong! 'Thank god for Ola's nerdiness.' Daniel thought gratefully.

Daniel headed towards the totalled, pink Beetle a few metres away. Stuck in the car's front seat, desperately trying to get eye contact, sat the car's driver. Daniel guessed the driver was a woman, but it was frankly not easy to tell. From her face—that was mostly a red-purple-and-black mixture of blood, dirt and tears—came a frantic scream for help. As Daniel got closer he heard her say. 'Oh my god! You're alive! He's alive!'

'I drive straight into her car and her reaction is that she's glad I am alive?' He felt contempt for such a weak person. How could her first reaction not be to be happy that she was alive?

She looked as if she needed help, but he just did not have the time. He would probably have tried to save her had the circumstances been different, but right now he had to get away before the Yangyang sent in a new Killer. He knew he had been lucky. But luck runs out. Daniel was not about to waste what luck he still had left on a random stranger, no matter how much she was bleeding to death. Most people would find this attitude harsh, but leaving her there was not inhumane. It was human. Most people in the same situation would also prioritize their own lives over a stranger's—even if most people would never admit it.

And there were others who could help. A couple of cars had already stopped jamming up the traffic on each side of the scene of the accident. The drivers hesitated to go up to the wrecked cars. But that was not Daniel's problem. Sooner or later the police and ambulance would come. But by then he would be long gone.

As Daniel passed the woman, she looked at him beseechingly, 'Help me . . .'

Disgusted Daniel replied, 'Oh, can you just stop?'

She looked at him in utter surprise as her last energy left her. Sure, that last remark had been uncalled for. He would blame it on still being in shock. And that woman had really been screaming a lot.

Manda, the Killer who had just sat in the officers' Volvo, evaluated the situation. It was she who had turned the steering wheel when the approaching truck was in exactly the right position to collide with the car. Everything had gone according to plan and she had survived. Manda had jumped out of the car just before the crash and curled into a ball to minimize injury. But she had been forced to leave her snake in the vehicle. The snake was dead. That was unfortunate, but manageable. There were many other snakes waiting to take its place.

The woman put the snake into a small cloth bag to bring her home. This evening she would eat it for dinner as a last tribute to their long and close partnership. She would give the snake's skin to the Queen. Eating her partner was a way of getting closure; of capturing the energy that had existed between Killer and reptile; of preserving it. Of using the energy instead of letting it go to waste.

She grieved her snake for a few minutes, but she would not grieve longer than that. Life should be honoured, not death. But it was the killing that she honoured the most. Not death—she hated it—but the killing. She could never get enough of it. And today she had even more reason to kill. The third man had somehow managed to get away. His Killer was lying lifeless next to the Toyota.

Manda quietly looked at her dead colleague. She swore to herself that she would avenge him. Promised to complete the mission that had somehow gone wrong. A person that was sentenced to death had no life. Daniel Johansen was as good as dead—they just had to find him. Manda would see to it that the mission was completed.

She signed a confused prayer—her way of screaming out her angst. A stream of tears fell from her black eyes.

I am the devil with wings. A Dark Angel.

I stand with no defence, conscious of the danger.

Always hunting.

My life contains no life.

Manda's slender body trembled when she was done. With her arms out in front of her, the head bent back until her neck muscles tightened, she shut her eyes. Then she collapsed. Her body cramped viciously as it curled itself into the fetal position.

Chapter 42

'He belonged to that army known as invincible in peace, invisible in war.'
– William Tecumseh Sherman

He was definitely on a roll. First he had been able to shake off a Killer—something that was apparently really difficult to do. Then he survived an accident, miraculously coming out of it with nothing worse than an injured collar bone, a sprained wrist and a collection of cuts. Then he had been lucky enough to get a new car. OK, the last part was perhaps less luck and more brashness.

One of the people who had stopped at the scene of the crash had left his car, a black BMW, with the engine running. Daniel had made the most of the confusion and 'borrowed' the BMW for an indefinite length of time. 'I have to get to the hospital. I'll get in touch later,' he shouted as he drove off. He figured he could use the car for two days before the driver reported it stolen.

Daniel had driven as fast as he dared for two straight hours to get as far away as possible from the scene of the accident. As far away as possible from the Killer.

Focusing on driving fast also helped him to not focus on what had just happened. Dwelling on the past was not Daniel's style. 'You can't drive a car looking through the rear-view mirror,' his father had always said when Daniel tried to get him to explain things that had happened when he was a child. Daniel thought he was becoming more and more like his father the older he got. His father was right: you drove by focusing on where you were going. Now he had to plan for the future; get control of the situation. Daniel Johansen would not be able to hide for long, so the only solution was that Daniel Johansen had to turn into someone else.

He stopped outside a hairdresser and went in. 'Shave off my hair. All of it.'

The barber looked at him suspiciously, as if he thought an escaped prisoner had just walked in. Daniel got nervous and quickly explained that he was the 'victim' of a stag party gone wrong. The cuts and bruises in his face came from having been forced to ride an electric scooter blindfolded, and now he was being forced to shave off his hair by his 'friends'. It worked. The barber relaxed, and after expressing sympathy for how the poor bride would be marrying a bald groom with scars, he offered to shave off Daniel's hair for half-price.

'Buy your future wife some roses to take the edge off the shock when she sees you,' he said when Daniel thanked him half an hour later.

Daniel left the barbershop and went into an optician's to buy a pair of sunglasses and a pair of glasses with thick, black frames and plain glass. Once again, he used the stag party excuse.

With a shaved head and prominent black glasses, he looked more like an artist than a doctor. And he looked at least five years older. But, more importantly, he did not look like Daniel Johansen any more.

Escape. Disappear. Disguise. The first three steps of his plan executed. Almost everything had gone better than he could have hoped for.

He should probably call his wife and tell her why he had suddenly vanished, but he frankly could not bother right now. Instead he had just written her an e-mail saying that he had suddenly been called away to a conference and he had to fly there immediately. That was all she had to know. He guessed she would be sad and disappointed, but if his mother could manage with his father being away on conferences for a long time, then so could Laura. Daniel had explained to his wife, even before they got married, that his career came first and that they would have to put up with the fact that some conferences might be booked at short notice.

He would call her later, right now there were so many more important things to do. Calls had to be made; tickets bought; meetings booked. If his plan was going to work, he had to be quicker than they were. Despite him being alone and them being an army. But Daniel was at his best when he was on his own. Alone against the world. He could do it. He would do it. And when he did, he would get the ultimate prize. You have to bet big to win big. Most people were afraid to take risks, but Daniel was not like most people.

He overtook another car in a slightly reckless manner.

The Killer's body had been carried home to the Vimana. Inside the giant open hall, they celebrated yet another life lived. Even though the Yangyang thought of the Yangyin as distant relatives rather than equals, they all knew that without the Killers their mission would not only be much more difficult. It would be impossible. And when a Killer had sacrificed his life for his mother's family, then it was only right to pay tribute to that deed. But while the Yangyang celebrated the life of the dead person inside the pyramid, the Killers gathered in a field outside where the corpse had been placed. Not even when he was dead was a Yangyin allowed to be a full-blown member of the Primary Queen's flock.

Manda took the dead man's arm and started to take off his armour. He would leave this earth as naked as the day he came into it. Shoes, shin pads, armour and helmet; everything was tied together with the Killer's robe and then fastened to his foot with the belt. Manda straightened out the man's arms and ordered the other Killers to fasten the man's bamboo pole to the back of his neck and both wrists. The edge of the pole had a lot of thin lines attached to it that the Killers now straightened out so that they lay flat on the ground around the man's head. When everything was ready, Manda signed to the Queen that she was done.

The Queen was carrying a bamboo construction in the shape of an upside-down pyramid. It was constructed with the same technology as the large pyramid: a bamboo frame with horse hides that created a tight structure, which was then filled with a gas that made the whole thing lighter than air. The little pyramid was a balloon for the dead Killer. The balloon floated above the Queen and was anchored with a rope around a stone that two Carers were carrying.

While Manda tied the Killer to the pyramid, the Primary Queen looked for the most experienced Watcher. When he reported that there were no humans nearby, she lifted up her hands. A hundred white doves soared out of the pyramid and circled the group. At the same time, a couple of hundred black ravens emerged from the forest. Manda stepped forwards and cut the rope anchoring the dead man and his pyramid to the ground. The other Killers raised their hands towards the sky and when the last of the dead man's equipment left the ground and floated up to the sky, the whole group yelled a single word. This was one of the very few times it was allowed to speak loudly outside the Vimana. The roar sounded like a mixture of wind and death. The word they screamed was, 'Revenge!'

As the body slowly rose up to the sky, the birds danced around it like dancers around a fire. If humans were to look up, all they would see was a flock of ravens flying towards the sky in an irregular pattern. The group standing on the ground, however, saw a funeral. The Killer would continue rising upwards until he disappeared. It was a beautiful and symbolic way to leave earthly life—and it was also a practical one. Burying an Unvisible would make transparent holes in the earth that people would not be able to explain logically.

The Queen looked up at the dead man floating naked in the sky with his arms extended. She bowed. The Killer had failed in his mission, but by dying, he had inspired the other Killers to complete it. The man who had killed the Killer would die. The Primary Queen was fully convinced of that.

Chapter 43

'Fear of things invisible in the natural seed of that which everyone in himself calleth religion.'
– Thomas Hobbes

Is there anything more powerful than a mother protecting her young? The powerful energy that Mary had mobilised from turning her worry into action in just a few days had surprised even herself. Waiting for the delivery of the cameras had been the hardest part. Once they arrived, she had installed the cameras in less than an hour and even managed to set the motion detection controls to only be activated between nine in the evening and seven in the morning. When she, after a few attempts, was able to work out how to control the cameras so that the one pointed at the door triggered the other two, she felt like a real hacker. Saga could now move around in bed without setting off the motion detectors and the cameras would only start filming if someone came into the room after Saga had gone to bed.

The idea of spying on her husband felt wrong, but the need to protect her daughter made it right.

She had to go away on a business trip the day after installing the cameras. The dinner with clients had ended late so she had been too tired to check if there were any recordings when she got back to the hotel.

The next morning, when she logged onto her computer to see if she had any e-mails, she had momentarily forgotten—or perhaps the right word was repressed—her suspicions about the unthinkable. So, she got a shock when she read the first heading in her inbox: HOMESECURE VIDEO. FILM 01—DATE: YESTERDAY. TIME: 23.15.

She stared at the link in the email and felt her stomach turn. 'Saga. My dear child.'

Unconditional hate mixed with unconditional love mixed with uncertainty and confusion. It couldn't be true, could it?

As she started to watch the movie, her first reaction was one of relief. The film did not show Thomas going into the room and assaulting their daughter.

In fact, the film did not show anything.

The door was never opened and yet the cameras had been triggered.

She finally saw what had activated the cameras. She saw it, but could not believe it. On the screen one of Saga's cushions moved. It was lying there on the floor and then it just rose up slowly in the air. Then it did a turn and landed back on the floor again.

She replayed the film and saw that the cushion really had moved. There was no one nearby and no one knew she had installed the cameras. It could not be a practical joke; it could not be Saga. It was not Thomas. So who was it?

She watched the film sequence over and over again. She finally came to the, for her, only logical explanation: it must be Saga's guardian angel who had come down to protect her. She had to tell Reverend Persson! It was a miracle. The deeply religious Mary had always known Saga was special. She had told the reverend as much.

She switched off her computer, called her boss and explained she had to go home earlier than planned to look after her daughter. Then she called Thomas. 'Can you contact Reverend Persson and ask him to come home to us at nine o'clock tonight? I'm coming home earlier than planned and have something to share with the two of you.'

Thomas asked her to explain. 'I don't have time. I'll tell you when I get home. Just make sure the reverend is at our house this evening. He'll understand. Everything will make sense. I've seen a miracle, darling. Promise me you'll convince the reverend to come. And make sure Saga doesn't go to bed before I get back.'

She re-booked her ticket and jumped into the first taxi she could find. When she got to the airport and was going to pay the driver she saw that the keycard to her room was still in her purse. She rushed home so fast she had forgotten to check out of the hotel.

Annoyed, she once again shooed away the flies that had insisted on landing on her thigh during the entire taxi ride. She didn't even wait for her change, instead she jumped out of the car to get away from the dirty taxi with its flies.

When Mary ran into the domestic terminal, she looked around to find the right check-in desk. It would turn out to be the last thing she ever did.

Mary's briefcase flew open when she fell to the ground and a few documents scattered across the floor. Her gray suit was a suitably boring colour to die in. A small group of people gathered around. A few more stopped and then moved on as others came to see what was going on. Someone called for help, got out a mobile phone and looked at it. But no one called an ambulance. A man tried to stop passers-by from stepping on the woman lying on the cold floor. But no one bent down to see if she was still breathing. No one undid her blouse or started CPR. The doctor who confirmed the death would, in all likelihood, write heart attack as the cause of death. All the symptoms pointed to this. And that was, of course, what it was supposed to look like.

A Watcher was observing the group from a distance. He knew that if someone had a heart attack, there was less chance of her being helped by strangers if there were a lot of people around. The same thing was true of people who were abused or who fell and hurt themselves. The more people around who could potentially help out, the fewer who actually did.

In the waiting area of a hospital in New York a while ago, a patient had collapsed and lay dead for more than an hour before someone came to see what had happened. Not even the nurses on duty reacted. It is only when a person was alone with someone in trouble that she would help. So it was best to kill people with fake heart attacks when they were in the middle of a crowd—for example in an airport—as there was a smaller risk of others intervening, no matter how paradoxical this might seem.

No one would ever know that the woman had not died from a heart attack, but rather from a snake bite on the inside of her cheek.

Next to the woman some big, black flies flew in circles. They were called 'Bangaw' and they were always found near the Killers. Like seagulls chasing fishing boats, they waited for death to strike so that they could feast. The Yangyang could have chosen to kill all the bangaw as the flies risked giving away the Killers. But they had deemed it unnecessary, as it was not enough that people noticed the flies: they also had to make the connection that the flies were a sign that a Killer on a mission was nearby. And the Yinyin had long forgotten this.

A few metres away stood the Killer who had sent her snake to deliver the kiss of death. Its first kill. The snake was once again coiled around Manda's shoulders and neck. It was ready to kill again. A few steps behind her stood a younger Killer wearing the same war attire, but without a snake. Today his job was just to act as back-up in case something went wrong.

Manda signed to her younger colleague. Every sign was crafted slowly and carefully. As if she was forced to think about how to get rid of her grief. Deep, black rings around her dark eyes made them look like hollow holes. Her eyes were more like a bottomless lake than a mirror to the soul.

The younger Killer interpreted the signs his mentor so laboriously signed.

'Flakes of ash, debris of joy for the sake of destruction. Gray.

Music that asks to be stopped.

In my path—doom.

Still crazy.

I am unpredictable.

My faces passionate and broken by the light.'

The younger man stood quietly and studied his master. He knew that it would soon be his turn to read a poem to a young apprentice about how he felt to be forced to take another person's life. He knew he would hate it. And yet he could not wait.

Chapter 44

'Philosophy and Art both render the invisible visible by imagination.'
– George H. Lewes

Shadow certainly did not give the impression of being someone who socialised a lot, so Alex was happily surprised when Shadow called and said she wanted to meet up. When Alex suggested meeting at Shadow's place, Shadow had sounded a little hesitant as if surprised that someone had actually asked to come home to her, but then she had given Alex her address.

With all the stress she had been feeling lately Alex had really appreciated a chance to meet up with another person. To be honest, she had been feeling very alone lately. At the end of the semester she had looked forward to the summer break like crazy, but now—after weeks without a daily schedule and after spending too much time alone with her thoughts—she cursed her off time. Will I go back to school? Should I? If not, then what should I do?

She bombarded herself with questions. At her age most people were in the middle of their careers, while she did not even have a profession. And worse, now she did not even have a direction. Perhaps talking to Shadow could bring some clarity to her confusion.

Next to the doorbell on the doorframe of Shadow's apartment sat a post-it note that read: 'Knock!'. Alex smiled and followed the instructions. A few seconds later Shadow let her in.

It was as dark as night inside. All of the windows were covered with black cloth and Shadow had painted the wallpaper matte black. The few pieces of furniture in the apartment looked as if they had been bought in a second-hand shop and they too had been given the same unsentimental going over with black paint. The unmade bed had black sheets and even the lampshades were black. A pink elephant lay in a corner, looking eerily out of place.

The apartment was not dirty, but it was messy. Alex felt at home although she guessed a lot of others would not. Shadow's home looked as if a darker version of Alex's soul had decorated it. Next to Shadow's bed, stood a computer and a really big computer screen. The light flooding out of the screen into the dark, black painted room was like a full moon on a clear night. The computer was clearly the centre of gravity for the apartment.

'Cosy, isn't it?' Shadow said with obvious irony.

'I actually like it,' Alex replied. 'But why the blackout curtains?'

'I tell the neighbours that I'm a photographer and use the room as a dark room, but it's really to keep the neighbours away; I don't want them snooping around. It's also a good way of shutting out the light so I can sleep during the day. I often work at night.'

'Why do you work at night?'

'Well, one reason is because that's when there is a demand for my services—but I also just work better when most normal people aren't awake. The quiet darkness protects me.'

Shadow went up to Alex and took her hand. 'You've had a pretty rough couple of months, huh?'

'You think?' Alex replied with a sigh. She sat down on the bed and tucked her feet underneath her.

Shadow smiled warmly, 'That's why I figured you could appreciate some company from someone who understands what you are going through.'

Alex's body relaxed when she heard that. 'How long will it feel like the world is falling apart?'

'Your world will never be the same. But in a few months, you'll accept the fact that you have to live with the secret for the rest of your life. The world is full of people carrying heavy secrets that they are not allowed to share. Grown men who try to forget that their parents were Nazis, families who know that their fortune was made illegally or immorally, or women who do not tell their husbands that the men are not the fathers of their children. The only difference is that you know a secret that is beautiful.'

'You make it sound so simple.'

'Life is not simple.'

'How long have you known about the Yangyang?'

'More or less my whole life. I was one of those kids who had imaginary friends. But unlike most, I continued to see The Unvisible even when I was a teenager. When I started school, both teachers and students bullied me when I refused to give up my stories about people no one else could see. Instead of supporting me, my parents sided with the teachers and made sure I ended up being examined by an army of psychologists. When nothing helped, I finally got a special education teacher from the church, who gave me extra tuition at home. My parents were very religious.'

'Were? Are they dead?'

'They are to me. Ever since they decided—along with our priest—to "beat the devil out of me". I ran away from home that night.'

'How old were you?'

'Thirteen.'

'And you've been on the run ever since?'

'I stole some of my mother's silverware and pawned it. Then I bought a train ticket with my father's credit card but threw it away as soon as I had bought it. It was just a way of misleading the police. Instead of taking the train, I hitchhiked for a couple of days until I felt they would not find me. That's when I became Shadow.'

'What's your real name?'

'Something else.'

'How did you survive?'

'At first, The Unvisible looked after me. But when I turned fifteen, I lost the ability to see them and . . .'

Alex noticed how Shadow stiffened.

'Is it hard to talk about?'

'Everyone regrets something.'

Alex interpreted this as a signal that she had probed too far into Shadow's private life. It was time to change the subject. Alex walked over to the computer and nodded towards the huge computer screen.

'What's with the computer?'

'That's my work station. I help newbies in World of Warcraft.'

'The computer game?'

'Actually, it's more of a world than a game. I get paid to teach beginners how things work. I get my customers by more experienced players recommending me. They don't want to be interrupted by curious newcomers that haven't yet understood how World of Warcraft works, so they refer the beginners to me.'

'How does it work?'

Shadow answered like a teacher. The mood had lifted now that the conversation was not centred on Shadow's dark past.

'There are two different sides: Horde and Alliance. On the Horde side, there are trolls, blood-elves, which are like the elves in the Lord of the Rings but with longer ears and shiny, green eyes, orcs, zombies and Minotaurs, although they're known as the Tauren in the game. And then on the Alliance side, we have humans, dwarves, gnomes, night elves—they are tall with either blue or pinkish-purple skin and long ears. The men have shiny, yellow eyes and the women have white. Then we have the Draenei. They have horses' hooves, horns and tails and their skin is bluish.'

Shadow scrolled through her messages while she was talking. 'This is me.' On the screen was an animated fantasy creature. 'I'm obviously a blood-elf Rogue; they can make themselves invisible. They're also assassins and belong to the Horde side, which is where most of the pros are.'

A question popped up on the screen from a character called Elin. 'Bob, why do so few players use their real names?'

'Bob?' asked Alex.

'That's my name here.'

Shadow fired off a reply to Elin. Alex leaned forward to read the text on the screen.

Chat text:

'No person plays just one character in life. You're one person in school, another when you're with your mum, a third with your friends and so on. Playing different roles is something people do all the time. By playing a different character than the ones you are in real life, you can explore other parts of your personality that don't have an outlet. Role-playing lets you develop your personality—or should I say, your personalities.'

Elin asked another question.

Chat text:

'But won't all these different realities make you schizophrenic?'

Shadow replied.

Chat text:

'Have you never watched a movie or read a good book and felt like some of the characters are actually real? My guess is that people with lively imaginations have healthier brains than those who don't. Unfortunately, moralists like to warn that young people will be damaged by these "dangerous" computer games. New things scare old people. It was the same with jazz, punk and skateboarding for example. When young people get excited about something that old people do not understand then the adult world tends to think it must be dangerous. Parents have to learn to let kids find their own worlds. Overprotective parents aren't just very irritating, they can also kill a child's potential.'

'I wrote that last sentence because I suspect Elin is really the worried mother of a child who has just started to play WoW. I don't have a lot of patience with overprotective parents . . .'

She turned off the chat feed with 'Elin' and continued, 'What people don't get is that, for a lot of people, digital worlds are the only way they can create a dignified life. It could, for example, be a single mum who is working double shifts to make ends meet. That moment at night after her child has gone to sleep, when she can go online and be the Ice Queen Saba for an hour, might be what keeps her going. Of course, it'd be better if she could live her dreams in real life, but many people never get the chance. Less than twenty-five per cent of all people think they have a dream job and, probably, even fewer think they are living a perfect life. So the chance to look like—say, a sexy fox—or have any exciting job, even if it's as an assassin, or to live in a penthouse on a deserted island is their escape. These are people with debts, family commitments, disabilities or people who can't do what they want in their ordinary lives. Or just people who are bored with life. While waiting for our dreams to come true, we want to escape life by disappearing for a while.'

Alex had the feeling that there was a time in Shadow's life when her fantasies were the only thing that kept her alive. Shadow broke her thoughts.

'This is perfect for me. I have a job where I meet a lot of new people, where they appreciate what I do. The money is great and I can work from home.'

'Isn't it lonely?'

'I meet hundreds of personalities without having to meet a single person. That suits me fine.'

While Alex watched Shadow running around in another world, she came to the conclusion that Shadow probably liked role-playing because she had spent her childhood living in two worlds at the same time. Perhaps experienced role-players would find it easier than others to accept the Yangyang as they comfortably jumped between different realities. Alex decided to sit quietly and study Shadow as she played. In some way, it felt safe to sit in the dark together with someone who knew how she felt, but who didn't bug her because she was too busy getting through her own trauma. They sat there together, more next to each other than together. Two people sharing the same secret but dealing with it on their own.

The Watcher sat on the floor next to the bed with the black sheets and looked at the two women. He guessed that Shadow felt his presence, but the other woman was probably unaware that he was there. Strange how people could think they were 'safe' from The Unvisible just because they were in someone else's home. He studied his subjects. There was something special about people who knew they were one of the Knowers. The burden of carrying such a big secret showed. You often saw it in their eyes, the windows to what lay hidden beyond. Shadow's eyes were dark and sorrowful. The Watcher guessed that this was not because she found the knowledge too heavy to bear—she had carried it for too long to feel its weight any more. The sorrow, instead, came from everything she had to endure to continue believing in the truth that everyone told her was a lie. A fight that had given her many scars.

The eyes of the other woman were not dark with sorrow, but with exhaustion. This was natural. Just as a computer needs a lot of power to create a 3D picture, so too is all the strength of a recent Knower ploughed into generating a new picture of the world. The Watcher was always impressed by how a person seemed able to repel all signals that her worldview was not true and then, at one point, accept a direct opposite world view as true. People could be both flexible and stubborn at the same time.

The Watcher looked at Alex again and wondered what emotions were running through her head. He knew that now that she had had a part of her worldview turned upside down, she would start to question many other 'truths'. Was she alive or was this all a dream? Did she have free will or was an invisible hand controlling her? When a storm hits only the things that are securely anchored remain stable. Everything else would tumble around. The woman on the bed probably had a few more tough days ahead of her before she once again would be able to trust the world.

The watcher was reminded of a text by Haruki Murakami: 'And once the storm is over, you won't remember how you made it through, how you managed to survive. You won't even be sure, whether the storm is really over. But one thing is certain. When you come out of the storm, you won't be the same person who walked in. That's what this storm's all about.'

Chapter 45

'If we don't know life, how can we know death?'
– Confucius

'Why did you kill my mummy?'

The little girl had tears in her eyes and sobbed quietly, in that proud way only very strong, or very sad, people cry. Sitting on the bed she looked at the Watcher opposite her. The Watcher knew that this was something he just had to do.

He listened while the girl asked the same question in different ways.

'My mother wasn't stupid. Why couldn't you just scare her? Now my daddy is all alone with me. My mummy doesn't really have to die, does she?'

The girl fell silent. 'My mummy didn't really have to die . . .' she corrected herself.

And then she was quiet.

It was time for the Watcher to explain.

'We have to respect all life, but most of all our own. Sometimes it's right to kill. Knowing that doesn't make the sorrow smaller, but it makes the killing easier to understand.'

'But the Bible says you shouldn't kill?'

Her mother had put Saga in Sunday School in an attempt to stop her from talking about her imaginary friends. At first, she had refused to go, but when the priest started talking about the holy spirit and white angels that flew up to heaven, she had made her own interpretation of what the Bible was all about.

Saga had quickly stopped talking about her theories when she saw her mother's reaction and had, instead, discussed them with her Watchers.

'It's not only wrong to never kill—it's not natural. But that doesn't mean you should kill someone just because you can. The Bible says, "You shall not kill", but the Bible is wrong. The rule is, "Respect all life, and most of all your own." People have a rule about not killing, but they kill all the time. You kill in wars, you kill animals you find ugly or annoying. You kill for no reason or for the wrong reasons. We have a rule that says we can kill—but that we must respect all life and, therefore, we only kill when our own lives are in danger. Because we have to respect our own lives more than anyone else's.'

'I don't understand.'

'Two dogs locked in a cage with no food will eventually try to kill each other to get food and to survive. It's only natural. It's okay to kill another animal if it means you'll get food and survive. In the same way, it's okay to defend yourself if another animal tries to kill and eat you. That's the way nature works. One animal tries to kill the other one to survive, while the other one tries to defend its own life above all else. All living creatures fight for their own lives.'

'But my mummy didn't try to eat you.'

'But she was going to tell others about us. If she had done that it wouldn't only be our lives in danger, but even the lives of all The Unvisible. Our whole race. Given the choice between all of us dying or killing one person, we were forced to kill one person. We are sorry it had to be your mother.'

The Watcher knew the girl would not immediately understand what he was telling her. She needed time to grieve and reflect. Instead of trying to explain everything in detail, he sat down next to the girl and got out a piece of paper and some crayons.

'Try not to ask too many questions right now. Think about your mother instead. Remember what a good mum she was. Why don't you draw something you did together so that you and your father can take it with you to church later?'

He knew the girl liked drawing. And it worked. The girl bent over the paper and started to draw, determined to make a nice drawing for her mother.

Some people who knew about The Unvisible were more dangerous than others. When a baby saw them it was more or less harmless as the baby had no way of telling anyone else. A small child was relatively safe as most adults would not believe her. A confident adult who could not keep quiet was, on the other hand, a potent risk. Most dangerous of all was a confident and religious adult. History was full of new Knowers who incorrectly made a connection between The Unvisible and angels. Religious fanatics were unreliable, confident and, well, fanatical. That combination was a powder keg that could explode when they got a glimpse into the world of The Unvisible. The Primary Queen still did not understand why born-again Christians had to go out and tell as many people as possible what they had seen. What she did know was that sending in a Wise One to whisper a message about keeping the secret a secret did not work on these people. It only ended up with the religious person telling anyone who would listen that 'angels had given her a message'.

The Yangyang had had to increase surveillance in places like churches, prayer meetings and other religious centres. When someone started to preach about invisible messages or unexplained signs from God, then they had to terminate the threat as quickly as possible. Revelations about invisible messengers spread like wild-fires within religious communities. That was potentially very dangerous.

And that was the risk here. Under no circumstances could Mary be allowed to tell a priest about her experience or be allowed to use the film as proof of guardian angels.

Instead of getting a chance to listen to Mary's message from God, the pastor would have to take care of her funeral.

Chapter 46

'If you can see, look. If you can look, observe.'
– José Saramago

Alex sat in the library, with Japanese pop blaring in her headphones. Listening to music performed in a foreign language made it easier to read what she had written without getting it mixed up with the lyrics.

The first draft of her essay was done and she was reading through it to check the flow. It was not a masterpiece, but she was proud of herself for having been able to focus enough on it to get it done, despite all the craziness over the last few months. Working on the essay had created a sense of routine in all the chaos. So had the Tuesday meetings with Carte Blanche. She was looking forward to the one tonight, and she hurried to get done before she would have to rush over.

Alex had printed out her notes and was now marking parts with a highlighter when the computer peeped. It was a message from Adam inviting her to chat.

Adam had written, 'What's the meaning of life?'

Alex just looked at the question. She was taken aback by its profoundness. After more than ten seconds, she wrote a simple 'What?' to win some time to think about how to actually reply.

'What's the meaning of life? And please don't make a joke of my question.'

Alex moved the computer so that she could write more easily. 'Hm—and there was I thinking I could answer with "to be the star of a reality show".' Alex used a smiley in case he did not understand she was being ironic, but regretted it the same second she pressed Send. Would he think it was immature to use smileys?

'Humour is often a defence mechanism.'

'Do you always have to be so wise?'

An animation of a pen showed that Adam was writing an answer. She started to write something several times, but always deleted the text again, unhappy with the result.

Finally, his answer appeared. 'Why are people so busy being stressed that they forget to live—even forget to reproduce? The birth rate in many developed countries is now lower than two children per family. And in many countries, like Japan, the population is shrinking. The richer a person is, the fewer children she tends to have; and the richer she becomes, the harder she works and the more stressed she gets.'

Alex noticed that Adam talked about people as 'she' and not 'we'. Was he distancing himself from other people in order to imply that he was better than them? It did not sound like something Adam would do. She had to confess that his questions provoked her, not because of how they were asked, but because of what answers they triggered.

Her thoughts wandered to a survey that showed people became five per cent less satisfied with their lives for every hour of TV they watched every day. And despite thinking that they spent too much time in front of the TV, people still sat there watching it.

Alex's thoughts often wandered from one subject to another, but she was used to keeping her thoughts to herself. Other people did not usually appreciate her rapid thoughts and associations. But Adam was different. She wanted to think faster, make even more connections and—this is what surprised her the most—share her thoughts with him. She loved hearing his point of view. It was as if their thoughts danced around each other. She loved it.

The most recent topics that Adam and Alex had worked their way through were questions about justice, honesty and values. Each time, she had learnt something new about the topic they were discussing, but also something new about herself.

Why was it so important to her that he listened to her thoughts? What was it that made her feel she had so much to learn from him without feeling like a student?

Once Adam had told her that he found her brain beautiful. That was the greatest compliment she had ever received. But if her brain was beautiful, then what would be the word to describe his? What did you call something that was more beautiful than beautiful? The more she met Adam, the more fascinated she became with his way of being; his way of looking at life. It was sexy. She had always thought that the brain was the sexiest muscle of a man. Alex had once had this idea that someone should open a 'Brain Gym' where men could do intellectual work-outs since mentally ripped men were much more attractive than physically ripped dittos.

Alex was shaken out of her daydreams by a series of question marks on her screen.

'?'

'?'

'?'

'?'

Adam had sent the question marks to see if she was still there.

'How ironic. Here I am thinking about how interesting he is to talk to and then I get lost in a daydream and forget about him,' she thought to herself.

A message popped up: 'Adam is no longer online.' She had waited too long to answer, forcing him to conclude that she was no longer there. She hit the screen as if it was the computer's fault.

Would he be annoyed at her for ignoring him?

The Watcher observing the woman left. When he came out of the library, a small group of younger Watchers were waiting for him. The group leader signed to the students to get up. When the Watcher approached, they stood in a row and bowed slowly. He bowed in return and motioned to them to sit back down and commenced to tell them about the purpose of the afternoon's exercises.

'Truth is fact, but fact is not truth,' he signed to his students. 'Today we are going to focus on deleting history. History is merely a series of stories, and those who decide which stories should be told are the ones who decide which history will be remembered.'

'Are we going to make books disappear?' one of the students asked.

'Not today. The need to get rid of books containing uncomfortable truths about invisible creatures is not as pressing as it used to be. Mainly because we have done most of that work already. And also because humans go to libraries less and less to look at old books. No, tonight our focus is the Internet. When the library shuts for the night, we'll stay inside and use their computers. We must rewrite and create alternative versions of history. We can't get rid of everything written about us on the Net, but we can drown the true descriptions with histories that make the truth look like fiction and the fiction look like truth. In the worst-case scenario, we'll have to write comments discrediting the most dangerous writers. A scathing remark in the comments of an article can make a serious blog post lose credibility. Think about what you learnt in your rhetoric classes.'

One of the students raised her hands and signed, ‘People want to be the rulers of their own history. Let people think they rule.’

‘Correct. Hide the truth by getting them to believe in their own stories. If people are faced with two versions of something that happened and one of the versions makes them appear strong, then people will assume this version is true. So always write alternative stories where Yinyin appear to be strong.’

The Yinyin had selected this location because the library’s computer halls lacked surveillance cameras which made their work so much easier. The small group sneaked into the library again and sat down to wait for everyone to leave so they could work undetected. It was going to be a long night.

Chapter 47

'Through the lives of all people there is (. . .) a thread, an invisible thread that shows we belong to God.'
– Hans Christian Andersen

Adam put his iPad back into Flight mode. He had just checked to see if Alex had sent him a message explaining why she had disappeared from their chat earlier. Maybe she was angry with him, or perhaps there was something wrong with her Internet connection. For some reason, she had not replied to his last message.

Adam had turned on Flight mode to save the battery. He needed the power to keep his screen on full brightness to be able to read the text. Adam used a white cane and dark glasses, but that did not mean he was blind. He was visually impaired.

Adam looked around the bus. All the seats in the bus were occupied except one—the seat next to him. Some passengers actually preferred standing in the bus to sitting next to him, and Adam knew why. It was because he was different. After a lifetime of albinism, he was accustomed to the feeling of being the odd one out. He knew people thought he was weird and abnormal—and therefore dangerous—because of the way he looked.

As an albino, Adam had always thought that the opponents of racism should be more interested in people like him as it would burst some of the prejudices and preconceived notions about exclusion and skin colour. Albinos were living proof that being white was not always a good thing. Adam was all too aware that really white skin was something people all over the world looked down on. In some countries it was particularly dangerous to be an albino. Only last year, the BBC had reported that twenty-five albinos had been murdered in Tanzania in one year. These murders were ordered by witch doctors, who used the hands and feet of albinos to make a brew that they claimed would give wealth and happiness to anyone who drank it. It sounded like something from the Dark Ages, but sadly it was the reality of today.

The white suit that Adam often wore made him stand out even more, but of course wearing the suit was a conscious choice. It somehow made him feel less odd when he was perceived as being different because he dressed eccentrically, and not because of some feature he was born with. If he was to be seen as being peculiar, he might as well dress the part.

What was it that made certain people—even entire groups—see themselves as different? There were more women in the world than men, but many women still defined themselves as if they were in the minority. A feminist would probably explain this by saying it was the fault of the patriarchy, but what made women throughout history insist on letting themselves be controlled by a minority? It was not a law of nature that men were the norm or that they should control women. There was an ethnic minority in China where the women were in charge and the children did not even know who their fathers were.

Sometimes Adam thought that if the entire human race were made aware of The Unvisible, then humans would come together as one. Perhaps this was what was needed to make people start seeing themselves as just people—and not merely as members of different sub-groups such as: Englishmen, Caucasians, Christians or Manchester United fans.

The potential of a collective humanity that defined itself as a group with the same values and goals was endless. Once upon a time, he had imagined a global movement, a kind of United Humans. A UH instead of a UN that was composed, not of united nations, but of united people who worked together for the best of everyone. If that did exist then how long would millions of people be allowed to starve and a billion people be allowed to live without clean drinking water? As attractive as the thought of a united human race was, Adam knew it was a dangerous idea. If humans started to identify themselves as one group, then it meant they would need another group to alienate themselves from. Manchester United fans needed a Liverpool as their rival. To strengthen their feeling of belonging to a group, Homo sapiens seemed to need an enemy to distance themselves from, and history was full of atrocities that people had done against other humans just because they were 'the others'. If the Yangyang were the reason humanity got together, then they would also be the threat that people would be forced to destroy. Adam knew what the result would be. A war of the races between Homo sapiens and Homo invisibilia. A real world war, a war of world against world. And the consequences would be devastating. It could mean the end of human civilization.

Adam's understanding of how humanity would behave towards an invisible and global group of different, strange—and therefore dangerous—human-like peers made him realize how important it was that the balance between the Yangyang and Yinyin was not disturbed. He knew he played an important part in this mission. It was thoughts like these that made it easier for Adam to accept that no one on the bus wanted to sit next him. If they knew what he knew they would look at him differently.

He activated his iPad again to see if Alex had sent him a message.

On the roof of the bus lay two Watchers who held tightly onto the handles of the roof hatch. Guard duty was divided so that the Watchers did not have to follow their Subjects all the time. For example, if a Subject commuted to work by bus or train, new Watchers took over when the Subjects got off at their respective stops. Whenever a Subject got off at a stop, one of the men on the roof signed to let the Watchers on the street know who should follow whom. A basketball player would probably call this strategy a zone defence rather than a person-to-person defence tactic. It was a flexible system and it worked well.

Chapter 48

> **'Love is not blind—it sees more, not less. But because it sees more, it is willing to see less.'**
> – Rabbi Julius Gordon

Alex and Shadow sat in Alex's living room drinking tea. Shadow had sat down on the sofa without even bothering to move the sweatpants that lay there out of the way. Having visitors in such a messy apartment would normally stress Alex out, but with Shadow it was different. She made Alex feel at ease; which was funny because when they first met Shadow had scared her. The harder it was to get close to someone, the more interesting those people tended to become as you got to know them. It was like a lot of things in life: a game that is too easy to learn gets boring after a while; you get bored with a challenge that was not really challenging. And a person that does not demand some effort to get to know often turns out to be a pretty meaningless acquaintance. Alex was glad she had given Shadow a chance.

'Can I ask you something?' Alex said as she looked Shadow in the eyes. 'Is there a connection between people who have mental health issues and the Yangyang?'

Shadow explained that there were some theories about how some people with certain mental conditions had a closer connection to The Unvisible. Many of the mentally ill had similar stories of hearing voices that asked them to do things. Some people thought that these patients had the ability to communicate more easily with The Unvisible thanks to their illness.

Others claimed that it was not the mentally ill who could hear the Yangyang but the opposite—that normal people became mentally ill because they could hear them.

Supporters of this theory said the Yangyang whispered words to people they wanted to get rid of. They did that because they knew that the friends of people who said they heard voices would soon stop listening to them. The people who said they heard voices might even end up in a psychiatric hospital 'for their own good'.

Shadow and Alex sat quietly for a while, enjoying their shared silence. Funny how you can feel uncomfortable sitting in silence with some people, while with others you feel so safe and at ease.

After a while, Shadow broke the silence. 'Did you hear the hypothesis that certain people can not only hear the Yangyang but see them as well?'

'Yes, that's what my essay is about . . . .' Alex was confused. 'Surely Shadow knew what she was writing about? Had she forgotten?'

'I don't mean kids. I mean adults.'

'Like you?'

'No. I could see them until I was a teenager, but I was still a child. And I don't mean seeing them with a yangsee.

There is a group of people that can see the Yangyang as well as they can see you and me.'

'What kind of people?'

'Albinos.'

Alex's soul was hit with a sledge hammer and all she could say was, 'Who?'

'Albinos. Albinos are a cross between an Unvisible and a human, between a male Yangyang and a female Yinyin.'

Alex's heart was racing. A thousand thoughts whirred around in her head and she found it difficult to say anything sensible. To get Shadow to tell her more, she repeated what Shadow had just said. 'A cross?'

'Yes—kind of like a mule is a cross between a horse and a donkey or a tigon is a combination of a tiger and a lion. It's like crossing different dog breeds to create new ones. Take a Labradoodle—it's a cross between a Labrador and a Poodle. Considering the differences between a Yinyin and Yangyang are very small, smaller than those between different breeds of dogs, it's highly probable that it's possible for these two races to mate successfully.'

'I thought sex between the races was forbidden according to some kind of ethical code,' Alex said. She tried to keep up with Shadow's reasoning, but all she could really think of was Adam.

'Rules around who can and cannot fall in love never work. Psychologists can fall in love with their patients despite ethical codes saying they're not allowed to, and people who are kidnapped often form relationships with their kidnappers. Watchers watch people all day long so it's only natural they should fall in love with their Subjects once in a while.'

'But how does it work physically?' Alex had tried to imagine having sex with an invisible man.

'You don't have to see each other to have good sex, right? It's not unusual for couples to make love in the dark.'

She had a point. If the lights were turned off then it did not matter if one half was invisible in daylight. 'But if the woman can't see the man, then how can she fall in love with him? Please tell me it's consensual.'

For a second Alex got a picture of an invisible Yangyang sexually assaulting a defenceless, unknowing woman. She pushed that image away as quickly as it had come to her.

'Yes, I would think so,' Shadow replied. 'I guess the Yangyang start off by talking quietly to the woman as she's sleeping and then they talk to her just before she falls asleep. If hearing voices doesn't drive her crazy, then she's become one of the people in the know. The step from knowing about The Unvisible to falling in love with one of them is not that big. Yangyang men are very handsome . . . .'

Shadow's got something dreamy in her eye. Alex remembered her walk wearing the yangsee. Shadow was right. They were attractive.

'If blind people can fall in love, or if two people who know each other through a dating site but haven't met can fall in love, then you must be able to love someone who is physically in the same room as you even if you can't see them. The World of Warcraft community is full of stories of people who are now married and have kids, but who fell in love without ever having met each other in real life. They fell in love through their avatars! I personally know a couple that fell in love when they worked together to slay a dragon. They had even decided on their children's names before meeting for the very first time,' Shadow continued. 'The problem is that these women aren't acknowledged as being in the know. If a Watcher and a woman get together, then it's in both of their interests not to tell anyone.'

Alex continued the line of reasoning. 'But if the result of these secret meetings is a child then there's a situation?'

'Right! And according to the theory, albinos are a big problem for the Yangyang, which is why they've spent a lot of energy creating myths about albinos that give them the low status that they have today. They don't want people to take Albinos seriously.'

'And albinos are a big problem because . . . ?'

'Because they're visible proof of the existence of Yangyang. They're also a problem because apparently they can see the Yangyang. Their eyes are often pinkish and their sight impaired compared to ours, but on the other hand, they can perceive the entire light spectrum. They inherit their pale skin from their fathers and are visible thanks to their mothers. Their eyes are a combination of both their parents, which means they can see our world and the world of The Unvisible.'

'So Adam is one of them?' Alex had to share.

'You're friends with an albino?'

'Well, I don't know about friends. He contacted me to talk about my essay. He'd read what I wrote about kids and their imaginary friends.'

The banging of a window interrupted their conversation. Alex had propped the window open to air the room before Shadow arrived and, for some reason, the window was now flapping against the outside wall. She shut the window and wondered how she could arrange a meeting with Adam. She had not heard anything from him for over a day, since they lost contact on that chat. She had to see him again. He had some questions to answer. What were his true intentions for getting in touch with her? Had he been using her? And the question that annoyed her the most: 'Had she misread his signals?'

There would always be security problems when a human knew a little too much about the Yangyang. That was the price that had to be paid to safeguard a certain amount of communication between the two races. But it could not be allowed to go too far. The Watcher sitting on Alex's bed had decided to sneak out and report back to the Queen. This message was urgent enough for him to take a small risk and undo the window latch. When the wind blew the window open, he jumped out.

Chapter 49

'Hope sees the invisible, feels the intangible, and achieves the impossible.'
– Helen Keller

After her conversation with Shadow, Alex considered different strategies for what she would say to Adam when she called. Should she be angry because he had not told her he could see the Yangyang? But could she really be annoyed at that when she herself had kept quiet about The Unvisible? Should she pretend that nothing had changed? But if it was true that Adam could see the Yangyang and that he was a kind of ambassador, how could they continue as before? Should she feel hurt that he only contacted her in a work capacity? But Adam had not made any inappropriate advances, hadn't flirted or been intrusive. So how could she accuse him of using her when he had behaved impeccably every time they met? Should she ask him to come over and tell her everything he knew? But was he really allowed to tell her and—if not—then was it right for her to pressure him to reveal his secrets?

The mysteries that were now surrounding him just made him even more attractive. And honestly, you could never know everything about a man when you were just getting to know him, so could she really blame him for not telling her his biggest secret?

Would her mother accept an albino as a son-in-law and what would Daniel say? He would probably just laugh. One thing was for sure, her father would be turning in his grave. Alex cursed her ability to paint such negative pictures in her head. She started to reason with herself. OK, first of all: why do you care about who your mum thinks you should marry? Second of all: you haven't even had a real date with the guy yet so perhaps you should stop planning the wedding?

She could not think clearly at the moment. The recent events had affected her ability to think straight. She sighed heavily and tried to clear her mind. But the stream of opposing messages clamouring to be heard gave her a headache. She lay down on her bed and looked at the ceiling.

'Alex,' she said out loud to herself, 'Don't think. Just feel. Yes or no?'

'Yes,' she heard her heart whisper. This time she would not let the voices of others control her. She felt that her knowledge of The Unvisible had made her stronger. More decisive.

She would ask Adam out on a date. What was the worst that could happen? That he would say no? She got out her phone and started to write a message. After a few attempts, she was pleased with what she had written. 'What are you doing on Saturday? How about a movie? I'll wear earplugs and then we can compare a film that I haven't heard and you haven't seen. What do you say?'

She hoped that her black humour would work on him. Those few seconds of waiting seemed endless. When her phone finally beeped, her heart started to race.

She read his message several times:

'I do not think that is a good idea.'

Alex flung her phone into a pillow and started to cry. Her tears dissolved the barriers that had kept her afloat during her recent turmoil. Now that all the barriers had disappeared, she collapsed. First she tried to control herself, but why should someone who was so alone look for reasons to hold back? Alex started to cry out loud. She cried for all the times she had not cried; for all the times she had held back the tears. When the first wave of crying was over, she curled herself up into a little ball. She took one deep breath and then let the rest of the tears out. Looking down at her phone she felt the next attack coming. When all her tears finally dried up, she cried tearlessly.

A person who lives alone tends to have quirky ticks and habits—like clearing the throat too often or coughing without covering the mouth. The problem was not that these people did more irritating things than others—the problem was that they did not have anyone to tell them that they should stop. Humanity had that same problem on a different scale. As a species, mankind had behaviours that they ought to let go of, but no one told them to stop. Sometimes, the Watcher thought it would be better if the Yangyang just let the humans know they existed. Then they could explain, once and for all, everything the Yinyin did not understand. But as great of an idea that was in theory, he knew it would not work in reality. The Watcher would have to focus on helping this individual woman instead. When she fell asleep, he would caress her. Nothing inappropriate, of course. Nothing that would get him into trouble with the Queen. Just enough to give her a much-needed release from her emotional frustrations.

Chapter 50

> **'What's invisible to us is also crucial for our own well-being.'**
> – Jeanette Winterson

It had been almost a week since their last communication when, out-of-the-blue, he called her. It took her a few rings to build up the courage to pick-up.

She let him talk first. 'Alex? It's Adam. Before you say anything, listen to me.'

Alex had no idea what to say right now, so she gratefully remained quiet.

'We have to meet. I know you know, and I'm going to answer your questions, but something has happened and I want you to come early to the meeting tonight.'

'Adam, there are so many things I don't understand. So many unspoken secrets.'

'I know. Sorry.' Adam's voice was weaker than normal. 'But your questions will be answered. I promise. Shall I come and pick you up?'

'No. I'll meet you there,' Alex said. She wanted explanations, not favours.

'Something has happened.' What did he mean by that?

A few hours later and Alex waited outside the locked door of the meeting hall. She had arrived early and spent the time reading the message boards in the corridor. She heard Adam's white cane in the stairwell and went over to greet him.

'Alex, you're here,' confirmed Adam.

'Wait, how could you know it was me?'

'I guess I have fine-tuned my fully functional senses.' He smiled. 'So, for example, I can recognize a person by their walking sound. Everyone's walk sounds different. Just as you knew it was me on the stairs because you heard my cane, so too can I tell who's approaching. But as I'm visually impaired, I'm much better at it. You walk fast, but a bit sloppy. As if you're always going somewhere and are a little late. Can we sit down?'

'There are some benches over here.'

Outside each door along the corridor, there was a bench screwed to the wall. Some of the benches looked new while the bench nearest them must have been there for decades. The wooden seats had dents in them as a sea of students had sat there during their breaks over the years. Adam took out a small, white shell and held it in his hand.

'Alex, I got this shell from my mother when I turned ten. "Whisper in it when you feel you have to tell your secret to someone," my mother told me. She meant well but she didn't understand how this shell came to symbolize the kind of loneliness that comes from knowing a secret no one else knows; the sadness that comes from not being able to talk about it with anyone.

'Every kid dreams of being extraordinary and they roll their eyes when their parents tell them that every child is special. The kids know that Harry Potter is more special than them. But I know I truly am special—special in the way that kids dream about. The most common superpower kids wish they had is to be invisible. And even though I'm not invisible, I was born with the ability to see invisible things. I know it's a gift—but it is a cursed gift. I just don't understand how they can put such responsibility on a kid by telling him about the greatest secret of humankind and then tell the child to keep it quiet. If you only knew how many times I wished I was like everyone else. To live in your world. Without all these expectations and demands.'

Adam went on to tell Alex how he was told, at age ten, that he was an ambassador between The Unvisible and the visible. That the man he called Daddy was not his father—but that he must never tell his 'father' that. That his biological father was a Yangyang, but that Adam would never know who that man was, nor never get to meet him, which meant never getting a chance to learn things about himself that might be inherited. He did not even know what his biological father's name was, and only used the generic name for all fathers of humans like himself: 'Distiya'. For Adam, his father was a Kalu Kumara Distiya: a dark, royal spirit. And yet, for the rest of his life, he was expected to help maintain the balance, to help Yangyang live close to Yinyin, but not close enough to be discovered.

Adam explained that it was a double punishment—first the curse of being born an albino, and then another curse, that of having to live with dual identities that he was not even allowed to reveal to anyone. He finished his monologue and turned to face Alex.

'Being a Mediator, as we albinos are called, has pros and cons. The pros are difficult to explain to an outsider—the best way to describe it is that my life is richer for being the son of a Yangyang. But the cons are easy to verbalize: I have to lie to the people I care about.'

He now looked deep into Alex's eyes.

'I am so sorry if you feel lied to. Or if you feel I have not told you the entire truth. But I hope you understand it was out of my control. And I hope you're not too angry that I had to distance myself a bit. My role is difficult enough as it is. Getting too close to a person I'm supposed to help will just complicate things too much.'

Alex did not say anything. In some situations, it was best to just be silent. She just wanted to hug him. She had probably been extra vulnerable lately and maybe that was why she had misinterpreted his friendliness for something else.

Alex saw Mr Williams enter through the main door at the end of the hallway.

Just before Mr Williams came up to them, Adam took Alex's hand and whispered, 'I hope you understand . . .' Her private moment with Adam was over.

After Mr Williams walked up to them and sat down on the same bench. Adam searched through a small, white bag and finally found what he was looking for. He took out two large shells. Their white surface was tinged with different shades of white that sometimes looked almost pinkish. The shells looked both fragile and strong at the same time. Alex could not help touching them with her fingers. When she did, her hand accidentally touched Adam's and a warm feeling came over her.

Adam placed one of the shells in Alex's hands and then gently closed her hands until they hid the item completely.

Then Adam put the other shell into Mr William's hand and covered it with the old man's hands. Finally, he sat up straight and put his palms together in front of his chest. Alex thought he looked like a Buddhist monk.

'You have been invited,' he said.

'Oh my God!' Mr Williams' voice was shaking.

'Invited where?' Alex wondered.

'To the Queen. Our Primary Queen.'

'This is what I've been waiting for my entire adult life. What I've . . .'

'The circumstances are not the best,' Adam said. 'You're being summoned to the Primary Queen to get a warning for letting Alex take Daniel to Carte Blanche without first doing an evaluation of his suitability.'

'So, you've known about this all this time?' asked Mr Williams quite surprised.

'We know much more than you think. Surely you've realized this by now?'

'But why should Mr Williams be punished for something that's my fault?' Alex thought it was unfair.

'Well, first of all, he's not going to be punished. He is going to receive a warning. And secondly, a leader has to take responsibility for his group. A chairman can't say he didn't know. With positions of responsibility comes responsibility. Missions of trust demand trust'

'He's right.' Mr Williams put his hand on Alex's leg, his hand silently asking her to stop pleading on his behalf. 'The responsibility is mine and I'm prepared to take the consequences of my actions, or lack of them.'

'Will I also get a warning?'

'Yes. Because you told Daniel. You have to understand the seriousness of your actions. The Queen can sentence adults to death for talking about The Unvisible. But as long as the person you've told doesn't tell anyone else the sentence is usually suspended. Instead a warning is issued.'

'I see,' Mr Williams said, looking anxious.

'Don't worry. The Queen bears you no ill feelings. She knows you mean well. That's why she's invited you so that she can personally deliver the warnings.'

'We're going to meet her in her dwelling!' Mr Williams exclaimed with shining eyes.

'Where does she live?' Alex wondered.

'She lives in a beautiful place,' Adam replied. 'If you had any plans for Saturday I suggest you change them. I'll come and pick you up in a taxi at 7 a.m. The others are arriving now—don't say a word to them.'

In the Vimana the preparations for welcoming the guests were already under way. The Yangyang were always looking for a reason to celebrate and having visitors was as good a reason as any. The Yangyang celebrated a lot of things: every full moon, for example. Or when it rained. When a woman got pregnant or when a child was born. When an animal was killed or when one of their own had died. They did not celebrate death, but honoured the life lived up until the time it ended. For without life, nothing can die. Death was the ultimate tribute to life, so why grieve when you can celebrate the life that the deceased had lived?

When the visitors came the Yangyang would dance. As a tribute to the guests. In praise of life. But also to get the visitors to reflect, get them to feel their hearts. And, who knew, perhaps the Yangyang would also soon celebrate the fact that a Killer had once again completed a successful mission.

Chapter 51

'We know accurately only when we know little, with knowledge doubt increases.'
–J. W. Goethe

'Hello?'

Daniel no longer answered the phone with his name. He saw it was Ola, but tried his best not to draw attention to himself by saying his name in case a Watcher was listening.

'Did you steal my yangsee at that meeting you came to?!' Ola said.

Daniel had indeed taken Ola's yangsee at the last Carte Blanche meeting he had attended. He had snatched it while Ola was in the bathroom and then quickly sneaked out before Ola came back. Daniel had decided to take the yangsee so he could bring it to the army the second time he went there. He guessed a lot of the messages on his voice mail were angry messages from Ola, but he had no plans to listen to them.

'I didn't steal it. I just borrowed it for a while. And I am afraid you can't get it back right now. Something came up and I am going away for a while so I will have to borrow the yangsee for a bit longer.'

'You're an asshole!'

'Don't worry, you'll get it back. I'll explain later. I've got to go.'

Daniel hung up. He did not have the time or energy to talk to Ola right now and Ola would eventually get his yangsee back. But only if he first promised to create a new one for Daniel.

Manda sat under a birch tree a couple of hundred metres away from the Vimana, the closest thing to a home she had. She did not live in the Vimana; she did not live anywhere. She called it her Vimana because it had been her mother's home and the place where she was born. But it would never be a place to call her own. As a Killer, she was expected to carry out the Queen's orders, but that did not mean she could expect her protection. She had to stay close, but not too close. Be available but not belong. As a Yangyin, she was not a part of the human world nor welcome in the world of The Unvisible. Except when the Queen wanted her services. Manda had learnt to live with it—just another load on her burdened shoulders. She did not need their group. She had her own. A group of one.

However, it still hurt. The wisest of the wise could do something stupid occasionally. The most beautiful of the beautiful had a bad hair day now and then. The kindest of the kind could have evil thoughts. And the Yangyin in her chaotic, frustrated, broken and twisted world could, if only for a short time, have a moment of harmony so why could they not invite her in on those days? It was as if the Yangyang did not want to see her moments of calm. As if they, and the Queen, would rather see that this powder keg that a human father and an Unvisible mother had created could not have any mitigating parts. As if an ounce of compassion towards a Yangyin would tempt the Yangyang to have more contact with the Yinyin. As if she was the cautionary tale. How the Mediators—the Yinyang—with their human mothers and Unvisible fathers, could move freely in both worlds without being rejected by the Queens was an insult to all Killers. It was pathetic how the Yinyang complained about being rejected by the humans when that was nothing compared to the rejection the Yangyin had to endure.

But Manda would not spend more time feeling sorry for herself. Sitting under her birch tree, near her flock, but not a part of it, she felt as peaceful as a Killer could.

Her pants were rolled up above her knees exposing her bare kneecaps that were positioned onto the rugged gravel on the ground. The longer she kneeled, the more the pieces of gravel cut into her skin. The small dents became deeper until they finally pierced through the skin and she started to bleed. The pain helped her forget her torment, cleared her head.

This was her tribute to her mother: the woman who had broken the holiest of rules. 'Respect all life, but above all, respect your own.' By becoming impregnated by a human man, her mother had known that giving life to a child would bring death to herself. And yet still had done it.

For this act of selflessness, or was it self-carelessness, Manda both hated and admired her mother, this woman she knew nothing about. No one who knew her mother or the identity of her father would tell her anything. Those were the rules. From the Yangyang's point of view, her mother had never existed. Though they had given her food and care until she was old enough to look after herself the Yangyang had been very careful not to let Manda get emotionally attached to her Carers. The Yangyang could not let the Yangyin babies die—they were too valuable as assassins for that—but The Unvisible did everything they could to distance themselves from the Killers. Yangyins were given food—but not love. The only hug Manda had ever received was the one she got as a newborn child when her dying mother gave her a farewell embrace. It was known as The Hug of Death.

Sitting there by herself Manda painted a picture in her head of something resembling a family—an alternative world where her mother was still alive. A world in which there was love.

A couple of Yangyang who happened to be walking by backed off when they saw her tears, trying not to interrupt her. But she had already heard them. *Run away*, she thought. *I'm here with my mother. We don't need you. We have each other.*

For a moment there was peace. But soon the anxiety reared its ugly head again, imprisoning her in its darkness.

When she stood up, some gravel was still clinging to her bloody knees. Manda did not wipe it away. As she stood there with her arms out and head bent backwards, she frantically signed the dark thoughts whirling in her head: the thoughts that made her who she most often was—not her mother's daughter, but her Queen's killer.

Mother.

I would do it for you a million times.

You do not believe me now.

Perhaps you never will.

Perhaps you never did.

But I would.

I am already a burnt-up heart.

Putting knives into you.

I never knew that I did.

I am doomed to a life of loneliness.

To a beautiful death.

I am waiting . . .

Let it come!

Her snake, which had been waiting for her to finish, slowly slithered up her leg. When it was coiled around her neck, she was ready. Manda was a Killer again.

Ready to kill to avenge her mother.

To honour her.

To forget her.

Chapter 52

'The privilege of operating a flying machine is great. The knowledge of flight is the most ancient of our inheritances. A gift from those upon high. We received it from them as a means of saving lives.'

– Haggadah, (Hebrew for 'telling'), a tenth century manuscript that sets forth the order of the Passover Seder

Adam was leading Alex and Mr Williams out of a clearing when Alex stopped and gasped. 'It's so beautiful!'

'Well, I guess it is,' Mr Williams replied unimpressed. All he could see was a field with some cows grazing and a small stream running through the landscape.

'I don't think Alex is talking about the view,' Adam said as he started to remove the yangsee from Alex's head.

They had agreed to wear the yangsee for fifteen minutes each as they only had the one. Alex's time was up. As soon as she took off the glasses, she saw the same field and cows as Mr Williams had. But Mr Williams also saw something else.

A gigantic pyramid hovered over the landscape. The tip of the pyramid faced the down and it had a door with a staircase leading from it to the ground. The pyramid was probably a hundred metres tall and its base facing the sky looked to be a hundred times a hundred metres.

Adam explained that these floating structures were called Vimanas and that they would now visit the Primary Queen's home, known as the Gaja Vimana. Each Vimana had a name and the one they were to visit was called Pushpaka. The structure looked solid even though it was floating above the ground and was only held in place by twenty or so thick cables tied to some large trees dotted along the banks of the stream.

The outside of the structure was covered in a material that made the pyramid sparkle in the sun, as if the walls not only reflected sunlight but made it brighter. A flock of birds—there must have been thousands—circled around the structure and played in the currents. There were lots of Yangyangs on the ground. Many of them were either going in or coming out of the pyramid. There were no queues or visible frustration though and it did not seem crowded. It reminded Mr Williams of an anthill where thousands of ants ran around in a controlled chaos. And just like ants, many of the Watchers stopped to sign short messages to each other before moving on.

'Tell me what you can see,' Alex begged.

'Horses! Lots of horses! They look like unicorns!'

What Mr Williams saw were large, majestic horses, each one with a dove on its head and a Watcher on its back. No saddles. They did not ride in formation; instead, it looked as if the riders let the horses decide where they wanted to go. The result was a random pattern of white horses that zigzagged through the forest. It was so beautiful that Mr Williams just stood there watching until Adam felt forced to take him by the hand to get him to start walking again.

While they were walking closer to the Vimana Adam explained, 'A couple of hundred years ago, an albino in Germany told his wife all about The Unvisible and the white horses with the doves on their heads—and she just couldn't keep quiet. After The Unvisible managed to kill most of the rumours, they let the myth about the horses live on, but said that the horses had horns. And that's how the fairytales about unicorns started. By strengthening the fake rumours, it was easier to get rid of the true stories that The Unvisible wanted to bury. More information, but less knowledge.'

'So, the stories about unicorns are myths, but the one about the invisible horses is true?' Alex asked Adam.

'Yes. There are hundreds of Unvisible animal species, a few insect and fish species, but most are tiny and somewhere between animal and bacteria. Most of the larger species have become extinct, except a few like doves, horses and, of course, people. Oh, and snakes. Once upon a time, there were even invisible elephants.'

Adam took the yangsee from Mr Williams. 'Time to hide this one before we get closer. We don't want them to become suspicious,' he explained. Sometimes he sided more with humans than with The Unvisible. Sometimes not. As a Mediator, he always had to keep a balance.

When they got to the pyramid, Adam led them up the stairs to the entrance. He smiled welcomingly at everyone they met, and most Yangyang returned the smile, often accompanied by a curious expression, sometimes accompanied with a look of caution.

'Welcome to Pushpaka—the Primary Queen's abode and the home of The Unvisible. Now you're going to find out what it's like to be blind,' he said as he took Alex by the hand. To Mr Williams he said, 'Hold Alex's hand and walk in a straight line behind me.'

Alex and Mr Williams saw Adam take a step straight into thin air. And then another.

'What?' Alex said.

'Ready to follow me?' Adam asked with a smile.

'Follow you where?'

'Into the Vimana. Without the yangsee, you can't see the pyramid or the stairs. But trust me—it's here. I can see it all and I will guide you.'

He grabbed her hand again and they began to climb. When Alex felt her toes bang into what must have been the stairs she carefully felt the outline with her foot and noticed she was standing on the first step. She then put her full weight down and felt the step hold. She repeated the process. Now she was standing a half metre above the ground without any visible support. The higher she got, the less confident she felt.

'How wide are the stairs?'

'About two metres. You're almost in the middle.'

Alex took a step to the right.

'Now you are closer to the edge,' Adam said and laughed.

Alex took a couple of quick steps in the other direction. 'This isn't funny.'

Alex shut her eyes and told herself this was like going up the stairs in the dark. That helped. She put her trust in Adam and let his warm hand gently guide her up each step. Behind her, Mr Williams had a firm grip on her arm.

For the rest of their time in the pyramid, they both kept their eyes shut.

They stood in a room with wide paths that wound their way upwards. There were no steps, just a steady slope. In the centre of the room, and from the very top of the ceiling, came a thick, white smoke that fell like a waterfall all the way to the floor. When it crashed onto the floor tiles the smoke created a fountain like effect, before flowing out through cracks in the walls. The walls were actually covered in small holes, and in front of the holes, there were different kinds of leaves and feathers, like small lampshades. The shadows created graceful patterns on the walls, floor and ceiling.

The visitors started to walk up one of the slopes. In all the rooms they passed, there were soft pillows and cushions, often against the walls. Small groups of The Unvisible sat there, signing to each other. Many of them were children. The older children seemed to be taking care of the younger ones and all the children ran around freely. Curious eyes looked out from the openings of almost every room they passed. The openings had no doors. Instead, thick cloths hung from the openings and were tied off to the side. The lack of furniture made the rooms look bigger than they were. Apart from the pillows and cushions, each room was filled with flowers and plants. The leaves were bluish-white, while all the flowers were gleaming white. All the plants were so bright that they almost shone.

'You have to tell us what you see!' Mr Williams cursed quietly that he was not allowed to have a yangsee now that he was finally going to meet the Primary Queen.

'Everything is white. There's no furniture, just cushions on the floor and lots of flowers. And kids. Lots and lots of happy kids. And a beautiful light. A natural light is coming in from the small holes in the walls and that creates cascades of shadow. And . . .'

Adam stopped.

'And?'

'They're dancing.'

'Who?'

'All of them.'

They had come to a large room where a hundred Unvisible of different ages danced a gentle and sensual dance in total silence.

'But there's no music?'

'There are no instruments, but there is music. They are dancing to the rhythm of their own hearts,' Adam explained.

He led them into the room and talked quietly so as not to disturb the dancers. 'Music exists in all human cultures. Even the most primitive tribes from the most diverse places on Earth use music. Drums and other instruments have been found in the excavations of long-gone civilizations. The feeling of wanting to move to music—to dance—isn't something we are taught. It's innate—something we're all born with. Like a sheepdog has to herd, a bird must fly and a dolphin wants to play in the water. It's not something they have to do to survive, but it is a part of what makes them what they are. A bird that isn't allowed to fly sings less. Is less of a bird. A dolphin that doesn't play is still a dolphin, but not as much of a dolphin as it could be. And a person has to dance. That's a part of what makes us what we are. We don't have to do it to survive, but it's something we do to feel alive. To be humans.'

'How can they dance without music?' Alex asked.

'They dance to their own heartbeat. The rhythm of the heart is the first sound we hear. While we're in our mothers' womb, we hear the soothing sound of her heart beating. All music is a reproduction of that sound. The closer to nature a culture is, the closer their music is to the natural heartbeat. I am sure you've heard African tribal music, which mainly consists of drums. These drumbeats are nothing more than heartbeats.

What modern cultures have done is to complicate things, and make things like electronic jazz. By doing that you've made the classic human mistake—complicating something natural in your eagerness to create something better than Nature. But the best solution is usually the least complicated one.'

'But how can they hear a heartbeat?' Alex asked.

'Oh, that's actually easy! If you were to find yourself in a completely quiet room, for example a well sound-proofed music studio, then you would also hear your heart beating. And with a little practice, you could hear this all the time. But just as urban people have lost the ability to identify edible plants, so too have you lost the ability to listen to your heart. It's sad, because there is nothing more beautiful, familiar, inspiring or full of life than the sound of a beating heart—especially your own heart. It's the sound of life.'

Adam raised Alex's hand and slowly put it inside his linen shirt and moved it towards his heart. He whispered that she should concentrate and she felt him take her second and middle fingers and press them against his chest. He helped her find the beat by carefully beating his fingers on hers. She could sense the music.

They stood like that for a while until Adam finally said, 'We have to get going. We do not want to keep the Queen waiting.'

Alex, Mr Williams and Adam entered a circular room, in the middle of which stood three women. The woman in the middle was tall. Her posture made her look even taller. It was the Primary Queen.

Flowers were stuck into an elaborate hair style of multiple braids intertwined with each other. Over a shiny, white, dress she wore a cloak that was sparkling in a million shades of white. Like a kaleidoscope.

The cloak was made of tens of thousands of scales sewn together by hand to create a stunning garment. The scales came from the snakes that had lost their lives in battle. They were gifts from the Killers.

The other two women were the Secondary Queens.

Behind them, the wall of smoke fell down and disappeared in a hole in the floor. It was almost fifty metres up to the ceiling. In the empty space, some doves soared slowly in circles. People were being led to cushions along the wall next to the Primary Queen.

'Come forth,' the Primary Queen said to Adam.

Adam approached and bowed to the three women. He kneeled and looked at the floor until the Primary Queen started to talk again. 'We have a problem.'

Adam did not say anything. He knew she would ask him to talk if she wanted to hear what he had to say.

'The problem is that, once again, we have certain people who don't understand what it means to know.'

The Primary Queen saw how her two visitors moved uncomfortably.

'You have to make them understand that they must be very careful who they speak to. The rule is to talk only to those people who are already in the know. To not widen the circle, but to make the circle stronger. We do not need more Knowers—we need better ones. The Knowers should work to keep the secret a secret. That is their duty. You have to make them understand.'

Adam nodded slightly.

The Primary Queen waited until she got eye contact with Adam and then switched from spoken word to sign language. 'An even bigger problem is the problem that this situation has created. We have someone who knows and who is determined to reveal the secret. We have to get rid of this man and we need the help of your friends. Can we trust them?'

Adam signed back. 'Yes, my Queen. We can trust them.'

The Primary Queen continued, 'Is it true that the woman is related to the man we're pursuing?'

'Yes, he is her brother,' Adam replied. 'I trust this woman. She knows what is right. She knows what is wrong. She is lonely and vulnerable; but in a crisis, she will make the right decision. I'm certain of that.'

'You better be right.'

The younger woman sitting next to the Primary Queen—she could not have been more than fifteen—signed that she had something to add. 'My reports confirm your statement. But it is important that we get her to see the world as it is. Can you talk to her?'

'I will talk to her,' Adam signed back.

These three women governed The Unvisible tribe living in the pyramid. The Yangyang had decided to have only women as leaders. Women had shown themselves to be better at making decisions that benefited the group rather than specific individuals.

To make sure there was a good balance between innovative thinking and tradition, the leadership was divided among three women. One girl—no older than fifteen who had shown herself to be wise beyond her years. One older woman—who was at least sixty but who had shown throughout her life that she was still in contact with her inner child. And one woman who had given birth. The mother was called the Primary Queen and the other two were her Secondary Queens. To enforce a decision, it had to be approved by the Primary Queen and at least one of the Secondary Queens. In reality, however, they tended to deliberate until they had absolute unity.

'The man we're chasing will die. Our mission is to find him. To liquidate him. Your mission is to make sure we get all the help we need from the two Subjects. Every second we wait increases the risk of having to kill additional people. And every time we kill someone, we create worry. Worry needs to be avoided. Do you understand?'

'I understand,' Adam replied in sign language.

The Primary Queen nodded and Adam bowed and got up. He walked backwards to where Alex and Mr Williams were sitting. When he sat down, he said, 'The Queen is going to hold a sermon. Listen carefully.'

The Primary Queen stood up and pressed her palms together in front of her chest. Everyone in the room followed her example. She spoke slowly, as if trying to listen to the words in her head before releasing them.

'There are no good or bad actions. Just actions. A soldier killing another soldier is—in itself—neither good nor evil. If that action prevents thousands of our people from dying, it can be seen by us as good. If the action is stopping our soldier from hurting our enemy we will see it as bad. And they will see it as good.

'An action can only be good depending on yourself and your perspective. You should never decide if something is good or bad based on another person's point of view. Only from your own. A lion will not stop itself from killing a zebra because it is bad for the zebra if it dies.

So when it comes to your decisions—do not listen to your Queen more than you listen to yourself. Do not listen more to your teacher, or your brother, or your sister, or your father or your mother, or your friends. Do not listen to anyone more than you listen to yourself. You have to respect all life. But most of all your own.'

When the Primary Queen spoke the part about not listening to her brother, she looked straight at Alex. She hoped she was not being too obvious. A message was best conveyed when the receiver put the last bits of the puzzle together herself.

The Primary Queen bowed to her Queens, who bowed back. Then they sat down and closed their eyes. Everyone else got up and left the room quietly.

Chapter 53

'There are children playing in the streets who could solve some of my top problems in physics, because they have modes of sensory perception that I lost long ago.'
– J. Robert Oppenheimer

Alex had not been able to stop thinking about Saga, the little girl who had given her the first drawing and warned her about dying. She wanted to meet her again. When she drew a blank trying to contact the girl's mother, she went to Saga's kindergarten to try to get an unscheduled interview. The principal was extra grumpy, perhaps because it was a Monday morning. The lady made it clear that she did not think it was a good idea, as the girl's mother had just died.

'I only want to return a drawing,' Alex said, holding up the sketch Saga had given her.

'Well, okay,' the principal said and let Alex into the TV room. 'But just five minutes.'

Alex went up to the little girl, and sat down next to her. When Alex looked into her eyes, she saw Saga was crying. Small, quiet tears.

'I heard about your mother. I'm so sorry.'

There was a TV in the room and the girl ignored Alex and kept watching the TV as she replied. 'My mummy deserved to die. She couldn't keep the secret. If you can't keep the secret, you can't keep your life.'

The girl's words 'keep the secret' flashed into Alex's mind and new pictures from the past flooded her consciousness.

People's darkest memories can remain hidden deep in the murkiest of corners for a long time. As if the memories decide to stay away so that their owner can get on with life. Then, one day, they decide to resurface. The girl's words had reminded Alex of how she, at three years old, had learned from The Unvisible why Elisabeth had to die. Alex now even remembered the Watcher's name—he had called himself Anaka—and how he had kneeled in front of her and told her that the Killers sometimes just could not help killing newborns because that was their nature.

When Alex asked Anaka if she could tell her parents why Elisabeth had died, he had looked at her kindly yet seriously and said, 'You have to keep the secret, otherwise you can't keep your life.'

Alex also remembered why she had been so sad when her father hit her at the funeral. It was not only because he did not believe her, it was also because she had broken her promise to Anaka. She had not kept the secret. When Anaka later had reassured her by explaining that The Unvisible were patient with little girls, she had thrown her arms around his neck and cried.

As Alex sat there now, looking at Saga, she remembered how grateful she had felt to be allowed to live. The last memories that came flooding back to Alex as she sat there on the floor were of how she had taken one of her dead sister's toys and buried it in the garden. Of how she had stood there with a spade in her hand and decided to bury, once and for all, the memory of the Killer's snake slithering towards her baby sister's cot. To bury that choked, whimpering sound that Elisabeth had let out. Never to tell anyone about the Killer's sad eyes that stared at her as life ran out of her sister.

Alex was startled out of her memories by Saga poking her in the side. 'Those who die should die,' the girl said.

The child's cold statement was in stark contrast to her sweet appearance. Alex did not know how to handle the child. She decided to give back the drawing. 'I just wanted to give you this. I don't think I should have it.'

Saga looked at Alex for the first time. 'I gave you the drawing, but it was you who accepted it. Giving it back won't help. You know what you know and you mustn't tell. Have you told?'

Alex nodded.

'Then you deserve to die too.'

Saga moved her attention back to the TV as a sign to Alex that she should leave.

Why had she come here? What had she hoped to get out of it? Perhaps she wanted to hear a child's perspective on being in the know so as to better understand how she had thought as a child. Perhaps she wanted someone to share the secret with. Whatever reason she had had for meeting Saga again, it had not worked. She had gone there on the spur of the moment, and it had turned out to be a mistake. Instead of leaving their meeting feeling relieved, she left the kindergarten feeling more haunted than ever.

The young children looked as if they were glued to the TV that had been rolled in on a small TV-table. To the teacher, it looked as if they were totally absorbed in the cartoon she had put on. But they were actually studying their other teacher. That is what they called him—the Watcher who came and spoke to them sometimes. It was the other teacher's mission to teach the children who still knew about The Unvisible why it was so important not to tell their parents.

The Watcher stood behind the TV and looked at the four children who sat in a semi-circle in front of him. By now, they all understood sign language so he could sign his message even if a teacher happened to come into the room.

'Your parents do not decide over you, because we decide over your parents. And that's why we decide over you.'

The children did not react. He had taught them not to nod or answer when he was teaching them during the day. They were to sit there and pretend they were watching TV.

'Every child who knows about us is a part of us. Everyone who is a part of us must follow our rules. We come before your parents. We come before your teacher. We always come first.'

It was time for the children to understand just how serious the situation was.

'Look at Saga. Her mother doesn't exist anymore. Her mother got too curious and that's why Saga no longer has a mother. Do you want to keep your mothers?'

The children knew they must not nod, so they quietly blinked their answers.

Saga sat up straight and blinked too. It was all right to cry as long as you did not say why. She let the tears stream down her cheeks. She was sad her mother was dead. Now she would do everything she could to make sure she would not also lose her father.

Chapter 54

'Where all think alike, no one thinks very much.'
– Walter Lippmann

Mr Williams sat in the taxi outside the house of his ex-wife. He had told the driver when they arrived to keep the metre running. The ticking metre acted as a kind of inverted countdown timer: the higher the sum he would have to pay, the more pressure on him to make a decision.

He knew he should not be there. Alarm clocks were ringing in his head. But just as there are certain things you have to do, there are also things you just should not do—but which you cannot help doing anyway. Mr Williams tried to convince himself not to go to the house, but for every argument he came up with for not doing so, he somehow managed to find another reason why he should do it anyway.

Was it not true that the yangsee had been handed down in his family for generations despite world wars, epidemics and revolutions? Was this chain to be broken because he could not convince his ex-wife to let him see the children?

On the other hand, the Primary Queen had expressly forbidden him from telling outsiders.

But hadn't he been good at both knowing about The Unvisible while also not letting them find out about the yangsee? Hadn't his ancestors managed this for generations? Shouldn't he be allowed to tell his ex-wife just a tiny bit of what he knew, if that could convince her to let him see his children again. He needed to see his children—he had to hand over the yangsee to the next generation. Mr Williams knew he was breaking a rule, but it would only be this once. Surely that was all right?

On the other hand, the Queen had expressly forbidden him from telling outsiders.

He did not want to be the one to break the chain. His father had chosen him to carry on Isaac Newton's inheritance. Mr Williams' children were born partly so that they would be another chain in the link. It could not end here. The legacy of previous generations weighed heavily on his shoulders.

It was not a good idea to go against the Queen's orders. He knew that, but alcohol was an effective anaesthetic for common sense. He took a few more gulps from his hip flask. The alcohol made him strong. The fog made him see more clearly. If the Primary Queen decided to warn him again, he would apologize and promise never to do anything like this again.

The taxi driver studied the man in the backseat. When Mr Williams felt his gaze, he paid and got out. He took a deep breath and went up to the door. He regretted pressing the doorbell the second he heard it ring. But what was done was done. When she opened the door, he met her irritated look with a smile.

'It's true.'

'You're drunk.'

'Yes, I am. I'm drunk. But that doesn't make it any less true.'

'What are you talking about?'

'I've seen their queen. Everything I've ever believed has turned out to be true! Even some of the stuff I did not dare believe. And you just laughed at it all.'

'We got divorced because you chose to live in another world to the one the kids and I lived in. You can do what you want with your life. But you're no longer a part of mine. In my world, there are no invisible people, no queens and there is no place for you. Leave me alone!'

'I'm going. I just want to tell my children. That it was all true. You have to let me see them.'

'Look—you really have to go.'

His response would be forever ingrained in the former Mrs Williams. Instead of leaving or becoming angry, he just stared at her with terror as he grasped his chest and fell hard to the ground.

'What's happening? Help!' she yelled.

The woman looked at her former husband in shock. He lay drunk and pitiful on the driveway to her new life and looked as if he was about to die. *You can't die here*, she thought, *It's not fair*. While the man lay dying, in what would be called a heart attack, his ex-wife just stood there and felt sorry for herself.

His eyes went from frantically trying to convince the woman, to suddenly becoming peaceful and calm as the water in a pond.

Mr Williams last words were, 'Tell our children that it was all true. Promise me that you will tell them. Tell them . . .'

The woman who looked down at him in disgust promised nothing.

Some people never learn! Manda stood behind Mr Williams and shook her head. Hadn't he been warned by the Queen only a few days ago? Hadn't she told him not to tell anyone who had not already begun to guess what the world really looked like? The Queen had made the effort to invite him for a visit and yet he still had not managed to keep quiet.

Manda looked at Mr Williams with contempt. *People are so weak*, she thought. *Always wanting to be right; always needing to win. To win all fights. All battles. So pathetic.* They deserved to die. Deserved to suffer as much as she did. But she knew that was impossible. No one could suffer as much as she did. Sometimes she wished that she could die instead of killing. That someone would take her life. But she knew that would not happen.

Manda released her snake and watched it slither to the man standing in front of the door and talking to the woman who did not want to let him in. When Manda saw the snake slide up the man's leg and wind itself around his chest, she raised her head to the skies and stretched out her hands. She waited for his cry of death, and when the little, surprised scream came, she shut her eyes and signed to her apprentice standing a few steps away:

'Total darkness.
Moon-like bitterness.
Flakes of ash.
Splinters of joy.
We are utterly unpredictable.'

She had killed again. She hated it. She could not wait to do it again. But the thrill was already gone before she had finished reading her monologue. A hunger that was never satisfied. It was time to feed it again. Manda picked up her snake and let it slither under her jacket while she walked away.

Chapter 55

'And now here is my secret, a very simple secret; it is only with the heart that one can see rightly, what is essential is invisible to the eye.'
– Antoine de Saint-Exupéry

'What is knowledge?'

Alex and Adam had once again met up for a walk. This time they had, on Alex's suggestion, opted for the botanical garden. During the walk Adam had once again asked a general question that at first glance looked simple, but which turned out to be more complex the more you thought about it.

'What you know that you know?' Alex tried.

Adam smiled.

'The problem is that people define knowledge as the ability to remember facts. To know things. You think that knowledge is being able to connect 1066 to the Battle of Hastings. In your eagerness to remember details, you miss the bigger picture. With such an attitude, you run the risk of not understanding what you already know. The brain receives an amazing amount of stimulation, but we can only process a very tiny part of it all. It's said that some autistic people lack filters and can, therefore, receive so much more information.'

Adam took out a copy of a drawing from his bag.

'This drawing was done by an autistic man who flew over London in a helicopter for half an hour. When he landed, he sat down and drew this. The drawing is correct right down to the number of windows in every house. Every single pillar is there. If you or anyone else were to ride in the same helicopter, you probably wouldn't be able to draw the right number of windows in a single house. Does that mean you saw less than the autistic man? No—you saw the same city, the same number of windows. The only difference is that your consciousness filters out most of what you see.

'In much the same way, you can look at a sea of faces in a big crowd and pick out the one face of a good friend in that big group of strangers. Have you ever wondered how you can do that? Your brain scans every single face and compares it with a database of stored faces. Then it lets your consciousness become unaware of all the faces that aren't relevant. Having a brain that acts like a filter is basically good; the problem arose when people, especially Westerners, started to think that conscious knowing and knowing was the same thing. By doing so, people—unconsciously—took away ninety-nine per cent of their potential knowing.'

'What's this magical way of thinking called?' Alex regretted asking when she heard how ironic it sounded.

'It's called intuition. And it's not magic. It's natural. Those times you've actually listened to your intuition, has it worked out?' He said it with a smile. In a way that made it sound as if he really wanted to listen to her answer

'Why must you always answer a question with a question?'

'She said by asking him a question in answer to his question . . .'

'Of course you're right. I'll listen to my intuition more. And my stomach. And right now, it's telling me I'm hungry. I have to get something to eat. How about you?'

'No, I think I'll leave you. It's easier to listen to yourself when you're alone. Turn off the TV tonight, get comfortable with doing nothing until the silence starts talking. And do me a favour—listen to what your intuition tells you.'

When she got home from the walk, she did as Adam had suggested. Sat on the bed and listened to the silence. Why had Adam started to talk about intuition? Before he had brought up the topic, they had been discussing Daniel. Alex had tried getting in touch with her brother the past few days, but had only got his voicemail. She was starting to feel worried and had shared her concerns with Adam. It was then that Adam had asked her to go home and listen to herself.

The Watcher who met Adam on the street waited until he had put in his earpiece. These days, when wireless headsets to mobile phones were quite common, reporting to Mediators had become so much easier.

Adam put on his headset, pretended to call someone and started talking. The Watcher was no more than a metre away from him as they walked. He signed his reply back to Adam.

'I think I got her to understand,' Adam said out loud.

The Watcher signed back. 'Understood. I'll report back to the Queen.'

'I don't think she really understands the grave danger her brother is in.'

'Has she understood that he will die?' signed the Watcher.

'Actually, I don't know.'

'Don't forget whose side you're on as a Mediator,' the Watcher replied.

'I'm not on anyone's side,' Adam answered. 'Or, more precisely I'm on everyone's side.'

'It seems to me you're very much on the side of your Subject. If you have additional intelligence on her that you ought to report, this would be the time to do it.'

'What are you talking about?' Adam gave the Watcher a harsh look.

The Watcher didn't flinch, 'I'm guessing you are aware that the Primary Queen is very close to ordering the liquidation of both siblings and not just the Subject's brother? If you have any information, then it's your duty as a Mediator to report it now.'

'She has a name,' Adam said angrily.

'As you know, while on a mission, we're not to call the Subject by name. To avoid the risk of getting too attached.'

Adam stopped and stood a few centimetres away from the Watcher. 'I am fully aware of what my role as Mediator is. And it's not up to you to tell me how to live my life.'

'I'm only informing you how the Subject might end hers,' the Watcher signed and turned away to get back to the Queen.

There was a lot to report.

Chapter 56

'The eternal mystery of the world is its comprehensibility.'
– Albert Einstein

Why was it so hard to find someone to talk to when you really needed to talk? Alex had tried to contact Mr Williams for several days but he was not answering his phone. She still could not get hold of Daniel. The fact that both of them had disappeared worried her. Mobile phones were a wonderful invention that really made it easier to keep in contact. In the pre-mobile phone age, weeks or months could go by before you started wondering why you had not heard from somebody, but now a mobile phone that was shut off could get you worried after only a few days. Going straight to voicemail without the phone ever ringing was a merciless reminder that something could be wrong. The easier it was to keep in contact, the harder it was to deal with not being able to.

She had called Mr Williams at least fifteen times over the past few days—and her brother's number even more often than that. Not even Laura was answering her phone and that was, perhaps, what worried her the most, because Laura was Mrs Happy Families. Both Laura's and Daniel's phones rang, so that probably meant they were only ignoring her. But why had Mr Williams turned off his phone?

Alex had gone to Starbucks to try and study, but she was too worried to concentrate. She could feel her heart pounding and found it hard to get any work done. Her books remained shut in front of her and every time she thought about opening them, she just had to try contacting them one more time. Why weren't they returning her calls?

Just then, her phone started ringing. She grabbed it and looked at the display hoping to see the names 'Mr Williams' or 'Daniel'.

It was Shadow.

'Have you heard?' Shadow asked. 'Mr Williams is dead. It will no doubt be called a heart attack, but I'm afraid Mr Williams didn't take his own warnings seriously.'

'What do you mean?'

'He died in front of his ex-wife's house. My guess is that he was there to tell her about The Unvisible again,' Shadow said.

Alex broke out into a sweat. Mr Williams was dead? A mountain of emotions and thoughts fell over her. Had he understood how important he had been to her? Had she even thanked him for all his help? She felt a sense of resignation at the thought of everything she could have, and should have, said to him. All at once she felt regret, embarrassment, guilt, sadness, grief, confusion, anger . . .

Then she felt fear.

She had to get out. She bumped into one of the waiters, but she could not even manage to say sorry. She had to get out of there. Into the fresh air. To breathe. Away from the place where she had just found out that the man who tried to warn her of the dangers of telling a relative about The Unvisible had just died for doing exactly that.

Once out on the street, Alex just wanted to keep on running. If she stopped, she was afraid her distress would overwhelm her. She heard Shadow shouting at her in the phone. But she did not want to hear more. Did not want to talk. She did not have the energy to care about what Shadow was feeling.

If Mr Williams had been killed for telling his ex-wife, then why wasn't Alex already dead for telling her brother? She remembered that someone had said the Primary Queen only gave orders to kill someone when she felt that the Knower did not respect the secret. Was it Mr Williams himself who had told her that? How could he go and tell his ex-wife directly after getting a warning for having sanctioned Alex and Daniel as Knowers?

She cursed him. She missed him. She mourned him. She broke down at a bus stop and burst out crying. Two passers-by looked nervously at her. They probably thought she was high. But she was not high. She was low.

The Primary Queen sat on a rock by the small lake near her pyramid. Close by Watchers and Carers went about their business and, in a forest clearing a bit further away, a Killer performed her ritual.

No one approached the Queen. It was not forbidden, but everyone knew that they better have a very good reason to approach her. She needed time to reflect and the others had to give her space. Give her time and space to think. A lake's reflection was the clearest when no wind disturbed its surface. A brain thought best when not disturbed by the thoughts of others. And the Queen had a lot to think about.

She thought about how the Primary Queens in generation after generation before her had faced the same challenges that she now faced. How their entire existence was at risk every day because of the possibility that one person was a little too curious or hungry for power. Or rather, how the Yangyang's existence relied on their own ability to constantly monitor these threats.

She thought about the Motherland; the island where all the Yangyang originated. The island in the middle of the Mother Sea between the Japanese islands and the Korean peninsula, where the Yangyang had lived in isolation long before they had understood their role in the bigger picture.

When the Motherland was destroyed in an earthquake, the Yangyang had been forced to leave the island and go to the mainland, from where they spread all over the world. Most of the bio-diversity from the Motherland had become extinct. They had only managed to take a small part of their animals—horses, doves, snakes, swans, sheep and a few more species. Luckily, they had even managed to save some of their bamboo plants.

From this invisible (to the human eye) bamboo, they could make everything from the strong but light structures of the pyramids to clothes, weapons, tools and food. It was a magical material that deserved to be celebrated. The Yangyang admired mankind's bamboo too and tried to place their Vimanas near the bamboo groves of humans. Strangely enough, people had forgotten the wonderful properties of this material and grew other crops like cotton, instead of bamboo—even though bamboo was much easier and cheaper to grow and you could make clothes that were just as comfortable and attractive.

In much the same way, humans used slow-growing wood for their buildings although bamboo grew faster and was more flexible for building. As so often before, people complicated things in their eagerness to find a solution instead of looking for simplicity.

The Queen thought about the risk that they themselves might become infected by the human outlook on life. It would not be the first time a group of people living near Nature saw their culture destroyed by a more 'civilized' one. It was easy to be temporarily dazzled by what was modern and lose the ability to see what was truly important.

The mission of the Yangyang—to create harmony by living in symbiosis with humanity—was important, but what if people, through their very closeness, brought some of their chaos to the Yangyang world instead? Was it possible to live so closely to humans without being contaminated by their worry? And with the population explosion of the past few hundred years, the Yangyang found themselves more and more at a disadvantage.

One of her jobs as Primary Queen was to make sure that her flock did not give birth to more offspring than Yangyang who died. Humans seldom had similar restrictions: instead they seemed to always strive for growth, even when it threatened their very existence.

Knowers often thought that there were as many Yangyang as Yinyin, but that was a false assumption based on the fact that a new Knower was surrounded by several Watchers. This made people in the know think that The Unvisible were everywhere.

The truth was that there had not been as many Yangyang as Yinyin for several hundred years. While humans had increased in numbers to around 8 billion, the Yangyang, with their 2 billion, had seen themselves become a minority.

Having so many people on the planet as now was not environmentally sustainable. The Yangyang knew that, and so did humans, the difference being that the humans did not seem to want to do anything about it.

Sometimes the Queen found herself wishing that a larger portion of humanity found out about The Unvisible so that they could liquidate a billion people or so. But she knew it would be impossible to stop the secret from spreading if so many people knew about them. Modern technology meant that it was no longer possible for a message to spread to only a part of humanity. The risk was too great that the rumour about the Yangyang would spread like wildfire.

So, they had to concentrate on finding people who knew about them in time. And on educating their own people on not letting the habits and culture of humans make too great an impression on their own way of life. The Yangyang would be a part of the Yinyin's world, but the Yinyin would never be a part of theirs. And luckily, she could always point to the Killers as an example of what happens when the two worlds collide. The Killers were not only a threat to humanity, but also a warning to The Unvisible.

Chapter 57

'Only he who can see the invisible can do the impossible.'
– Frank Gaines

Daniel had not had the courage to use the yangsee at the airport. Partly because the security guards might think it was some kind of weapon. And partly because he guessed that The Unvisible, just like humans, would have extra security details posted at the borders. But everything had gone smoothly and when he sat in the airplane and the 'Fasten seatbelt' sign was turned off, he pressed the service button and ordered two gin and tonics.

After taking a few sips, he got out his computer and looked through his presentation again. He felt more and more convinced that he would soon take the world by storm.

On a whim, he turned off the computer and put on his yangsee. There couldn't possibly be any Yangyang on a crowded plane—could there? He scanned the cylindrical cabin but saw no signs of any Watchers or Killers.

'I am getting paranoid,' he reflected. But then again 'only the paranoid survive' as the famous book had stated. Daniel wrote in his notebook: 'Make presentation shorter.' Ten minutes would have to do. He made a mental note that he had to find somewhere safe to stay. It would all sort itself out. Linda would see to that.

Linda was one of Daniel's former classmates from Med. School. One of all those he had had sex with—and more importantly—one of those who had let themselves be photographed. You could get the most prudish of girls to agree to a few 'fun pictures' in the heat of passion. The next day they would either ask him to send the pics to him or order him to delete them. Either way, he had, of course, saved copies in another folder. You never knew how valuable some silly, sexy seconds in front of a camera could be one day.

Several years later, when Daniel saw that Linda was responsible for booking speakers at a prestigious medical conference, he had put a red mark next to her name in his little, black book. A red mark meant 'important hold'—that is, someone who had a powerful position and would probably be more than willing to do him a favour in return for not revealing some awkward moments from their past. He had not really been sure how he would use Linda, but he knew that sooner or later it would be useful to have a contact at the conference. Now he was happy he had waited to use her. Fate had decided that Linda would give him the platform he needed.

When he had contacted her and demanded she give him a keynote slot on the main stage during the last day of the conference, she had first laughed at him before hanging up. When he had called again and explained that if she did not listen to him, he would be forced to upload some 'interesting' old photos on the Internet, she had laughed at his threat. When he had mailed over one of the most embarrassing shots with the caption 'One of the least embarrassing photos' she had cursed him. But Daniel knew these were just the different stages of defence she was going through. And the last time he had called, she had sighed and said he could have fifteen minutes on the last day if she shortened the chairperson's closing remarks. But he had to promise never to call her again and to delete all those photos. He had, of course, promised to do so, but he could not help crossing his fingers as he did.

'He has few close contacts.'

The Watcher whose job it had been to watch Daniel wriggled in embarrassment. He knew the Queen did not want excuses, so it was important that what he presented was perceived as facts and not as an excuse for why his Subject was so hard to find. He also knew that it was much harder to find a missing Yangyang once they had lost him. A Yangyang on the run had a tendency to run away, and as soon as they left their home city they were much harder to find. Each Vimana was a tight knit society and that was its strength, but it also meant that Vimanas in different parts of a country often had very little communication. And Vimanas in different countries had even less. The Yangyang had no central, national government, and no international organizations like the Yinyin had the UN for example. So if a hunted Yinyin was just able to escape to another city or country they were relatively safe as long as they did not start spreading the secret again. That was why it was so crucial to never lose track of a Suspect. And the Watcher standing in front of the Queen knew that that's what they had done this time. It was not good. They had failed. Thankfully most Subjects on the run actually decided to stay close to home for some reason, perhaps because people feel comfortable with the world they know. The Watcher was praying the Subject they had lost track of this time was one of those who did not run far.

He carried on. 'Even though the Subject has an unusually large number of social contacts, most seem to be acquaintances and work contacts, and only a few are friends.'

'Family?' asked the Primary Queen.

'We haven't noted any sort of contact with any family members.'

'Relatively unusual,' the older of the Secondary Queens reflected.

The Watcher continued. 'He has more than one hundred and fifty phone numbers in his mobile and a black notebook with even more numbers and descriptions of people he has met. Mostly women. But the people he actually calls are few. And those who call him are even fewer. That makes it difficult to predict his next step.'

The Primary Queen nodded. They had an Unaccepted who was difficult to find. That was a problem. An Unaccepted was someone who knew about the Yangyang, but could not keep quiet. A Knower who had to share. The mission of the entire network of the Yangyang with its Watchers, Killers and the Wise—and even, to some degree, the Mediators—was to identify, localize and neutralize the Unaccepted before they made too much trouble.

When someone in the know became an Unaccepted and decided to tell others about the secret, then the correct strategy was to increase the surveillance on the Subject's family and friends. When people wanted to confess something, they tended to turn to their nearest and dearest.

The Primary Queen glanced down at her cloak and studied the oval bits of serpent leather. An untrained eye would see a sea of scales. The Primary Queen, quite literally, saw tens of thousands of individual pieces. The differences might be minimal, but they were there. She saw one piece that was chipped. Another thicker piece reflected the light in a bluer shade of white. A third piece was hiding in the shadow of a fourth and was therefore not as bright. And there was the fifth piece, where the white thread holding it together was lying on top of the scale in the shape of a little eight. For more than two minutes, she let everyone else wait while she focused all her energy on identifying the uniqueness of each and every one of the seemingly similar objects.

There was a pattern to everything. An interpretation for all situations. Even those who did not want to be found could be found. You just had to know how to interpret the details. There were always signals. There was always a pattern to be found.

When she was done the Primary Queen looked up at her group again. 'We have to stay calm. Panic breeds panic. The man is a hunted animal and he knows it. He will make a mistake. Yinyin always make mistakes when they are stressed. That's one of their biggest flaws.'

They had to find him. It was essential. It was even urgent. But there was no stress. To help her subjects understand the value of never letting a situation get control of the calmness of the mind, the Primary Queen turned her back on them and walked to the fall of smoke. Her Secondary Queens joined her. The three women, one young, one middle-aged and one old, and all with an important and big decision to make, stood with their hands at their sides and admired the smoke falling down into the room. The three women studied how the smoke wall kept transforming itself. It was always the same wall of smoke, but it was never the same; constantly changing, renewing and reshaping itself.

They stood there in silence for more than twenty minutes. Letting their senses be present. Letting the impressions come and go.

When the Primary Queen finally turned around, a sense of calm had descended on the room. A calm she knew would spread throughout her Vimana and out to all the members of her flock—perhaps even to the Killers.

'So solid. So fluid,' the eldest woman said, looking at the smoke.

'Like life,' said the girl.

'Like the hunt,' finished the Primary Queen.

And then, in a louder voice so that no one would miss her message, she added: 'No human who wants to reveal our secret can keep himself hidden forever. Watchers watch. Killers kill. Find he who is in hiding.'

Chapter 58

'If only we could pull out our brain and use only our eyes.'
– Pablo Picasso

Alex was waiting for the bus when her phone buzzed. It was a text message from Shadow. 'Your brother has stolen Ola's yangsee. Did you know?'

Alex looked at her phone in surprise. She was just about to call Shadow and ask her what she meant when she was interrupted again by another call. This time from Laura. Alex hesitated. After a few signals, she decided to accept the call.

'Alex. I'm sorry I haven't called you back, but there's been a lot going on.'

'Is everything okay?' Alex asked.

Laura was silent.

'Laura?'

'I've left him. The kids and I are moving in with my parents. I'm filing for divorce and I want sole custody of the children. Just wanted you to know. I've been waiting for an opportunity when he's gone for a long time so that I can organize everything before he comes back home.'

'But what about the kids?' Alex regretted saying it in a tone that made her sound like her mother.

'They'll be happier with me.'

'What?' Alex could not believe what she was hearing.

'I'm trying to save myself, Alexandra. Your brother isn't well. There's something wrong with him. I've really tried my best, but I can't do this anymore.'

'What are you talking about? What's wrong with Daniel?'

Laura lowered her voice and answered slowly. 'I'm really very sorry, Alex. So sorry. But I just can't go on like this.'

She hung up. Alex called her back at once. Surely Laura couldn't just end a relationship like that. Not when there are children involved. But Laura did not pick up. Alex called again. When she phoned for the third time, her phone buzzed. It was a text message from Laura.

'Don't be angry with me. I've done my best. Please don't call again. I'm going to change my number and stay away until all the paperwork is sorted out and your brother has calmed down. It's best this way. P.S. I haven't told your mother. Just can't. Sorry.'

Alex stared at her phone.

It seemed like all the people around her were crumbling. She tried calling her brother again.

No answer.

Alex went and sat on a bench. What had started out as a wonderful secret was turning into a nightmare. Her own brother's arrogance put him and The Unvisible at risk—and quite possibly Alex too. She knew just how determined Daniel could be when he set his sights on something and how forcefully he could chase something he wanted.

Somehow she had to figure out what he intended to do, and she had to do it before The Unvisible caught up with him.

She broke out into a cold sweat at the thought of what a Killer would do to her brother. But the one thing that scared her the most was not knowing what her brother intended to do with a yangsee. A flash of insight came to her: 'I am the only one who can fix this.' And then, like thunder to that flash, came a second insight: 'But I have no idea how.'

But a seedling of an idea started to grow inside her head. Alex picked up the phone and sent one last message to Laura: 'Thank you for telling me. I think you did the right thing. Do not worry about my mother, I will talk to her. P.S. You said he had gone away. Do you know where?'

That line about 'you did the right thing' had been a lie, but Alex knew Laura would not answer her question if she did not think Alex was now on her side. Laura had said something about 'before he comes home' and Alex needed to know if Laura knew where Daniel might be.

After a few minutes her mobile phone pinged with a message: 'Some medical conference.'

That last message from Laura triggered an idea. In her notebook Alex wrote down what she knew:

- Laura has left him.
- He has Ola's yangsee.
- He's gone to a conference.

Alex looked at the list At least it was something. She typed in the day's date and 'medical conference' in the Search box on her phone.

When she saw the hits her feelings of helplessness and frustration turned into decisiveness. She now thought she knew what he was planning to do. It was completely crazy—and so like him. She might be wrong, and if she was, the trip she was now planning would be in vain. But it would be even worse to stay home and just wait. He was obviously going to the medical conference and it was equally obvious that Alex had to go there and stop him.

There was a minute chance her plan would work: that she could save her brother and keep the secret too. She had to get there before The Unvisible. The fact that he seemed to be alive must mean that The Unvisible did not know where he was. So, she had an advantage. Perhaps she could limit the damage. It was worth a shot. But she needed help. She got out her phone and called Adam.

'Adam, I hope you're not scared of flying. You and I are going on a little adventure.'

Chapter 59

'There is both visible and invisible labour.'
– Victor Hugo

Alex and Adam stood in the queue to the security control. About fifty people stood in front of them. The progress of the process was excruciatingly slow.

'I'm fed up with these security checks. Completely pointless.' Alex shifted from foot to foot in frustration.

The man in front of Alex turned around and looked down at Alex with contempt. He was almost two metres tall and must have weighed about 120 kilos. He spat out his words. 'I couldn't help overhearing your bullshit. My cousin died in a bomb attack in the London underground—and you think we should let terrorists go onboard with liquid bombs and create another 9/11.'

'I'm sorry your cousin died, but . . .'

'I don't want your pity!' the man snapped.

' . . . but as I was saying,' Alex said, ignoring the man's interruption, 'A terrorist could just leave their bottle of explosives in the trash cans at the security control itself and let it explode there. After that people would be terrified of standing in-line in a security check . . . And what do you think we should do about that? Have a security check before going to the security check?'

'Is there a problem here?' One of the guards had noticed that Alex was raising her voice, so he went over to investigate.

Adam turned to the guard. 'There's just been a little misunderstanding. Tell me, could my assistant and I go to the front of the queue? Don't you have a rule about prioritizing passengers with disabilities?'

The security guard pointed at Alex and Adam, 'You two—come with me.'

As they walked past the queue, Adam whispered to Alex, 'Am I right if I assume that it's not uncommon for people to see your fearlessness as obnoxious?'

'Oh, where should I start? Let's see . . . my mother, my father, my priest, and many of my teachers, to name a few?' She smiled and continued, 'But what they all don't realize is that if there weren't for people like me—people who question rules—then the most idiotic rules would be enforced. We are the reality check of a sane society. We are the last defence stopping mankind from regulating itself to death.'

The last part she said in a pompous voice.

After a brief pause she added, 'And yes, some people find that annoying.'

Adam replied calmly, 'I find it captivating.'

When Manda went through security control, the machine buzzed angrily. It was her amulet that had set it off. The amulet was a gray and bland round piece of jewellery that all Killers wore around their necks. It was not very pretty, but it was the finest thing a Killer owned. It symbolized how the Killers were half Yinyin and half Yangyang—how the white and black in the yin and yang symbol had melted together to create a gray mass. The amulets were made from the leftover magnetic stone that the Yangyang had taken with them from the Motherland before it sank into the sea. There was only a small quantity of the stone left and the Queen had decided that it would be used to make amulets for the Killers. It was a sign of gratitude for the sacrificing work they did for the Yangyang.

Manda did not care that her amulet set off the security control machine. She had walked right behind a businessman who she knew would get the blame. By the time the security guard had searched the businessman, Manda had already left the area and was walking towards the gate.

Chapter 60

'I see the world through my eyes. It's sometimes a strange world.'
– Keira Knightley

After a couple of hours' flying, most of the other passengers had fallen asleep.

But Alex was awake. She did not plan on wasting precious hours with Adam by sleeping. They had not talked about it, but when this mission was finished and they had, hopefully, stopped Daniel, then Adam would most likely move on to another mission. Would that mean that she would lose him? Since meeting Adam, Alex had thought of him as someone who would always be a part of her life, but what if that would not be the case? Best to use whatever time they had left together talking, not sleeping.

Alex turned to Adam and nudged him with her elbow.

'I've been wondering about something. When angels get sick, what do they do? Do they use our hospitals when we're not looking?'

Adam had explained that she must never talk about The Unvisible in public so she had suggested using the word 'angel' instead and that they would pretend that Adam was a priest That way they could openly discuss the Yangyang without anyone else understanding what they were actually talking about. If anyone asked, Alex could always say she was writing an article about angels. Adam had been hesitant at first, but finally given in—as long as he could pause the conversation at any time.

'No. They have very few doctors,' Adam replied.

'No doctors? But can't angels get sick?'

'They can. But it doesn't happen very often, so only a handful of doctors are needed. A doctor mends people that break down. But for something to be mended, it first has to break. Instead, they have Maintainers, people who make sure the angels take care of their bodies and souls so that they don't break down.'

'And by doing that, they don't get sick?'

'A good engineer can mend a machine when it's broken. But an excellent one takes care of the machine so that it doesn't break. So you could say that instead of doctors, they have service technicians.'

'Since when did you start talking in metaphors?'

'We priests often talk in metaphors.' Adam winked at Alex. 'As I've tried to explain, angels are much better at listening to their bodies and souls than we are. And they've developed methods for preventing illness and healing injuries in a natural way over thousands of years. They don't get sick because their immune system is strong, and their immune system is strong because they do not stress. And stress is—directly and indirectly—probably the biggest reason why people in the Western world get sick so often. If we stressed less, we would need fewer doctors. And fewer pills.'

Alex knew all too well what he meant. Two of her best friends had developed acute allergic reactions due to stress. Alex thought about the stress she herself felt over trying to balance her own dreams with the demands of her parents. A quiet, grinding stress that made itself felt as a stinging sensation in her heart—a pain she tried to repress, something that only added to already high stress levels.

Alex got stressed by all the talk about anti-stress. She whispered to Adam, 'Only eat animals that eat other animals, live in big families, work as little as possible to have as much time as possible for the children, hardly getting sick . . . I'm sorry, but it's all too Utopian. Why are The Unvisible so bloody wholesome?'

'Don't let them fool you: they can be ruthless when it comes to protecting their own interests. And not all of them are 'bloody wholesome'. Some are just bloody,' whispered Adam in reply.

'Who?'

'The Killers.'

They leaned towards each other and talked quietly. The engine noise made it impossible for anyone to hear what they were talking about. They sat way back in the plane so there was no one behind them. The man sitting in the middle seat had swapped places when he noticed they knew each other and that there were free seats elsewhere in the plane.

'A Killer is the last person you want to meet because there's a big risk that he or she is the last thing you'll ever see. If the Queen deems someone a threat, then she commands her Killers to kill.'

'So that's all they do—kill?'

'Almost every country has professionals whose only job is to kill or to be trained how to kill. So why shouldn't The Unvisible have the same?'

Alex hoped she would never meet a Killer again. The mere knowledge that there was a merciless group of Killers among The Unvisible, whose job was to murder humans who knew too much, made her feel ill. Daniel must be stopped. Tomorrow was a big day in many respects. She had to make sure she was well-rested in order to carry out her plan to the best of her ability.

'I'm sorry, but I have to get some rest now,' she apologized, and pushed back her seat as far as it would go. 'Be sure to wake me up if some terrorist decides to blow the plane into pieces.'

Adam smiled. When she shut her eyes, she felt her left leg resting against his leg. Her first reaction was to move her leg away, but then she realized that she did not want to. She felt his warmth spread to her. Alex cautiously moved her elbow until it touched him. She felt safe. She could relax. The roar of the engines did not scare her—it was soporific. Within a few minutes, she was asleep.

Chapter 61

'Life is to be lived, not controlled; and humanity is won by continuing to play in face of certain defeat.'
– Ralph Ellison (from Invisible Man)

The main hall of the medical conference was packed. There was an air of expectation in the room and everyone felt it. Linda had been forced to rename Daniel's presentation to 'The Greatest Discovery in the History of the World?' in order to get her boss to shorten his own closing speech. And Daniel had, for some strange reason, asked her to put the speaker's name as just 'Dr Johansen', instead of using his full name. She knew that no matter what Daniel presented, it would not live up to the hype of the title. She desperately hoped that it would not be a total failure. That when this was all over, she would still have a job. Linda had consistently refused to give out any more information about the presentation to avoid fuelling people's expectations any further. Instead she had referred all questions back to Daniel.

But for some reason, Daniel had kept away from the conference for the first two days, so no-one had been able to get in contact with him. The aura of secrecy that lack of information had created had fuelled a storm of rumours and the conference hall was boiling over with anticipation. People were even standing in the aisles.

The sound technician, who had just put a headset on Daniel, smiled when he saw the sweat on Daniel's forehead.

'Stage fright?'

'Yes, maybe a little,' Daniel gave a forced smile in return.

But the drops of sweat on his forehead were not from stage fright, they were from death fright. Daniel knew there were Watchers in the hall, an unusually large number. He had seen them when he had quickly put on the yangsee backstage. He also knew that after a few minutes of his presentation, they would understand what was going on. After he had delivered his message he would have to get away quickly before they could catch him. He really wanted to wear the yangsee during the presentation, but he knew no one would take him seriously if he did.

He would just have to take a risk. To increase his chances, he had persuaded the guards to show him the quickest way out of the building. He had even hired a car and chauffeur and had them standing by outside. The plan was to be driven to a remote cottage in a forest which he had rented. That way it would be harder for the Watchers to find him. There he would spend the next three weeks and handle all communication via the safety and anonymity of the Internet.

The noise in the hall quietened down as if on a given signal. 'Sounds like they want you to start.'

Daniel shut his eyes for a couple of seconds. This was the moment he had been waiting for his entire life. He had always wanted to be famous for something, but never in his wildest dreams had he thought he would be known as the man behind the discovery of humanity's invisible cousin. In a few minutes, he would deliver the news that would guarantee him a Nobel Prize in physics and maybe also one in medicine. He smiled at the absurdity of the situation.

The host of the conference introduced Daniel using the script he had given her. To boost his credibility, he had tweaked the truth a little. Everyone lied a little in their speaker résumés, didn't they? When the host had read the texts from her cards, she turned to Daniel and smiled. 'And here he is. The man who's going to give the last presentation—Dr David Johansson.'

Of course, she would get his name wrong, but he would ignore that detail. Soon she, and everyone else in the world, would know his name. He walked out and stopped in the middle of the stage, squeezing the remote control. With feet wide apart and his gaze fixed on a point just above the heads of the people sitting at the back of the hall, he took a deep breath.

It was show time.

'Ladies and gentlemen. Humanity develops through discoveries: it could be via a voyage like that of Columbus discovering America or Armstrong's journey to the moon. Or it could be a mental expedition like Copernicus realizing that the earth was not the centre of the universe or Darwin's uncovering of the origin of the species.

'It is rare to actually be there when discoveries like these are presented for the very first time. But all of you here today will be part of the revelation of the greatest discovery humanity has ever made.

'Ladies and gentlemen. I give you—"The Unvisible".'

He clicked up the first picture with the heading: 'The Unvisible'.

In the very back of the main hall of the medical conference sat a very bored Watcher. He understood why it was important to attend industry conferences, since that was where people tended to announce big discoveries, but he also knew that it was very rare that anything around Yinyin's understanding of Yangyang would show up at a conference. The Yangyin had a tendency to have been called in way before someone got to present at a conference.

After attending this specific conference for days, the Watcher was very excited that it was over. They should really be called 'Waiters', since ninety-nine point nine per cent of what they did was to just wait. But no reason to complain. Waiting was the main activity for many professions, from fire fighters to life guards and all kinds of military personnel. And soon this shift would be over and he would be back watching his regular family again.

The Watcher looked up when the moderator came out on the stage to present the last speaker. She read from a script and ended her introduction with the words:

'And here he is. The man who's going to give the last presentation—David Johansson.'

The Watcher switched his attention away from the stage towards a window where he was able to see the clouds dance.

Chapter 62

'I don't think we did go blind, I think we are blind, Blind but seeing, Blind people who can see, but do not see.'
– José Saramago

Just being in a room with hundreds of doctors made Alex feel queasy. Doctors, like lawyers and architects, had this annoying habit of thinking they were better than other people. That they were a little smarter. No, obviously not all of them, but many of them. Individually they could be irritating, but in groups they were downright insufferable. As soon as she entered the grand conference hall, she had been struck by the know-it-all energy in the room. In spontaneous self-defence, she had dragged Adam with her to a couple of seats in the middle of the last row of the room. When Daniel started talking, she saw why this was a bad idea as they were forced to push their way past everyone in their row to get to the stage.

Strange how people who are seated can still look down on people who are standing up, thought Alex as she apologetically pushed past the row of seats accompanied by demeaning glares from the people they walked by.

'We have to stop him!' Alex tugged Adam's arm.

'You'd better get started then,' Adam answered.

Alex dragged Adam to the front of the large hall.

At first, the audience sat quietly in reluctant surprise over Daniel's presentation. But after a few seconds, scattered boos could be heard. After a couple of minutes, a lot of people started laughing at the absurd story of an alternative human race that was superior to man. Absurd or not, many in the audience could not help but be drawn in by Daniel's rhetorical reasoning. After a while, even the sceptics found themselves fascinated by the elaborate picture Daniel's storytelling was creating.

'Only ten years ago, most experts laughed at the idea of there being water on Mars. Today we know for a fact that the red planet is full of it. Before the discovery of atoms, the idea of such tiny parts was completely unbelievable; but nowadays, we know that atoms are far from the smallest, indivisible building blocks that we though they were.' Daniel slowly carried on building up his argument.

For every minute that went by, the laughter died down. His biggest critics became louder in their criticism, but instead of the rest of the audience joining in, they started to hush those who were interrupting Daniel's presentation. Some people got up and walked out in protest, but most stayed and listened.

It was then that they saw a woman get up on the stage.

The Watcher at the back of the hall could not believe his ears. Was the man really planning to talk about Yangyang while standing on a stage in front of hundreds of people? Did he not understand that he was about to sign a death sentence, not only for himself, but for everyone in the room? What was he thinking? The Watcher ran out of the hall to get back-up. No matter how much he wanted to stay and listen, he had to get a message to the Queen. The Killers had to be called in immediately.

He wrote a quick note and went out onto the balcony, which stretched along the side of the building. He had left his dove there as he had misjudged the risk of anything being revealed on the last day of the conference. It was, no doubt, a decision he would be criticized for later, but right now he had to send off his message and run back to the room so that the man did not escape. Within ten minutes, the man would be dead. The Watcher's job was to decide how many others would meet the same fate.

Chapter 63

> **'The only difference between me and a madman is I'm not mad.'**
> – Salvador Dalí

Alex knew she had less than a minute to get Daniel on her side and then another two to three minutes at the most to get her message across. As soon as she was on the stage, she ran over to Daniel and tore off his headset. Daniel was so surprised that he did not react until she was standing there with the headset in her hand.

'This isn't his discovery. It's mine!' she pointed at Daniel with a straight arm and her index finger resting accusingly against his head.

'What are you doing?' Daniel muffled the microphone with his hand and whispered as loudly as he dared. Alex held the microphone away and leaned in. 'You have fifteen seconds to make a decision. Either I reveal that you've lied in your presentation and didn't discover The Unvisible at all, but stole the discovery from me. In which case, you'll be seen as an unreliable liar who steals ideas and no one will ever want to work with you again. Or, you confess that I am a part of the project, that I was the one who found out about them and that we are in this together. And then you agree to share any future Nobel Prize with me, as well as give me half of all future earnings you get from selling the secret I told you in confidence.'

Daniel stared at her in confusion. His eyes flickered from side to side as he weighed his options.

'Ten seconds left.'

'So, it's about money?' Daniel seemed to have come to a decision. 'I'll give you thirty per cent.'

'Forty,' Alex countered.

'Deal,' Daniel confirmed. 'Forty per cent of the profits.'

'Deal,' said Alex and handed back to the headset. 'Get back to your presentation.'

Daniel had regained his composure and introduced Alex with an open hand. 'Ladies and gentlemen, let me present Alexandra Johansen.'

The audience was following the drama that was unfolding on the stage with great interest. This was turning out to be one of the most unusual endings to this conference ever.

'This is my sister, Alexandra—the woman who is the brain behind "The Unvisible". She was the one who helped me understand that they really do exist Without this woman, there would be no greatest discovery in the history of the world.'

He paused and smiled at Alex.

Alex did not smile back. Instead she grabbed the headset again and pulled it off him. She purposefully put the head set a little crookedly on her head. Then she started to talk. She was addressing the people in the audience, but she wasn't looking at them as she burst out her words in anger; she was looking straight up into the ceiling.

'This is just the beginning. The gods are going to punish us. The flood is coming. Judgement is here. No one will be spared. The time for confession and atonement is past.'

She banged her head with her hands after every sentence. When her hands hit her forehead, a loud thumping sound was heard in the headset and the sound made her shake her head as if in shock.

Daniel went up to Alex and whispered, 'What the hell are you doing?' Alex slapped him on the cheek. A murmur of surprise rippled through the room. Alex continued to preach.

'Everything is falling apart. The aliens will invade again. The angels have stopped hugging. The world is ending. We have to admit that Karl Marx was right or the heavens will split in two. Our children will turn against us. And what about all those poor, homeless cats?! Who will take care of them?'

The part about the cats was probably a bit over the top, but Alex reckoned that it was better to be perceived as too crazy than as not being crazy enough. Pretending to be a crazy woman who worried about abandoned cats was the perfect way of making sure no one would take her seriously.

There was only one way to get the audience to stop believing Daniel—and that was to make them feel that the ideas he was presenting were mad. And if there was one thing she had learnt from working with the mentally ill, it was that a wise thought from a crazy person was never more than just a crazy idea.

Shadow's stories about how certain psychiatric patients might be connected to The Unvisible had given her the idea. If the audience thought that Daniel had been tricked into believing in a conspiracy theory conceived by a lunatic, then the discovery he was presenting became ludicrous as well. After working closely with Gunnar, Benjamin and her other patients, Alex had no problems copying the body language of a mentally unstable person. In her performance, she combined a little of Gunnar's aggression with Benjamin's absent look and cold voice.

Her performance as a crazy woman seemed to work. The boos from the audience got louder.

Time for the 'Grande Finale'. Alex went over to Daniel and hit him on the head one last time. Then she started to hit herself, over and over again. A couple of security guards finally reacted to what was happening and ran onto the stage to try and stop her. She whacked one of the guards on the ear. The effect was what she had hoped for. Instead of leading her gently from the stage as they had planned, they grabbed her legs and lifted her up. They carried her off the stage like a rolled-up carpet. To increase her craziness, she spat in the face of one of the guards. As soon as they got backstage, she stopped the kicking and the fighting. The show was over. The audience had got up and left. She might not get great reviews, but she was happy with the results.

Daniel approached her and slapped her. 'You bitch! I'll never forgive you for this!'

'Daniel—listen to me! You've got to escape. Just hide! Then get in contact with me when you're safe so we can work out a plan. But you have to get out of here before they get you!'

'Don't tell me what to do. I had a plan! Why did you have to ruin everything?'

'I would never have forgiven myself if I hadn't.'

A couple of flies buzzed around Daniel's head. One of them landed on his hair; another on his shoulder. Daniel became distracted and jumped back, trying to wave them away. When the flies landed again, there were four of them. He looked at them in disgust.

He did not have time to deal with Alex—that would have to wait. The audience might not have believed him, there was nothing he could do about that now. He had revealed the secret and he had revealed himself. He had to escape.

The Killers must be nearby. He ran out into the corridor and towards the emergency exit. When he came to the door leading to the car park, he paused. The next moment was critical. If he could get out of the building and into the car without being seen, then he would be safe.

He tore open the door, ran to the car and jumped in. No invisible power stopped him. It had gone well.

The driver had left the engine running and, as soon as Daniel slammed the door closed, the driver put his foot on the gas. Once in the car, Daniel turned around to see if the door had opened again. It had not. Perhaps he had managed to shake off the Killers. He told the driver to go faster. The car was clean on the outside, but the floor next to the driver was littered with empty Coke cans and crumpled packs of cigarettes.

A whole swarm of flies buzzed in and out of the cans. The driver did not seem to care. Daniel looked at the flies. They were so black that they looked blue. Their wings were transparent. Their eyes unpleasantly eerie because you could not tell what they were looking at. Daniel was engrossed by the sight of the persistent, swarming flies. Both ugly and beautiful. For a second, all worldly problems disappeared. But only for a second.

In the backseat of the car that sped away from the conference sat two Killers. The Yangyin rarely worked in pairs, but special cases called for special arrangements. This time there was no room for failure. When the car neared a suitable location, the male Killer signed to his colleague.

'Now?'

'Soon,' Manda signed back. 'Soon.'

Chapter 64

'Life is a beautiful bubble. Death shows what an empty bubble man is.'
– Carl Linnaeus

The driver never really understood what happened. He felt a hard blow to the head and he almost lost consciousness. Everything was spinning. When he looked up, he saw that the car had skidded on the bridge and when it hit the railing, he knew it would not hold.

Is this what it is like to die? he thought, disappointed. *No angels singing? No flutes playing beautiful music?*

His head was flung to the side and he made eye contact with the doctor. He looked terrified. Eyes wide open, he waved his arms around and screamed. The driver then figured out that the other screaming voice he heard was his own. They would die like two screaming babies.

When the car hit the water, both men were thrown against the windscreen, crushed by the impact. Water gushed into the car, which slowly sank in the flowing mass of water.

'Mission accomplished,' a Killer standing on the bridge signed. His role had been to intervene if the Subject somehow managed to get out of the car. But it had not been necessary. Two Watchers stood next to him and looked down at the spot where the car had just sunk beneath the surface.

'Finally!' one of them replied before leaving the bridge.

A small group of people had already begun to gather and it would soon get difficult to leave the bridge without banging into anyone. Manda stood next to them. She quickly prayed.

A mysterious story.

To carry out the murder gray.

Oh, to long to fly.

No one close. No one near. No one to light my fire.

In the conference hall, Adam managed to squeeze his way to Alex. When she had been carried off the stage, most of the participants decided it was time to go home. He had to fight his way through the stream of people heading for the exits. Most people he met blatantly ignored his white cane. When he finally got to Alex, she was already lying on a stretcher. A woman who had taken offence by how Alex had been treated by the security guards had offered to help. The woman's brother was schizophrenic and she knew how to treat someone going through a psychotic attack.

Right now, she was shouting at the guards for having been too rough. 'Don't you realize that a sensitive soul like this woman only gets worse if you use violence? You have to speak calmly to her. Make her feel safe.'

'Why don't you try speaking calmly to someone who is spitting in your face! We got her onto the stretcher. Isn't that enough?' said the guard holding the towel.

The woman continued her lecture, but they were not listening. Instead they carried Alex to the ambulance. When the stretcher passed Adam, Alex put out her arm and tried to reach him. Adam took her hand. For a second, their eyes met.

'I love you,' Alex said quietly.

Chapter 65

'The positive thinker sees the invisible, feels the intangible, and achieves the impossible.'
– Benjamin Franklin

She had to play her part. While she pretended to fight for her life, Alex screamed as loudly as she could. 'They are going to kill me!'

Adam went up to Alex and tenderly stroked her hand. Alex looked at him and tried to sound frightened. 'The voices. Can't you hear them? They are here!'

'It's all right, Alexandra. We can hear them. Of course we can,' Adam said in a soothing voice.

Alex played along and gave him a confused look. 'You have to let me go. Listen to me—they are here. And they know that I know! That I've revealed the secret. That I've revealed them. That . . .'

The two nurses leaned over Alex. One of them straightened her left arm, while the other got a syringe out of the bag around his waist.

'No! No injections! I'll calm down. I promise!' she begged.

The nurse found a vein on the inside of her arm and plunged in the needle.

Alex lowered her voice and said quietly, almost in a whisper. 'They are here. Save me . . . Please save me . . .'

Her eyelids grew heavy. She fought against the tranquilizing effect of the medicine but did not stand a chance. Slowly, but surely, the world around her became blurred.

Alex's head fell forward and her eyes closed. Just before losing consciousness, she opened her eyelids and, with a look that was fully alert, stared into Adam's clear, blue eyes. Their eyes locked in a moment of mutual understanding. She winked. Adam squeezed her hand and smiled back. A look that only a loved one could understand, speaking more than a thousand words. A look that said everything.

Just outside the door, stood two people. A man and a woman. They felt reverence for the fact that a Yinyang had taken a job at a psychiatric hospital to be near his beloved. And they felt gratitude for the woman who would need to stay locked up in the hospital for several years to protect The Unvisible.

Many of those in the know ended up here. On a psychiatric ward. Those people who were mentally the healthiest, those who knew what the world was really like. They had to spend life behind bars while the rest of humanity lived on the other side in utter ignorance.

The two observed the group.

The man whispered to his colleague, 'The sane have no idea, whilst the aware are seen as insane.'

The woman nodded in agreement.

Author's Note

Thank you for reading *The Unvisible.* I hope you enjoyed it, and that it made you look at the world in a new light.

If you have experienced any events which feel as if they could in any way been inspired by *The Unvisible*, do let me know. I would love to hear them.

Do also share any ideas, thoughts and/or feedback with me.

I love to hear from my readers.

You can write directly to me at Fredrik@fredrikharen.com.

If you know of people who might appreciate getting to know the story of *The Unvisible*, please do share this book with them or encourage them to get their own copy. Help from readers to spread the word is invaluable for an author!

Thank you.
Fredrik Haren.

P.S. Let's connect.
You can connect with me at:
Linkedin: https://www.linkedin.com/in/fredrikharen/
Instagram: https://www.instagram.com/the.unvisible/
Facebook: https://www.facebook.com/TheUnvisible
Official website: www.theunvisible.com